ALLIANA
GIRL OF DRAGONS

"UNRAVEL YOUR OWN TALE."

ALLIANA
GIRL OF DRAGONS

JULIE ABE

Illustrated by Shan Jiang

LITTLE, BROWN AND COMPANY
New York Boston

Text copyright © 2022 by Julie Abe
Illustrations copyright © 2022 by Shan Jiang

Cover art copyright © 2022 by Shan Jiang
Cover design by Karina Granda
Cover copyright © 2022 by Hachette Book Group, Inc.

Little, Brown and Company
Hachette Book Group
1290 Avenue of the Americas, New York, NY 10104
Visit us at LBYR.com

First Edition: August 2022

Little, Brown and Company is a division of Hachette Book Group, Inc. The Little, Brown name and logo are trademarks of Hachette Book Group, Inc.

Library of Congress Cataloging-in-Publication Data
Names: Abe, Julie, author. | Jiang, Shan, illustrator.
Title: Alliana, girl of dragons / Julie Abe ; illustrated by Shan Jiang.
Description: First edition. | New York ; Boston : Little, Brown and Company, 2022. | Audience: Ages 8–12. | Summary: Alliana spends her days tending to her stepfamily's inn at the edge of the abyss, but when she rescues an orphaned nightdragon and later helps an apprentice witch, she seizes her chance to escape her stepmother's tyranny and find her own happily ever after.
Identifiers: LCCN 2021031397 | ISBN 9780316300353 (hardcover) | ISBN 9780316300568 (ebook)
Subjects: CYAC: Orphans—Fiction. | Stepfamilies—Fiction. | Dragons—Fiction. | Witches—Fiction. | Magic—Fiction. | Fantasy. | LCGFT: Novels. | Fantasy fiction.
Classification: LCC PZ7.1.A162 Al 2022 | DDC [Fic]—dc23
LC record available at https://lccn.loc.gov/2021031397

ISBNs: 978-0-316-30035-3 (hardcover), 978-0-316-30056-8 (ebook)

Printed in the United States of America

LSC-C

Printing 1, 2022

FOR MY DEAR GRANDMOTHER MARI–
for inspiring me with your strength
in the most trying of times
and your unconditional love.
I miss you.
Although you will never see this, thank you.

AND FOR YOU, READER:
May you find your own path,
and unravel your own tale.

CONTENTS

PROLOGUE

There was only one set of crossroads on the dusty outskirts of town. Four paths converged and diverged, sending travelers to utterly different fates.

Alliana paused, squinting through the bright overhead sunlight. Worn signs hung from the pole in the center of the paths, creaking tiredly in the muggy summer wind. The parched dirt was marked with her bootsteps; she was often sent out on errands along this road. And always, she stopped to look at the signs, as if something might change. But they were always imprinted with the same words:

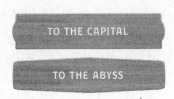

TO THE CAPITAL

TO THE ABYSS

To Alliana, however, the signs reminded her of possibilities:

Those words flitted around in her heart each time she passed by, like a pair of traveler's dice about to reveal its final roll.

Today was a normal trip: *The path to others.* The small town of Narashino awaited her, with its handful of shops catering to the adventurers who dared to explore the depths of the nearby abyss to seek their fortunes in gems and gold.

But as Alliana turned toward the sleepy buildings, she glanced longingly to the right, at the path to dreams. Her heart fluttered, like it was growing wings, tugging and aching to soar. Maybe, in a few years, she could explore that path. Maybe, in a few years, she'd finish repaying her debt to Stepmother, and she and Isao could begin to make their fortunes, shedding Narashino like the exoskeleton of the shadowsnakes that were known to crawl through the abyss. Perhaps, even, she would receive an invitation for the Royal Academy—though that was a dream sweeter than spun sugar.

The young girl didn't notice as she walked away, but a crystal pigeon landed on one of the signs. The iridescent white-and-pale-gray bird—a magical cousin of the common soot-black wood pigeon—chirped knowingly, looking between the small girl and her future path—if only Alliana would be brave enough to claim it for herself.

The road that led to the capital...

The path of dreams.

PART ONE

CHAPTER ONE

THE TOWN OF DUST

The weary border town of Narashino was a strange place for dreams. With nothing more than a general store, a diner, and an empty, never-used schoolhouse, it wasn't much of a town, either. Amidst the sparse waste-land of the South, it was as close to the abyss as the residents dared set up shop.

"Watch where you're going!" a grizzled old man barked, and Alliana roused herself from her daydream of where the other paths might lead.

"Sorry, sir." She dipped into a quick bow. Even as the man tsked with annoyance, she kept her head tucked down. Stepmother would be furious if Alliana got on the wrong side of their potential customers.

Alliana darted around the grouchy man and his friends, a noisy troop of adventurers gathered outside the

general store, their canvas knapsacks heavy with food
and purchases. The men and women smelled like sludgy
squab curry, too strangely sweet yet bitter, a telltale sign
they'd stayed at her stepmother's inn the night before. She
resisted the urge to gag; even a whiff of her stepmother's
cooking was a punishment in itself when she scrubbed
down the greasy pots at the end of the night.

Gritty travelers like these were Narashino's only
visitors—they alone dared to venture into the abyss to
hack away at the rocks, hoping for a speck of gold or a
glimmer of gems. They were dreamers, of a sort, though
they always came back more dirt-stained and empty-
handed than when they had first left. The last big gold
discovery had been five years ago, and the abyss seemed
to have dried up ever since. She glanced over her shoulder, eyeing them wistfully. The adventurers, even if they
didn't find riches, were able to go back to their home-
towns and away from this spell-forsaken place.

Alliana paused in front of the rickety diner. Early
afternoon light hit the window, casting a glow on the
handful of patrons taking a quick break before heading
out to the abyss, like the group Alliana had seen moments
ago.

The owner, a thin, stringy-looking man with a dirty
apron laced around his waist, looked up, as if sensing her,
and she ducked into the side alley. Alliana had no coin for
Mister Leo's ridiculous prices; she was never welcomed

inside. But more than that, the proprietor liked to stick his nose in places it didn't belong, so if Stepmother caught word of her taking a break even for an *instant*...

She shuddered, thinking of the heavy purple ledger.

Behind the diner was a dried-out wasteland: empty except for the piles of rotting remains of barely touched meals. Like Stepmother, Mister Leo was not particularly talented at cooking, though he believed his dishes were fit for the queen. Alliana snorted. Queen Natsumi would *never* eat his cooking, much less travel to a middle-of-nowhere village like Narashino.

"Psst, Alliana!"

She looked up, grinning. "Isao!"

"Hurry up!" her best—and only—friend called cheerily from the rooftop. The edge hid him too well, but Alliana could picture him likely lying out with his hands cushioning his head, his dark hair and tanned skin slightly lighter than hers, without the smattering of freckles that dotted her nose and cheeks. He was eleven years old, just like Alliana, but with a steady, easygoing nature that reminded her of a placid running stream. Though it seemed almost still on the surface, the water was rushing and moving underneath, full of energy and life as he cooked up another dish for the diner or took care of Hiroshi, his younger brother. Alliana and Isao had been friends since birth, it felt like, even though it wasn't as if Alliana could remember being born. She had tried, though—because if she could remember that far back, then she would remember her mother, who had passed away hours after her birth. Or her father, who'd remarried the clerk at the town's general store when Alliana was only six, and died that same year, when he'd fallen during a trip to the abyss hunting for gold.

There were the gritty travelers, who were able to chase their dreams, and then there were the handful of townspeople, who were stuck in Narashino. Isao, like her, was stuck. He worked at the diner, and even picked up extra shifts running messages within the abyss, to scrape together enough coin for him and his younger brother to keep a roof over their heads, but he dreamed of becoming a baker, of creating sky-high confections and croissants as light as air, yet irresistibly buttery.

Alliana clambered up the side of the diner, using the grooves that Isao had carved into the wood panels. He was indeed lying out under the warm sun like she'd expected, and Alliana plopped down next to him, making sure not to catch the hem of her knee-length skirt on the rough clay tiles. Stepmother would only add to her debts if she tore another set of clothes, though her stepsister's cast-asides couldn't be worth more than a copper. She nudged her friend. "So, were you able to make it?"

Isao shook his head solemnly, and Alliana's heart dropped.

"You should've seen me last night," he said. "Making your order of cloudberry cookies made me feel like one of those wizards from the Guild of Magic."

"I wish I could be part of the Guild." Alliana sighed just at that thought. "What happened?"

"Mister Leo was snoozing off 'cause of his yuzu cider, over in the dining room. I crept around the kitchen, stoking up the fire again real quiet, mixing things up, mashing the berries...." Isao winked. "Almost like magic. I was putting the cookies in the oven, and I was in the clear...until that darned hinge squealed. He snorted and fell onto the floor."

Alliana's eyes widened. "He caught you?"

Isao rubbed his forehead. "I tried warming up some fernleaf cider—you know how he is about that stuff. I pushed it in front of him—on the floor, mind you, because he hadn't gotten up. No good. He drank it all and started waking up again, this time trying to head to the kitchen. I hadn't washed down the bowls. I was done for."

"Oh, no," Alliana groaned. "I'm so sorry."

Her friend lifted one flour-dusted finger. "But I had a scrap of batter left. I wrapped that around my remaining fernleaf, and stuck it in the oven where it's real hot. A minute later, I served it up to Mister Leo." Isao grinned. "He ate it, singed edges and all, and went back to snoozing."

"You did it, then?" Alliana exclaimed. "You made the cloudberry cookies?"

Her friend grinned, pulling a small newspaper-wrapped bundle from his pocket. The tangy-sweet smell of the red-orange berries wafted up, mingling with the buttery aroma of Isao's mouthwatering cookies. "Just as requested."

"Oh, Isao!" Alliana grinned. "This is perfect! You know they're Grandmother Mari's favorite. Thank you." She pulled out the red coin purse Grandmother Mari had sewn for her, matching the slightly faded fireblossoms on her blouse, and fished out her lone copper.

"Take the cookies as my gift to Grandmother Mari. Tell her happy birthday from me." Isao tried to wave the coin away, but she insistently pushed it into his hand.

"For your future bakery," she said, and her friend finally put it in his pocket. "You'll have to let me be the first customer."

"Promise you'll eat a cloudberry croissant on the house?" Isao asked, and she nodded eagerly. If Isao had his bakery, that meant they'd be free of Narashino. She'd eat all the cloudberry croissants in the realm if they were out. Then he sighed. "If only we had magic. I bet those witches and wizards don't have to sneak around like I do—they'd just magic themselves away from this place with a flick of their wand."

Neither of them had a drop of magic; if they did, they wouldn't be in Narashino. The witches and wizards didn't even stop by the town, because they flitted back and forth from the capital on their fancy broomsticks and magicked up all the supplies they needed. They had no reason to visit this dusty town.

Alliana clutched the tiny bundle of cookies in her hand. The heat of the overhead sun made her collar itch. That copper coin she'd given Isao had been two moons of gathering herbs by the abyss. Which had meant she was a whole copper coin further from getting out of Narashino, and away from her stepfamily. "We can't wait for a spell. We've got to do something."

"I want to find some way to get out of here as much as you do," Isao said, and Alliana was reminded of gentle yet strong currents of water. Except, unlike water, she and Isao were stuck. "But who would take us as apprentices?"

Neither of them had an answer for that. Isao had paid his gold coin admission fee to the bakers' guild, so that he could send out letters across the realm to see if any bakers would accept him as an apprentice. But after they'd found out that Hiroshi, Isao's younger brother, would be joining, they suddenly no longer had space; they didn't want to feed two mouths. And Alliana...there was no way Stepmother, as her guardian, would let her enter an apprenticeship—not unless it was an invitation to the Royal Academy—not even Stepmother would refuse the law. They leaned against each other, Isao's thin shoulder bumping against hers, and stared out at the dry, sad town around them. Together, they let out a huge sigh.

Alliana let her mind drift to the crossroads. To the path that led far away, to a coastal town, where she could catch a boat heading to the capital. And Okayama, the capital city...where the queen lived. A place bursting to the brim with fairy tales come true, of possibilities being plucked out of thin air like a dusklight flower, where—

"Isao!" A shout broke their companionable silence.

Alliana and Isao jolted upright in horror. They'd been too busy daydreaming and letting time fly away without them. Alliana was surely late to pick up the supplies from the general store, and Stepmother would have yet another fit. Then dread pricked her spine. Mister Leo was stomping out, huffing with fury.

In a flash, Isao scrambled off the building, motioning for Alliana to hide. He stepped in front of Mister Leo. "You called?"

The old man wheezed in shock, stumbling backward. "Where in the abyss did you pop out from?"

Isao smiled smoothly. His rooftop hideout was a secret; even his little brother didn't know about it. "I was just cleaning out the waste bins, sir." He motioned to the tin pail he'd somehow managed to pick up.

"Customers are waiting! What took you so long?" Mister Leo craned his neck, looking around suspiciously. "If I see that orphan girl around, I'm going to tell Mistress Enokida and dock your wages."

Mister Leo loved to tattle on Alliana when she

stuck even the corner of her pinky toe out of line. Any infraction—any *second* she was caught in town chatting with Isao instead of tending to her endless list of chores like a mindless automaton—Mister Leo instantly told Stepmother. And that was when the ledger made its appearance, pages got added, and the debts Alliana owed her increased and increased, like a lock clicking into place and sealing her future here in Narashino.

Anger swelled in her chest. Mister Leo had added more than ten moons of dues she owed to Stepmother. "You're hardly paying him as it is," Alliana muttered.

Mister Leo snapped upright. "What did I just hear?"

Her heart nearly stopped. She flattened herself on the rooftop, urging every fiber of her being to stay still, even the tips of the flyaway hairs escaping her braid.

Below, Isao stammered, "I—I said nothing, sir. Maybe it was the wind."

Alliana's heart thumped as she gripped her fingers against the roof tiles. *Don't look up, don't look up—*

"Did you know that we're almost out of fernleaf?" Isao blurted.

"What?" the proprietor spluttered. "How can we be low? We still had two bunches when I looked a day ago."

"Yes, sir," Isao said solemnly. "And then you asked for me to make you some fernleaf cider and fernleaf cookies last night."

Well, Mister Leo hadn't quite asked. Alliana grinned.

"I'm going to check the pantry. There better not be any sticky fingers around here." Mister Leo stomped inside. Alliana peeked over the edge. Isao looked up, winked, and hurried back in after the proprietor before the old man yelled again.

Find some way to get out of here. Isao's words rattled around her head as she picked up the inn's latest shipment from the general store, skirting around yet another boisterous group of adventurers. Her arms burned from the weight of the burlap sack as she lugged it back to the inn—*the path to misery*—and she wondered if there really was a way for her to leave Narashino.

CHAPTER TWO

LAST STOP INN

Alliana turned the corner into the inn. It wasn't as if she could miss it. In the barren flatlands before the abyss, the inn was the last—and only—stop. She glanced over at the white barrier in the distance, the protective shield maintained by the witches and wizards of the Guild of Magic—it was the only sign of a spell anywhere near Narashino.

Beyond the glowing light, a cavernous rift stretched from east to west; the abyss ran through the land as far as the horizon. The depths gaped like a deep scar on the land that no one dared to cross, for fear of meeting the creatures that would crawl out from the darkness. Grandmother had said that, in the time before the abyss, Constancia, the realm to the south, used to trade openly with its neighbors, and Rivelleans would travel to visit its lush, oasis-like cities amidst its stretches of grassy plains. Constancians often spent moons in Rivelle, to explore the powdery snow at the Sakuya Mountains or test their luck hunting phoenixes in the Walking Cliffs. Back then, magic thrummed through the land; a child could easily levitate cookies off the rack and out the window with a wave of their hand (much to the dismay of the local baker), or a traveler could cast away the clouds instead of trudging through a storm.

In a history tome that an inn guest had left behind, Alliana had read that the merchants' guilds of Rivelle and Constancia had gotten into a disagreement over a contract, and it combined with other petty spats, spiraling out of control. The tipping point was generations ago, when the emperor of Constancia had tried for the queen of Rivelle's hand in marriage, only to be utterly rejected. In a magical fit, the emperor broke down the bridges over the river that once flowed between the two realms and tore the land asunder, creating the abyss and transforming peaceful creatures into monsters that stalked the dark. Ever since, Constancia's borders had been closed and blocked to all other realms, and the magic in the seven realms had dwindled, year after year. But most dangerous of all—especially to those living at the border— were the cursed beasts.

Alliana shuddered, wondering what monsters were

stirring as midday shifted to early evening. Nightdragons—
the near-mythical beasts that had once amicably flown
the skies over Rivelle and Constancia—had been banished
into the darkest depths of the abyss and could breathe fire
hot enough to melt an adventurer into thin air. Shadowsnakes, the nightdragon's supposedly less deadly companion, grew more and more venomous with each encounter.
Even the most intrepid adventurers stayed at the very edge
of the abyss, near the pulleys operated by workers who
sent down messages as soon as any beasts were sighted,
and within close reach of the protective shield that they
could rush to for safety. Though the Royal Guard offered
bounty to those brave enough to slay a creature, few were
foolhardy enough to dare.

Years ago, according to Grandmother Mari, Alliana's
parents had built the inn after they'd met here, attracted
by their love for adventure—there was no better place
for that than the abyss. With a baby on the way, though,
they couldn't rappel down like they used to, so instead,
they set up the inn as close to the cavernous rift as they
could get.

Alliana always tried to find some trace of her parents in the once white, now dirty wood slats of the
squat building. But nearly five years had passed since
Father had died, and Stepmother had sold off everything that might've sparked a memory, to use on expensive dresses and lacquer jewelry to impress Stepmother's

family, who never came by. Alliana only had a few treasured recollections—the days spent wandering the hidden meadow next to the abyss, searching for herbs with
her father and recording their discoveries in his dog-
eared notebook. He'd tell his stories about fighting—and
sometimes befriending—creatures in the dark abyss, and
they'd make plans for the day that she was old enough
to accompany him. Though, when she asked, he always
said, "Not yet, not yet. I have lost your mother, and I cannot bear for you to be in danger."

Now, her long days were spent sweeping the tatami
floors or laundering sheets for Stepmother. Sounds of the
dinnertime bustle drifted out of the kitchen window, and
Alliana's steps quickened. She was late, and Stepmother
would have some choice words about *that*. Alliana ducked
under the window as pots and pans clanged.

"Get out of my way!" a cold voice snapped.

Alliana jumped, but Stepmother was inside, chastis-
ing one of her stepsiblings—likely naive Reina, who, when
given a knife to cut simple things like potatoes, was a
danger to others far more than a threat to the vegetables.

When Alliana hurried over to the side door, the inn's
crystal pigeon trilled from its roost on one of the nearby
thin, sickly-looking trees; the call, somehow, felt like a
warning. Alliana glanced around, but no one was nearby.

The late afternoon light reflected through the bird's
glass body. A long time ago, Grandmother Mari had

explained how crystal pigeons were enchanted versions of witches' and wizards' letters, except these carried wishes. Any non-magical person could pay a silver coin to the Guild of Magic and request a crystal pigeon to carry their hopes for a dream that might come true. It was said that the crystal was a manifestation of a wish in that one could feel it and almost see it, but it wasn't quite all there yet. When the wish was complete, the crystal pigeon would flutter off, never to be seen again. This crystal pigeon had come from a wish that Alliana's mother and father had made on the day of her birth— but she didn't know what it was. Stepmother had tried to chase it away countless times, in the same way she'd cleared out the inn of anything else that had belonged to Alliana's parents. Stepmother even tried to capture the pigeon once—likely to sell off to the highest bidder— but the bird nearly pecked her nose off. Alliana felt a rush of relief each time she saw the crystal pigeon had returned.

Right now, though, Alliana had no time for wishes or crystal fancies. She hurried into the narrow, dark hallway, and eased the burlap bag of provisions off her aching shoulder.

For a second, she jolted—her stepbrother stood at her shoulder, glaring down.

Then she breathed out. It was only the newest portrait that Stepmother had framed of her son, commissioned from one of the traveling artists who had stopped by the inn. The entire hallway was plastered with illustrations of Stepmother, Reina, and Reizo glowering over Alliana and all the inn's guests.

For being part of the "family," it was peculiar how, according to these drawings, Alliana didn't exist. And the only portrait of Grandmother Mari was facing the stairway, for the rare times that the old woman descended from her attic and Stepmother pretended to fawn all over her. Even when Reina went through her wanting-to-be-an-artist phase, Stepmother had used the one picture she'd painted of Alliana as a fire-starter.

"Is that girl trying to hide from her duties? She should've been back hours ago. Why, after all I do for her!" Stepmother's shout echoed through the inn, over the clamor of guests in the main room. Before Alliana unlaced her boots, she hastily pulled out the bundle from Isao and unwrapped a corner to check on the half dozen cookies.

Her gift to Grandmother Mari was still safe. She breathed out in relief. Her friend had used the edges of an empty can to cut the buttery cookies into circles. The tangy-sweet vanilla aroma eased away the strangeness of the noxious-smelling dish that Stepmother was attempting to make.

"Well, there you are," a snide voice snapped.

Alliana jumped, shoving the cookies back into her pocket, and spun around.

The real Reizo stood near the stairs, leaning against the wall with his arms crossed. His broad, muscled shoulders and wide face made him look like he was carved out of the cold rocks lining the abyss, and his stony, unforgiving temperament only added to that resemblance. Reina, his twin, on the other hand, was like a scatterbrained sparrow who often playfully acted half her age. "Where have you been? It's almost the dinner rush, and Ma's trying to cook."

Reizo *knew* she'd had to go into town to pick up supplies from the general store—he'd been the one who sent her out for a bag of gingko nuts. Which might've been because Alliana had fed the last handful to the pigeon so she'd have an excuse to get Grandmother's cookies, but her stepbrother didn't need to know that.

"Smells like she's doing a great job," Alliana said brightly, shifting her burlap sack to cover the bulge in her pocket.

Her stepbrother narrowed his eyes. He hissed, "Are you trying to be funny?"

Then Reina stuck her head out of the kitchen. "Oh, there you are, Alliana. Mother is mixing up the cabbage pancakes." The girl let out a shudder, her two braids swinging emphatically. "I nearly fainted from the fumes when she doused the pancakes with vinegar. Again."

Reizo groaned, rubbing his forehead. For all that he snapped at Alliana, he was protective of Reina, as if any consideration he might have given Alliana was given to his twin instead. "Get to work, Alliana. Or I could ask Mother to pull out the ledger?"

Alliana raised her chin. "I *have* been working."

Then, as if those words had cast a summons, heavy footsteps pounded in the hallway, and Alliana paled.

Stepmother.

The older woman pushed past her children with a clash of expensive enamel bracelets, and stared down at Alliana. Her narrow face—sharp as a pair of scissors that constantly snipped—was permanently pinched; the motherly look she'd had when she coerced Alliana's father to marry her had faded the instant she'd realized Father always put Alliana first—ahead even, to her rage and shock, of Stepmother herself.

Sharp retorts faded on Alliana's tongue, replaced by the scent of cloying incense and the sour, poisonous cabbage pancakes.

"You?" Stepmother spat. "Working? Hah, I expect Mister Leo will tell me you were visiting that useless, dumb assistant of his."

Alliana was used to being berated, to being told she would never amount to anything. But Isao was *off limits*. "Isao is *not* useless! He's going to be the most famous baker in the realm, he—"

Stepmother grabbed the ledger and a stub of charcoal out of her apron pocket. "Oh, what were you saying?" She licked a finger—it was dirty, Alliana noticed with disgust—and thumbed through the pages. "Your tardiness adds two coppers to your dues. Doesn't that sound about right?"

Alliana's heart dropped. She was already thirty gold coins in debt. She'd be working at the inn for the rest of her life. She couldn't let that happen. She survived her dreary days by thinking of her dreams: traveling to the Constancia Sea, a day spent wandering through the winding paths of the capital city.... Most of all, she wanted to attend the Royal Academy. And she couldn't go to the Farmlands Ball without Stepmother's permission.

Alliana swallowed her pride. "I'll be in the kitchen as soon as I take off my boots." She dug into the burlap sack and lifted up the bag of gingko nuts toward Reizo. "Here, as you requested."

"Finally," he muttered, seemingly somewhat appeased.

But Stepmother narrowed her eyes, her charcoal stub still poised over the ledger. "And?"

Alliana tipped into a deep bow, and said hoarsely, "I'm very sorry I was late, Stepmother."

Stepmother sniffed. "Don't you forget your place, girl."

Fiery responses burned in Alliana's throat, but she swallowed them down. *Dreams, dreams, don't forget about your dreams*, she told herself.

She didn't raise her head until Stepmother and Reizo had sauntered back to the kitchen. Reina, following in their wake, asked, "Wait, Ma, do you promise your cooking won't make me faint anymore?"

As Alliana rose, she took a deep breath, looking longingly toward the stairs. She'd have to wait until later to give her gift to Grandmother Mari. She slid off her boots, tucked the cookies behind a stack of dusty baskets, and hurried to the kitchen.

Stepmother wasn't satisfied with Alliana just salvaging the cabbage pancakes. After serving the late-night patrons, wiping down the tables, cleaning out the chicken coop, and scrubbing all the dishes—including dumping out the poisonous sauce outside—Alliana had finally finished the list of chores that Stepmother had tasked her with before the woman had flounced off to her bath.

As Alliana wiped down the sink, her heart dropped as she looked out the window. It was so late that the thin sliver of the waning moon was starting to sink back toward the horizon. It was far past midnight, and Grandmother Mari was likely asleep.

Still, she filled up a canteen with the elderly woman's favorite roasted green tea and hurried into the hallway. Alliana hadn't had time to stop by earlier, only to set a dinner tray in front of her door. Perhaps she could catch Grandmother Mari before she nodded off over her embroidery, and wish her a happy birthday.

At the entrance, Alliana dug her hand behind the baskets to pick up the cookies. Dust filtered down as she nudged the woven straw rounds to the side. Stepmother had bought them at a discount at the general store and marked up the price for the inn's guests. The woman was certain she'd snag a wealthy buyer someday, though no one had touched these baskets in over a year.

But Alliana's fingertips met empty space.

The weariness of the full day and night of work dropped away in an instant. Had she pushed it further than she remembered?

Her heart pattered as she hurriedly unstacked the baskets, one after another until—

Nothing.

Bare floor, just the woven straw mat.

The steps creaked, and Alliana spun around. She clung to a wild hope that perhaps...perhaps Grandmother Mari was inching down the stairs, and she'd give Alliana one of those warm, eye-crinkly smiles—

The shadows shifted like rocks tumbling down, and Alliana's heart dropped.

Reizo sat down at the foot of the stairway, lazily biting into a familiar pink-red cookie.

Grandmother's cookies.

Alliana's eyes darted to the unfolded wrapper next to him. There were two cookies left. Two wasn't as nice as six, but it was better than none at all.

Reizo followed Alliana's gaze down. "Looking for something?"

"I...I..." This was a trap. Reizo had played this game far too many times before. With her dinner she'd been looking forward to eating, with her tunic that she'd just hung up to dry, with the dishes she'd just finished washing...she'd spent as long as she could remember, losing Reizo's games. "No, nothing."

"Nothing. Especially nothing to do with that good-for-nothing old woman's birthday, I suppose." He jerked his chin up at the ceiling, toward Grandmother Mari's room in the attic.

"She's not good-for-nothing! She mends clothes and sews tapestries and—"

Reizo stretched his leg out and ground his heel into one of the cookies.

She let out a startled yelp, and then pressed her lips together, her hands curling into fists in the pockets of her skirt. She refused to let Reizo win. But if she stood up to his bullying, it would only get worse. Her stepbrother would tell Stepmother, and that would add another tally to the ledger. She knew all the possible outcomes of this game. If she didn't say anything, perhaps he'd get bored and go to sleep.

Still, it hurt. The fury welling up in Alliana hurt so much her eyes stung. Grandmother Mari was Alliana's only companion in this inn. And Alliana was the only one who truly cared about the old woman. Stepmother piled on syrupy words when she saw her mother-in-law, but she complained the instant Grandmother returned to her room; all Stepmother wanted was Grandmother's crystal necklace.

Reizo leaned forward, his thick eyebrows raised. "You said you're missing something?"

Slowly, Alliana raised her chin, like she was Queen Natsumi out of one of Grandmother Mari's tales, her face as still as could be. "No, I'm not missing anything. Thank you for your concern, Reizo."

"Nothing at all?" His foot hovered over the last cookie. She wanted to dash forward and snatch it away.

Her heart ached. "Nothing."

Reizo brought his heel down and crushed it into dust.

Alliana kept her eyes trained on him, steady as she could make them. Like she herself was the queen, though the idea of that was pathetically laughable. But she would *not* let Reizo see her cry.

When Reizo growled, frustrated that he hadn't been

able to get a rise out of Alliana, he spun on his heel and stalked upstairs.

She listened for his footsteps to fade and for the telltale slam of his door.

Finally, when she was sure he was gone, she slipped down to her knees and gathered the crumbs in her hands, watching the remains sift out like sand.

CHAPTER THREE

THE ATTIC OF DREAMS

Alliana climbed up the ladder to the attic and tapped softly on the door, clutching the canteen of tea with her other hand. Grandmother Mari was likely asleep, but...

"Alliana?" A gentle voice drifted through the cracks in the wood. "Is that you? Come in, dear."

She pushed the door open. Despite her age, the old woman still sat up straight at her low sewing table, her swirls of beautiful midnight-black and faint-morning-gray hair spun into a bun at the nape of her neck. In the gentle candle glow, Grandmother Mari's favorite necklace, with the crystal droplet at the end, sparkled like a light beckoning her forward. "I didn't think you'd visit tonight."

Alliana's heart constricted; of *course* she would want

to see Grandmother Mari on her birthday. The old woman
waved her off the ladder and into her attic. It was a small
room, no bigger than the pantry of the kitchen. But it was
a homey, cozy place, with the clean straw floor, plenty
of handmade cushions, and the familiar sight of piles of
shirts to be mended or trousers to be hemmed. Balls of
crumpled paper overflowed the waste bin; Grandmother
refused to let Alliana near it, for the old woman had
said she was writing something for Alliana. She even
was fond of that mess, because it was something from
Grandmother to her. But most of all, Alliana loved the
twelve tapestries that hung on the walls, depicting scenes
from the old tales she loved to hear so much. The star-
crossed lovers, Orihime and Hikoboshi, stretched their
arms toward each other across an inky blue-black sky,
fated to always be in love yet apart. On the other wall,
Kintarō, the brave boy raised by a mountain witch, faced
off with a vicious nightdragon threatening to burn down
a town in the foothills of the Sakuya Mountains. Grandmother and Alliana had painstakingly embroidered each
piece together as the old woman told her its story; Alliana
knew each line just as well as she knew each thread of the
tapestries.

Alliana settled on the thick floor cushion at the
low table in the center of the room, across from the old
woman. Made by Grandmother Mari herself, the pure
white, puffy cushions were laced with gold stripes; the

fabric was scraps from other projects, but like the tapestries, with Grandmother's craftiness, it was fit for a
queen.

"I wouldn't have missed seeing you, even if I'm late,"
Alliana said, pouring out a cup of tea. "Happy birthday,
Grandmother Mari."

"Thank you, dear one." The old woman moved aside
the shirt she was mending for one of the inn's guests and
wrapped her knobbly fingers around the steaming clay
mug. "It's been another year, already. How strangely
time blurs as I age. There seem to be no markers between
this year and the last."

Alliana's shoulders sank. Last year, she'd spent the
evening with Grandmother, helping the old lady catch
up on mending and work on embroidery. But she hadn't
had the coin to give her a proper present. First, Alliana's
embroidery box had gone missing, the beautiful tradi-
tional box made of thick, reinforced washi paper that had
been one of her prized possessions, and a miniature of
Grandmother Mari's precious red-and-gold embroidery
box. She suspected Reizo, because he had demanded Alliana go outside to clean the yard before it had disappeared
from her tiny room behind the kitchen, but she didn't
have a shred of evidence.

Alliana had used the three coppers she'd saved up to
buy replacement needles and a thimble instead, so she
could continue helping Grandmother Mari. And then

Grandmother had one of her dizzy spells and a head-ache, so Alliana spent her only silver coin to buy a pair of glasses at the general store for the elderly woman to see the thread, even though the new owner at the time had raised the prices twofold. When the old woman had pro-tested, saying it was far too generous of Alliana, she'd lied and said the glasses had come from Stepmother, Reizo, and Reina, too. But if she'd given Grandmother Mari an actual present, like the cookies, would this year's birth-day have been finally memorable? She blurted out, "I had a present for you."

Grandmother turned her head, sensing a deeper story, and the crystal on the long silver chain clinked. Alliana took a slow breath and started. "I ordered a half dozen cloudberry cookies from Isao, and—"

Grandmother Mari squinted, rubbing at her fore-head. She'd been having more headaches and dizzy spells lately, and without a healer in town, there was little help she'd be able to get until the traveling healer came by in three moons.

A line from one of Alliana's favorite Queen Natsumi stories came to mind. *Straight and tall; not above all, but see the truth.*

It was a truth that Grandmother didn't need to see.

So Alliana smiled as brightly as she could, curling her hands into fists under the table, her nails indenting her skin. "But I tripped and crushed them on my way back."

Alliana couldn't add to Grandmother Mari's burdens, and risk harming her health. Most of all, she couldn't bad-mouth Reizo to his own grandmother.

Mari Sakamaki wasn't her family by blood. She was the mother of Reizo and Reina's father, who had died before the twins were born, back when Stepmother had lived in the far west with her family. Stepmother was polite enough to Grandmother Mari; after all, the elderly woman brought in good coin mending the guests' clothes and sewing up handkerchiefs and small goods that Stepmother made Alliana sell to guests upon check-in and checkout. But most of all, Stepmother always eyed Grandmother Mari's crystal necklace, the slim, shimmering gem tucked under her blouse; Alliana had heard her claim to Reizo and Reina that Grandmother would give it to her after she passed, as payment for taking care of the elderly woman for so many years, and that she'd sell it right away and raze the "ugly" building she'd received upon Father's death to build a bigger, better inn, with hired servants so she could lounge around all day like she deserved.

Grandmother often asked after Stepmother and Reizo and Reina, though none of them bothered to visit her. Alliana had spun up stories about how they'd had dinner together as a family—on nights when her stomach ached with hunger—or how she and Reizo had happily hunted herbs together near the abyss—when he ridiculed her whenever he finally did go.

Because if Alliana told Grandmother Mari the truth, then the old woman would worry about her. And with her faltering health, she already had enough to take care of. Worse, what if Grandmother didn't believe her?

Alliana shrugged off her thoughts, trying to ignore how pinched and tight her shoulders were. "I didn't want to give you cloudberry crumbs, of course."

"Oh, Alliana." Grandmother Mari set down her mug and reached out, taking Alliana's hands in her own. Grandmother rubbed warmth into Alliana's cold and weary fingers. The old woman's skin was papery, mottled with age, and wrinkled like just-washed clothes. But Grandmother's hands filled Alliana's soul with a contentment that was better than any cup of tea. "Are you okay? Didn't the fall hurt?"

"Me?" Alliana blinked. Grandmother's brown eyes were turning gray with age, but those eyes studied her inquisitively. For a moment, Alliana felt like that cup of tea inside her was going to spill over and pour out as salty tears. What if she told Grandmother Mari the truth, instead of spinning stories about how much she loved her days?

But Grandmother Mari was too old now; she couldn't just up and run away from the inn. And Alliana had debts to pay; Stepmother would hire mercenaries or, worse, pirates to hunt her down. She couldn't go on the run with a seventy-year-old grandmother in tow. The only way out was if Alliana earned her admittance to the Royal Academy, but that was as likely as Grandmother Mari finally finishing up that letter to Alliana. Or as likely as Alliana paying off her mountain of debt.

Instead, Alliana shook her head quickly. "I'm fine! Just a little dusty."

Grandmother Mari continued to study her thoroughly; Alliana kept her smile bright. She'd practiced her expressions, after all, for many years in front of Stepmother and Reizo and Reina. Stepmother always pretended to dote on Grandmother Mari when she ventured out of her attic; the old woman thought Mistress Enokida was a "lovely" daughter-in-law. "Lovely" didn't match how Stepmother had screeched at Alliana for ten minutes straight for not bringing in her sweet bean cakes with the afternoon tea, though the woman had asked for the tin of sable cookies. Still, Alliana would *not* ruin Grandmother's birthday.

"Well, then," Grandmother Mari said finally, seemingly satisfied. "We'll have to have a little special treat today. Go on, take a look. But don't you dare go near my letters."

Alliana pushed off the cushion and made her way to the window, careful to circle wide around the waste bin. From here, she could see Grandmother's thin, careful handwriting—though she was too far away to make out the message—and her favorite gold-brown paper. "Are you sure I can't read it, Grandmother Mari?"

"No!" the old woman said, pretend-scolding, with a laugh. "Alliana, my letter to you isn't ready, not yet. Besides, we've got a full year until the Farmlands Ball. I've got until then."

"You're so well-versed with your words, though," Alliana protested. "Even with just a line of your stories, I fall straight in."

"Those kind words of yours are beyond precious." Grandmother Mari smiled. "We think we trade in gold and silver, but words are the true currency of our lives. Words are what connect us through time and distance, whether expressing troubles or joy. I hope this letter will be something for you to carry close to your heart as you rise through the ranks of the Royal Academy, a reminder of where you've come from, and the future you have yet to unravel."

One more year until the ball. Alliana's heart hummed with hope. No one in the Farmlands had been chosen for the Royal Academy for as long as she could remember—though Alliana would certainly try.

Next to the cold glass, there were wood panels, just like all around the rest of the attic. But this one was different. She pushed with her fingertips, and the board slid to the side, revealing a narrow hideaway. It was Grandmother's hiding spot, and Alliana was proud that it was a secret they shared together. The old woman loved little secrets in plain sight; even in the tapestries, she would embroider a favorite line or two from the story onto the cloth, and then stitch the illustration on top of that. The star-crossed lovers' line was *Though you may be far, you are always near in my heart.* For one of Queen Natsumi's tapestries, Alliana had seen *My dreams may be great, but my resolve is greater.* Alliana wondered what Grandmother Mari would sew for her—not that her particular ordinary life was likely to become worthy of a tapestry.

The recess was filled with a small box with a miniature tapestry that Grandmother wouldn't even show Alliana—the old woman swept it away and into the box whenever Alliana came close, which made her wonder if it was a Year-End holiday present for her—but this time there was also a round metal tin.

"Now, don't you sneak a peek at the tapestry. I know you've been trying," Grandmother said teasingly. "Tonight, we want the tin. An adventurer was particularly gracious after I mended her knapsack."

Alliana fetched it out and returned to the sewing table, opening it to reveal round, golden rice crackers. As Grandmother Mari took a cracker, Alliana couldn't help but notice how the woman's hands shook more these days. "Let's enjoy these."

The crackly, toasted crackers were as salty as the tears that Alliana could never cry in front of Grandmother.

But the saltiness calmed her, reminding her of the sweet-
ness of every night spent with the old woman. And, at the
end of another day stretching out the thin porridge Stepmother gave her—barely substantial even after adding in
herbs she'd collected from near the abyss—the crackers
were a welcome treat. As they ate, Alliana helped Grandmother start mending a pile of traditional-style shirts like
Alliana's, the front tied with a bow on the right side—
albeit none were as threadbare as hers. More and more
often recently, Grandmother had trouble threading the
needle even with her glasses on. So Alliana helped whenever she could, and Grandmother Mari paid her well with
magical fairy tales.

"Ah, my bones ache more and more these days." The
old woman settled back into her white cushion with a
sigh, returning to mending a tear along a shirt's wide
night-black sleeve, the fabric woven with lines of faint
silver. The shirt was clearly owned by a traveler who had
already made some amount of fortune and was only at
the abyss for a week or so of fun before they went hurry-
ing back to the capital to regale their friends with stories
of swashbuckling adventures. Likely, this mended shirt
was meant to be proof of their tales. "So, what story shall
we explore tonight?"

Alliana looked around Grandmother's attic. The
twelve tapestries shimmered in the moonlight, beckoning

Alliana to dive into their threads and get wound up in the tale.

Years ago, Stepmother had tried to coerce Grandmother to sell the tapestries, but that was the one time the mild-mannered old woman put her foot down. "No," she'd declared so firmly that even Stepmother hadn't had the courage to ask again. But a few weeks later, Alliana had heard Stepmother grumble to Mister Leo, "After that old woman dies, I'll sell those stupid tapestries for a fortune. I can't wait."

Alliana couldn't imagine a day without Grandmother Mari's kind smiles, the cozy attic, or her nighttime stories. It was like a fairy tale with an unhappy ending—it simply couldn't exist.

"How about the tale of Queen Natsumi when she was just a student, stepping into the Royal Academy for her first test? Or perhaps the story of the star-crossed lovers? Ah, let us finish the mending tomorrow," Grandmother Mari said, drawing Alliana away from her thoughts. Then the old woman slid the pile of shirts to the side, shifting in her seat to take out a broad stretch of thick linen from a box next to her—the tapestry they were working on. "Oh, I know—the tale of Queen Natsumi's birth."

"Of course." Alliana lit up as she hastily tied up one last knot on a shirt and took up the black embroidery thread. Carefully, with weaving, smooth stitches, she began filling in the sleek black of Queen Natsumi's hair, brushed off her forehead in a single braid just like Alliana's, like a crown. Grandmother's stories about Queen Natsumi wove together tragic beginnings with majestic destinies. Alliana knew every word by heart, but it felt different, more *magical* when Grandmother Mari spun her tales in her warm storyteller voice:

Once upon a time, on the coldest day of the coldest year, a little girl was born to two nobles. Her mother was the Royal Advisor to the capital city; her father was the Royal Advisor to the merchants' guild.

But little Natsumi did not know who she was, because on the coldest of nights, a wicked witch stole her from her crib. The witch harbored a deep and terrible anger toward Natsumi's father for his poor leadership in the guild, which had led to the merchants ignoring the poor and only catering to the nobles.

Her parents desperately searched high and low for their daughter, but she was nowhere to be found; the witch's curses were too strong. They mourned their daughter, believing her lost forever.

But this witch had a plan in mind, and bright, clever Natsumi grew up in the wild forests in the foothills of the Sakuya Mountains, unaware of her noble blood, and raised by the evil witch....

Alliana's heart thumped as Grandmother Mari created an entire world with just her words. The tapestries fluttered in the faint breeze drifting through the small window, bringing in more of the muggy summer heat. But with Grandmother's storytelling, the hot air felt like the icy winds from the day Queen Natsumi was born. The slightly musty straw of the floors turned into the sharp sap-scent of the evergreen trees in the forests of the foothills. As the story unraveled, Alliana felt like she was Queen Natsumi, sneaking through the witch's cottage and uncovering her secret past.

The tapestry seemed to sew itself magically. After finishing Queen Natsumi's braid, Alliana returned to the mending, flying through the pile until, as always, Grandmother said, "And then Queen Natsumi lived happily ever after."

Grandmother lapsed into a peaceful silence, knotting off a thread. Slowly, the magic of the fairy tale faded away. Alliana was still in Grandmother's attic; she hadn't traveled to the stone castle in Okayama, the capital city, like Queen Natsumi had.

Alliana had to tamp down the urge to ask, *Another story, please, just one more.* Grandmother's eyes were drooping with tiredness from the late hour, and her brow was wrinkled; her headache hadn't subsided. The young girl let out a wistful sigh. "If only we could live in a fairy tale."

Grandmother Mari smiled as she folded the tapestry and slid it back onto the shelf. "Sometimes, we may be

in a magical tale but not even know it until far, far afterward. But you'll have to unravel your own tale, dear."

Unravel your own tale.... Grandmother Mari said
that all the time, but Alliana knew the truth. "There's
nothing close to a fairy tale to be found here, not in dry
and dusty Narashino."

"Only time will tell," the old woman said cryptically,
as she always did. Outside, the crystal pigeon cooed,
loud and echoing in the quiet night. "Besides, it won't be
long before you'll have a chance to go to the Farmlands
Ball. No matter what, don't close the door on a good
opportunity."

The Farmlands Ball was one of the annual balls that
occurred in the twenty-three regions around the realm,
right before the Year-End holidays. There, non-royal-
born twelve-year-olds met the area's Royal Advisor and a
scrying witch or wizard. With a quick spell, the children
would learn if they were invited to attend as a pupil of
the Royal Academy to be schooled in everything from
inter-realm diplomacy to the proper way to bow to the
queen versus a Royal Advisor. And only the top students
were allowed to take the final exam and vie for a chance
to serve the queen. The Farmlands Royal Advisor's estate
was two hours away by carriage, but even just seeing the
elegant mansion and ballroom would be a delight. And
the possibility to become part of the Royal Court? A
future beyond Alliana's wildest dreams.

"But I wouldn't want to leave you to mend all these shirts," Alliana protested. "Besides, I doubt Stepmother would let me go." As her guardian, Stepmother had the final say in what Alliana could do. She sighed, knowing it was a certain, cold *no*.

"No matter what, you *must* go. It's a step toward unraveling your own tale; I'm sure of it." Grandmother Mari raised her chin. "I'll talk with Fusako."

Alliana's heart sang with hope. "Thank you, Grandmother Mari."

"Ah—and I know just how I want to celebrate my birthday now. This is just as good as any adventure from a fairy tale: Let us travel to that hidden meadow of yours, sometime this moon."

Stepmother never let Alliana visit the abyss alone; it was her one remotely motherlike concession toward Alliana. Though, perhaps, she was just worried Alliana might try to run away. Usually, Reizo or Reina accompanied her on the herb-gathering trips, both of whom were difficult to go with. Reizo never wanted to venture near the abyss, so Alliana could never collect the herbs she needed, and Reina wandered far too close. Just last moon, Reina had traipsed off—and into a nest of shadowsnakes. Alliana had had to use a valuable pouch of katori chrysanthemum—which had taken her more than two moons to collect and would've sold for a full silver—to distract the venomous snakes from biting her stepsister.

And that wasn't one of the times that Reina had almost fallen straight *into* the abyss.

"An afternoon of gathering herbs with you at the meadow? That will be the best present," Grandmother Mari said decisively.

Alliana's eyes blurred; it wasn't from the late hour or the weak lamplight flickering over their faces. Her heart felt warm and soft. "Grandmother, what do you dream of?"

The old woman hesitated, pausing in the middle of folding one of the mended shirts. "That is a curious question...." Then Grandmother Mari pressed at her temple: another pounding headache.

"Do you have any more shokyo roots? I'll steep some tea—"

But the old woman had her eyes squeezed shut; this headache seemed to be especially bad. Alliana dug through Grandmother Mari's basket of medicine tins, but the square box for the tan root only had a thin, wrinkled shred.

"I'll get a batch of shokyo now—"

The old woman folded her hands back on the table, blinking as the headache dissipated. "It was just a small one. You cannot take care of an old woman like me if you cannot nurture yourself." Grandmother focused on Alliana. "Promise me you'll rest first?"

She nodded, though she was already calculating the

hours of sleep needed before she could slip out to the hidden meadow.

As she clambered down the ladder, resolve filled her, strengthening her weary steps. One day, she promised herself, she would leave this dusty town behind. She would make her way to the Farmlands Ball, and by earning her place in the Royal Academy, she'd finally be able to get proper care for Grandmother Mari. One day, she would be able to seek the life she'd always wanted.

CHAPTER FOUR

THE HIDDEN MEADOW

"Polish the teacups! No, again! Boil up more hot water for my tea. Faster!"

Alliana could recite Stepmother's demands in her sleep. She also knew that there was no way she could heat up water faster—the stove was crammed to the edges with crackling firewood. It was late afternoon, and she still hadn't had a chance to visit the meadow with Grandmother today, as she'd hoped. But, hopefully after this last chore, Stepmother would be in a good enough mood to let her go. If only the water *could* boil faster.

Alliana shoved at the shimmering flames with the cast-iron rod that had been broken off an old wheel rim. Stepmother was too stingy to cough up the silver coin for a proper set. The beautiful red-white fire didn't deserve her frustrations. But even the flames had more freedom than her; the embers traveled up the chimney and away, flying off to new horizons.

Sometimes, we may be in a magical tale but not even know it until far, far afterward.

Grandmother Mari's words danced around her, warm and bright as threads from one of the old woman's tapestries. Maybe *Alliana* was in a fairy tale. Maybe she was like Queen Natsumi, and she and Isao would one day escape from Narashino. Maybe she could get into the Royal Academy, and she'd spend her days traveling through the realm, discovering all of Rivelle's treasures.

Working at the inn felt like reliving one of her favorite tales: *The Queen of Thieves.* Queen Natsumi had faced down an angry mob of villagers, ready to burn down the castle of their local ruling Royal Advisor over a rise in taxes so sky-high it was like thievery. The queen—though she'd been only a princess then—had managed to quell their shouts and curled-up fists by negotiating new terms with the Royal Advisor that were finally fair for all. If Queen Natsumi could do that, surely Alliana could face down Stepmother.

When she'd asked Grandmother Mari why nearly all of the realm's Advisors were chosen by birth and not merit of their own—those in the Academy from commoner origins only seemed to become stewards, not Royal Advisors—the old woman had laughed, her wrinkled hand squeezing Alliana's. "Oh, dear one, you see things as they should be, and that is a gift you should share."

Alliana hadn't understood what Grandmother meant by that, but Grandmother's laugh, no matter the reason, was a sliver of sunshine that beamed through the darkness.

"*Where* is the tea?" Stepmother snapped, cutting through her fairy-tale daydreams.

"The water's just boiled." Alliana spun around, a smile smooth as Queen Natsumi's. She wrapped a rag around her hand, grabbed the pot, and poured the bubbling water into the ceramic teapot. Slivers of tea leaves—the nice kind that she'd never gotten a chance to try—swirled through the hot water like dancers at the balls that she'd never get invited to.

Still, Alliana gathered her strength—*just like Queen Natsumi*, she told herself—and lifted up the tea tray with the politest of smiles. "All ready, Stepmother. Shall I carry this over or—"

Stepmother grabbed the tray, rattling the delicate teapot and cups. "You've made me wait long enough," she snarled. "Wipe that smirk off your face. I'll be with Mister Leo in my tearoom. Don't bother us."

Alliana brightened. "Would you mind if Grandmother and I went to the abyss? I can collect more fernleaf; I think Mister Leo will be placing another order soon."

Stepmother's forehead pinched, likely trying to

calculate the value of finding more chores for Alliana to do, compared to what she'd get as a cut of Alliana's fernleaf earnings. "Fine," the woman spat out, her love of coin swaying her. "But one thing."

What demands could Stepmother have now? Alliana had already wiped down the entire entranceway, register, kitchen, *and* main room; changed all the bedsheets; done two vats of laundry and hung it all up to dry....Surely there couldn't be more?

The woman leaned forward, the sour scent of vinegar plums wafting from her teeth. Alliana had to quell the urge to gag. Stepmother's eyebrow rose, like a hand drawing up a dart to aim straight for the bull's-eye, and she spat out, "Mistress Sakamaki is *my* mother-in-law. *Reizo* and *Reina's* dear grandmother. She's not your family. Don't forget that."

Alliana watched her stepmother flounce off to the tearoom, her heart sinking with every step. She knew she didn't have any real family. She *knew* she was alone, even in this crowded, bustling inn.

But having Stepmother grind those words into her as a reminder felt like fresh salt in an already stinging wound. Alliana turned toward the stairs, to head to Grandmother Mari, the only family she'd ever wanted, but the family she'd never have.

Alliana led Grandmother Mari by the arm, keeping an eye on her stepsister in front of them. "Turn to the right!" she called.

They slipped through the rocky crevice that was barely visible from the main path; Alliana's father had first taken her here years ago, when they'd hunted for the elusive fernleaf together and spent the rest of the afternoon adding more entries to his notebook. The dusty road continued on to the main entrance to the abyss, the one that had a door through the shield and allowed adventurers to rappel down to lower platforms in search of treasure. Isao worked there on the days that the diner was slow; he operated the pulley system for messages, so that adventurers on all platforms could get warnings of monster sightings. But Stepmother would probably lock Alliana up forever if she tried to go into the abyss, so this special spot was the closest she ever got.

"Oh, that's where this place is!" Reina giggled, flashing the gap between her two front teeth. "I always forget." The girl ran ahead, dragging her hands along the stone cliffs until they were coated in dirt. Alliana would have to make sure Reina washed off before Stepmother saw her—especially since Stepmother hadn't known that Reina would come along. Then again, Alliana hadn't known, either.

Her stepsister had popped her head out of her bedroom window the instant Alliana had pushed open the side door, helping Grandmother out. "Can I go, too?" she'd chirped. The old woman's eyes had brightened, and Alliana hadn't had the heart to say no. Neither did she have the gumption to ask Stepmother, who was locked up in the tearoom with Mister Leo, his sawlike laugh echoing through the hallways as Stepmother told him not-at-all-funny tales.

Still, today was one of Grandmother Mari's good days. The old woman chatted brightly as she waved her hands around, emphasizing parts of her stories about Queen Natsumi and the other precious tales. The anecdotes were strangely out of order—Grandmother jumped from a story about Queen Natsumi's coronation straight to a tale about Queen Natsumi's parents before the girl was born—but Alliana bathed in the warmth of Grandmother's arm and the happiness ringing with each of her words.

All too soon, they arrived at the hidden meadow, a little oasis nestled against the shield. It was filled with tall, silky grass that hid the curly fernleaf Mister Leo was willing to pay a pretty copper for. This place was so out of the way from the main path that none of the adventurers had discovered it. If she craned her neck and looked through the shield, she would be able to see the long wood structure that made up the first platform and a few adventurers in the far distance: small little dots rappelling into the darkness on their way into caves or down even further to the second platform. She shuddered; even being next to the shield was unsettlingly close.

"Granny, Granny!" Reina had already run ahead to pick a few plants.

"What is it, little one?" Grandmother Mari asked. Though Reina was the same age as Reizo and Alliana, she called her Granny; she didn't use the formal terms that Alliana stuck with, out of respect for the older woman.

"Isn't this pretty?" Reina danced in front of them, clutching a bouquet of leaves with bright red, hard berries.

Alliana's jaw dropped. "Curses, drop that!"

Reina drew the bundle to her chest, her lip sticking out in one of her usual pouts. "No, it's mine! I found it first!"

"Yes," Alliana said, trying to muster up the semblance of calm to reason with her far-from-reasonable step-sister. "That's a very wonderful bouquet. How about we trade?" She looked around wildly and pulled out a square of pretty red fabric from her knapsack. "Have this, and place that bouquet down on the ground, okay? You're holding on to poisonberries, and it might get you sick."

Reina grumbled as she reluctantly placed down her bouquet. The instant the girl let go, Alliana pushed the cloth into her hands. "Wipe your hands down." The tiny square of linen was soaked in beech tar; it was a useful all-purpose tonic for everything from drawing out poison from needle gnats to easing pain from stomachaches.

As she had many times before, Alliana wished for her father's notebook on herbs and natural remedies. She was certain he'd had a page on things that the berries could be used for, but it was impossible to recall the exact recipe. Poisonberries weren't quite something that she could experiment with, either, unlike fernleaf and katori chrysanthemum. But when her father had fallen into the depths of the abyss, his notebook had gone with him.

Reina didn't seem deterred by the encounter with the poisonberries. "Alliana?"

She was busy trying to kick the toxic herbs away without cracking any of the small red fruit. "Yes?"

"Will you and Granny make my gown as red as poisonberries?"

Alliana paused. "Didn't we just make you a new dress?" The day before Reina and Reizo's eleventh birthday, Stepmother had bought yards and yards of vibrant yellow-orange fabric to make a kimono—and had guilted the old woman into finishing it as a gift.

Grandmother and Alliana stayed up all night to sew Reina's birthday dress, and when Alliana brought the kimono downstairs, Stepmother had snatched it from her grasp without a word of thanks. The woman announced, "Here's your present, darling!" as soon as she had sashayed into Reina's bedroom.

The girl's voice had drifted out. "Didn't Alliana and Granny make that?"

"It's from me. Now, don't you like this color? I chose it for you."

Stepmother wouldn't even allow Reina to give credit to Alliana and Grandmother Mari, a nicety that would've been free. And for Alliana's birthday, just three moons after, she'd only received a list of chores.

"I want a red ball gown." Reina pouted, inching back toward the bush teeming with poisonberries. "I want to be chosen as one of the princesses of Rivelle at the Farmlands Ball!"

Alliana's heart clenched. She could only *dream* of a future like that…becoming a princess, attending to *the* Queen Natsumi.

Grandmother smiled. "Ah, but you'd have to get the approval of the local Royal Advisor at the ball, wouldn't you? That's quite a feat….Do they judge by dancing? That doesn't seem quite fair."

"The newspapers say the Royal Advisor has a scrying witch or wizard with them," Alliana blurted out. "And you have to go through years of lessons at the Academy before even getting a chance at the final exam to become a princess of the realm and a potential Royal Advisor. Though, truthfully, all the princesses and princes I've read about have been royal-born. Commoners who go through the Academy just seem to become stewards, other than Queen Natsumi, of course. Well, technically, she is of royal blood, but no one knew that until the end."

Grandmother blinked. "Oh?"

"I...um, just was reading, the other day," Alliana said, trying to force an edge of nonchalance into her voice, as she turned to search for fernleaf amongst the tall grass. She always took in the beat-up books and newspapers that travelers left in their guestrooms after they'd checked out. When she had a spare moment, she scoured them from cover to cover, searching for a mention of Queen Natsumi or the world outside the narrow, dusty limits of Narashino. And the Farmlands Ball was a ticket out, but she'd *never* be allowed there, even if Grandmother asked Stepmother on her behalf.

"Here, another bit." Grandmother stuffed a handful of the curled herbs into Alliana's basket, and then shook her arm. "Ah, my arms feel wobbly as one of Alliana's fresh puddings. What dress shall we make you, Alliana?"

From a few feet away, idly yanking at the grass, Reina frowned. Alliana knew why; there'd be no chance Stepmother would ever let Alliana go to the ball, even if she was of age. Further, there'd be no way Alliana could afford fabric for a dress of her own. But, thankfully, Reina's eyes widened from a distraction. "Ooh, I'll be over there!" Her smooth gown of russet-brown linen sashayed tauntingly as the girl skipped away to the other end of the meadow, after a butterfly.

Alliana looked down. Her "uniform" for the inn— leftovers from her stepfamily's wardrobes—was all she had. The high-waisted black skirt that went down to her knees was comfortable and easy to move around in, whether for carrying baskets of laundry outside to hang up to dry or scouring the kitchen of grime, but it was already becoming threadbare. Her traditional-style shirt, tucked into the waistband of her skirt, had been star-tlingly pretty new, with vibrant fireblossoms dyed onto the creamy white fabric. Stepmother had worn it for one day before she'd soiled the hem. The woman had tossed it in the waste bin, but Alliana had scrubbed the shoyu stain out, brought in the hems—with room to grow—and kept it as her own. All in all, her clothes worked. But they were nothing close to the dreamy, floating dresses or suits that attendees at the balls wore. And she only had her two feet; she'd never be able to ride in the frilled-up horse-drawn carriages she saw in the newspaper.

But she couldn't let Grandmother find out about all the things she didn't have.

"Oh, I still have more than a full year before I'm of age to go to the ball."

"One year is a wink of time," Grandmother said. "At least, it is for little old me, being a hundred times your age."

"A hundred times?" Alliana squinted through the sunlight, calculating it out. "So you're more than a thousand years old?"

"Give or take a few years." Grandmother winked.

Alliana smiled at that; to her, a year, no, a *moon* felt like an endless stretch of dirty dishes to be washed and shirts to be mended. But she was glad Grandmother seemed to find time passed quickly, even when she spent most of her day stuck in the attic.

From one of the trees edging the meadow, a bird trilled a sweet and lonely melody. Grandmother looked up and smiled. "Ah, the crystal pigeon is giving us some lovely company. Even its voice is magical."

"I don't think they're really magical." Alliana eyed the white-gray, plump bird sitting on a thin branch. As much as she cared for the crystal pigeon and the sparrows and doves that fluttered down from the branches whenever Alliana brought out some crumbs for them to eat, the bird didn't seem particularly enchanted; she figured it was just hungry, like the others. "When's the last time you've seen a pigeon cast a charm?"

"Magic takes many forms. I've enough respect for myself to say I carry a bit of thread-magic, and creatures seem to be particularly fond of you, perhaps through some form of magic of your own. It's not always wands and flashes of spells, as you know from the oldest of tales." Grandmother ran her hands through the tall grasses, searching for the fernleaf in the same way her fingers swept along the tapestries, checking for loose threads.

"Besides, crystal pigeons carry the deepest hopes of the wish-maker. I'm most certain that your parents made a wish for your future, Alliana, and that wish combined with your skill with creatures of all kinds is why it stays particularly close to you."

Alliana wished that her parents were *here*. "But pigeons aren't part of the Guild of Magic. They're *birds*."

"Well, they're always quite good at getting your attention." When Alliana looked at her doubtfully, the old woman added, "After all, that pigeon knows exactly when to poop."

Alliana cracked a grin. "I can't argue with that."

Earlier in the morning, Reizo had been stomping around as Alliana cleaned out the chicken coop, scaring the birds, when the crystal pigeon had swooped down, plopping a *meaningful* message onto Reizo's head. Grandmother, who had been resting from that headache she just couldn't seem to shake, had woken to his enraged shout—as had most of the inn. Alliana had commented to the pigeon that the wish didn't seem to be related to relieving itself on Reizo, since it had stayed. Reizo had overheard and locked her in the coop. She'd had to wait for one of the adventurers to come by and let her out, but seeing Reizo finally get part of his due was worth sitting in the dark with the pecking chickens, who all clamored to sit in her lap, coating her in feathers.

They lapsed into a comfortable silence, searching through the tall grasses to pluck out more fernleaf. Before long, they had a sizable mound piled up in the woven basket. *This is one step closer to earning another coin. One copper closer to freedom!*

Alliana cleared her throat. "Grandmother, if you could have anything in the world, what would you dream of?"

The old woman was silent for a moment, musing over Alliana's question, as her hand drifted to cup a tightly closed dusklight flower; the pale purple bud was a rare find in the shadows of the abyss. According to *Foliage and Flora*—the thick, dusty book she'd recovered from a waste bin—these vines grew only on the cliffs of Auteri, one of the port towns of Rivelle Realm. But that was the odd thing about the abyss. Like the creatures that roamed within, the plants also seemed to thrive as if in a world of their own. And like a dusklight flower, time with Grandmother felt just as precious and rare.

"I thought you already knew," Grandmother Mari said. Her eyes drifted over Reina, who was chasing a glowing butterfly that—hopefully—wasn't venomous, and then back toward Alliana. Her eyes creased in that whole-heart smile Alliana cherished. "Happiness for my family, that's everything to me." And before Alliana could have time to think over that answer, the old woman added, "What about you? What brings you joy?"

She froze. *Happiness is life away from Narashino's drudgery. Joy is chasing dreams, even seemingly impossible dreams of traveling to the capital city or seeing Queen Natsumi.*

But how could she tell Grandmother—who was perfectly settled into Narashino—something like that? She couldn't leave the old woman; Reizo refused to bring up her meals and Reina would simply forget. What would Grandmother think of her and Isao's plans to leave? Maybe Grandmother would want to join them. Alliana's heart soared at that thought— they could disappear in the shadows of night, traveling far away from Stepmother.... Between the coppers Alliana earned selling her herbs and remedies, and what Isao brought in from the diner and the odd shifts he took managing the messenger pulleys at the abyss, they should have enough coin scraped together. Perhaps Alliana and Grandmother could earn their keep by embroidering in the capital city while Isao pursued his apprenticeship in one of the realm's top bakeries....

"Grandmother," Alliana said. "Would you want to go to the capital city?"

"Oh, my." The old woman laughed lightly, plucking another fernleaf and adding it to the basket. "Me, go to

Okayama? Alliana, this is my world, here. It makes me happy to spend time with my daughter-in-law and my grandchildren, I—"

"Right. I should've known."

Grandmother was quiet as she ran her hand over the silky soft grass, searching for another hidden fernleaf, and then she paused. Instead of picking up another herb, she put her hand over Alliana's.

"Dear one," Grandmother Mari said, "you must listen carefully. Though you're very good at that—it's one of your talents: to hear the truth...to see more...to believe in more....I have written that letter to you that you shall read someday. I have written it time and time again, trying to get the words just right. But, one day, when you read it, I hope you will agree. I hope you will know how much you can do in your future."

Those were riddles that Alliana didn't understand; she turned to face her. "What do you mean, Grandmother?"

The old woman's hand wrapped around hers. "You... you are meant for more. Look inside..."

There was something strange about the desperate way Grandmother clung to her. Alliana fished in her pocket for her handkerchief. It was too hot out, with a cup of iced barley tea, she'd be fine—

Grandmother Mari faltered, her voice strange and distorted. "You are meant for..."

The girl laughed shakily, dabbing at the old woman's wrinkled forehead with the cloth; she was sweaty in the late afternoon heat. "Grandmother..."

Alliana's words faded as she stared, her hands trembling.

Grandmother Mari's eyes were unfocused, staring at something beyond the girl, something impossibly out of reach....

"Alliana," the old woman whispered. "My family... Take care...my family..."

"Grandmother." Alliana's words were quick and sharp. "Let me take you back to the inn. We'll get you a slice of fresh contomelon and sprinkle on plenty of salt. It'll make you feel right as rain. I—"

"Alliana..." Then—

She tried to grab the old woman, but Grandmother slipped down—

Crumpling to the ground like all the air had been pulled out of her, like she was deflating, and Alliana's heart thundered. *This couldn't be.*

Reina screeched out from somewhere behind them, "Grandmother is dead! She's dead, dead!"

And there was another voice screaming, *No, no, no...* Alliana didn't realize until she bit her own tongue, the blood metallic and hot on her teeth, that the strange, strangled voice was her own....*No, she can't be dead.*

But Grandmother Mari—no matter what Alliana shouted, as she and Reina half carried, half dragged the old woman back to the inn—she didn't wake, her eyes shut, the heartbeat in her wrist far too faint.

As if...as if Grandmother was already gone.

Alliana's arms burned, but she didn't rest—not even when Reina stumbled to a stop, sitting on the side of the path. Alliana lifted the old woman onto her back and rushed her all the way back to the attic, Grandmother Mari's favorite place.

As soon as Alliana laid the old woman gently down on her bed, she looked up at her stepfamily; Reina might've not been able to carry her grandmother, but she'd brought her brother and mother.

Stepmother and Reizo stared down. Even Alliana, despite the pain coursing through her veins, knew that Grandmother's body looked too shrunken and small. Grandmother was as colorless as moonlight, and Alliana's heart felt as bleak as the empty flatlands around the inn.

Reizo knelt next to Grandmother Mari, checking her pulse. Only moments later, he stood and wiped his hands on his trousers as if brushing off the sensation of the old woman's skin. He turned to Stepmother and Reina, who were hovering behind him.

"She's gone," her stepbrother said. "Gran's dead."

The coldness of his words slapped her in the face. Alliana slid to the ground, her knees scraping against the cold tatami. Silent tears of disbelief ran down her cheeks...until she felt Grandmother's ice-cold hands.

The one person who had cared for Alliana like a true guardian...was gone.

CHAPTER FIVE

A FINAL WISH

Alliana knelt at Grandmother Mari's bedside, her heart brimming with sorrow so deep and fathomless that it felt like she had fallen into the abyss, with no light in sight. *Come back. Come back. Come back.*

But the old woman didn't hear, not anymore.

Stepmother clapped her hands, jolting Alliana. "Well, then. I shall take what's mine. Reizo, Reina, let's look for the crystal necklace. That stone should be worth ten gold coins at least. If we melt the chain down, the silver in the chain should amount to another full coin's worth. As a necklace, it's completely out of fashion, unfortunately. You too, Alliana. If you find it, I'll erase your debts to me. Isn't that so kind?" The older woman began rummaging through Grandmother's pockets.

Burn it down? Hot, red anger seared through Alliana,

like Stepmother had stoked the coals in the fireplace. Her voice started as a wobble, but grew steadier, fueled by rage. "She just passed. How *dare* you try to search her body?"

The older woman snorted. She had no qualms, not if there was a crystal necklace to be found. "It's not in her pockets. Reina, you look through the fabrics. Reizo, check those drawers."

"No!" Alliana burst out, but her stepfamily didn't listen.

"Look at all of this!" Reina grabbed a basket of fabric pieces and began digging through it, scattering scraps all over the floor. "There's so many colors!"

Reizo was yanking out all the metal tins and prying the lids off, one by one. Grandmother's precious rice crackers tumbled to the ground, scattering onto her cushions. "Nothing. Everything's worthless."

"Those are her favorite!" Alliana cried, pushing Reizo away.

"Guess what? Gran's *dead*. She doesn't need them anymore," he said, and shoved her back. She tumbled to the ground with a thump, her eyes watering.

Isao's head popped in through the doorway, his forehead knotted with concern. He was carrying a basket of bread: the week's delivery for Stepmother's meals. He opened his mouth, but Alliana quickly shook her head, putting her finger to her lips, and willed for him to understand her plea. *Get help.*

Alliana couldn't stop her stepfamily from ransacking Grandmother's room. But if she'd learned anything from the old woman's tales, heroes were never as alone as they'd thought. True, she was no character from a fairy tale, but for the old woman who she'd loved, she had to try.

She snatched Grandmother's precious embroidery box out from under Reizo's heel. "That's full of needles!" Alliana cried out. Even if Reizo didn't see the worth in it, perhaps reasoning that he might get hurt could save it from being crushed.

Reizo's eyes shone with glee as he took in Alliana's concern. He yanked out one of the small drawers, sending strips of ribbons fluttering through the air. "I guess I'll take my time dismantling this one, piece by piece, to make sure there's no needles or necklace. Right, Alliana?" His fingers poised at the edge.

"Stop, stop, *stop*!" Alliana shouted, but Reizo only grinned wider, and yanked straight down.

Rippp. The noise tore at Alliana's heart.

"Hello, there!" A sudden, loud voice from the doorway startled Reizo, making him drop the drawer. Alliana swooped in, clutching the broken drawer to her chest, her eyes smarting with tears.

A tall, broad-shouldered adventurer stood at the top

of the ladder, looking around curiously with her sharp, bright eyes. "I'm...I'm here to pick up my mending." Then her eyes went straight to Grandmother's body. "Oh, my! Grandmother Mari, are you okay?"

"She passed away," Alliana sobbed out.

The woman let out a cry of shock, particularly loud, and clamored off the rungs and into the attic. Her knapsack shoved Stepmother away from Grandmother's nightstand, where she'd been snooping inside. "Isn't this terribly sad, Innkeeper?"

"Why—why—" Stepmother spluttered, shoving the thin books back. "I didn't expect visitors so soon. I—I was just cleaning things up. Yes. Very sad, so sad." Hastily, she grabbed her children, pulling them to her side.

The adventurer's commotions drew more attention, and more guests came by to show their dismay for the old woman's passing. And from below, Alliana spotted Isao, peering up at her worriedly.

Thank you, she mouthed.

Mister Leo clambered up the ladder, huffing. "Grandmother has passed?" He sidled over to Stepmother. "I'm terribly sorry, Fusako. So sorry. You must be feeling poorly, but I'm here for you."

Stepmother's eyes shifted, looking around at everyone paying their respects. With a dramatic cry, she pulled out a frilly, bright purple handkerchief. "Oh," she wailed, "I can't believe that my *darling* mother-in-law is gone!"

The guests, Mister Leo in particular, patted her back and piled on syrupy condolences for Stepmother, who had never given her mother-in-law a moment's attention unless it was to get a pile of mending done.

"I can help you make arrangements," Mister Leo said. "I can go by the Royal Advisor and file the paperwork to receive her will."

Stepmother's beady eyes peeked out from behind her handkerchief. "That's right. Her *will*. We shouldn't linger, let us do that—"

"We'll get her cremated straightaway, and then buried. By then, the Royal Advisor's secretary should be able to send over the will, and I can help read it out. I'll try to speed things up, so you can get on with your lives, of course."

"But I am so despondent! Mistress Sakamaki! Dead!" Stepmother broke into another chain of sobs, likely saddened that she couldn't receive the will straightaway. Her fingers inched toward Grandmother's embroidery box, to check it again.

"Poor Mother!" Reina cried, misreading her gesture, and piled two dirty handkerchiefs she'd pulled from her pocket into her mother's hand.

Alliana didn't believe Stepmother's dramatics for a second. She watched the older woman's eyes dart around one more time, searching for the crystal necklace and trying to appraise the rest of Grandmother's belongings, before resigning herself to fake-sobbing on Mister Leo's shoulder.

Grandmother's body was taken away for cremation; her ashes would be sent to a grave in the eastern Farmlands, where the rest of the Sakamaki and Enokida family were buried. It all happened so fast: One moment, Alliana was holding Grandmother Mari's hand; the next, she was alone in the attic, curled up on the floor, clutching the plush white cushions Grandmother had sewn. Alliana hungrily breathed in the slightly musty scent of straw and cedar and linen. Her last trace of the old woman.

As day inched into night, Alliana tried to sleep. Stepmother had tried to command Alliana to tend to her chores, but for once, Alliana had snapped back. Stepmother had retreated, anger simmering in her stiff shoulders. No amount of threatened debt could take Alliana away from Grandmother's attic, nor pull her out of the deep darkness of mourning.

This can't be true, she repeated to herself. *This can't be, this can't...*

All that answered her was the crystal pigeon, cooing from the windowsill. She cursed at the bird, shooing it away with flapping hands. It fluttered with a squawk and returned moments later.

Maybe—maybe it was a sign. Alliana brushed her hand against the wood panel next to the window. Perhaps Grandmother had left the crystal necklace for her to find.

She slowly pushed the board to the side, her breath caught in her throat.

Nothing.

Grandmother's secret spot was bare and empty, cleaned out. Even the wood box with the tapestry was gone.

The girl fell into a restless sleep, hoping with all her heart that when she woke, Grandmother would push over a cup of green tea and smile, laughing and saying she'd overslept. Alliana wished fiercely for a morning that she knew would never come again.

In the early hours of the next day, Reina shook her shoulder. "Alliana. *Alliana.*"

"I will not work today—"

Reina shook her head. "It's Granny's will. You're in it."

Then Alliana heard the thump of Stepmother's heavy tread on the stairs, followed by Mister Leo's greasy chatter. Alliana had barely scrambled to her feet before Stepmother burst into the room, Reizo and Mister Leo in her wake. The older woman stomped into the center, and Alliana could sense the way her greedy eyes were calculating the worth of everything, from the bolts of muslin to the jars of pearl buttons.

Mister Leo patted down his pockets and pulled out a thin scroll.

"What does it say?" Alliana blurted out. She didn't want anything for herself; all she wanted to hear was Grandmother Mari's precious words one more time.

Stepmother's face soured, wrinkling like a salted plum. "Ah. Alliana. Did you finish your chores for today? You've got other things to attend to—"

"Complete. *All* of them." It wasn't as if Stepmother would go through the effort of walking back down to check.

The woman narrowed her eyes. She snapped her fingers at Reina. "Go. Inspect."

"Aw, I just got here!" the girl huffed. Reizo shoved her toward the door.

A few tense minutes later, Reina popped her head into the attic. "Mother, I checked, and the silverware looks polished enough, and the tin of rice crackers was full, so I went outside to look at the laundry lines. But then I dropped my cracker in the well and I couldn't fish it out and—"

"Oh, shut it!" Stepmother snapped, her fingers pressing

on her temples. She waved her hand at Mister Leo. "Go on, read it."

THE WILL OF MARI SAKAMAKI
as confirmed by
Royal Advisor Kenzo Miwa
❋ ❋ ❋

For Fusako Enokida—thank you for taking in an old woman like me. All that is mine is yours, except for:

Reizo Enokida—my leather wristwatch, from your late grandfather. Shall it help you always understand the right time.

Reina Enokida—my brass compass. I once traveled far with that, and I hope it may accompany you, too.

Alliana—may you take the memories of the times we spent together and my embroidery box. May you always spin new tales.

Mister Leo cleared his throat. "That's it."

Reizo snorted. "Memories! I hope that feeds you well. And what good is a few spools of thread going to do?"

Alliana wouldn't trade her inky midnights with

Grandmother for anything; they sparkled in her heart brighter than a star-studded sky. Still, she steeled her spine; truthfully, there was something she wanted to take. "If no one wants them...I'd like just one of the cushions." She glanced down at the soft white-and-gold pillows that she and Grandmother had sat on, for countless sewing sessions. It might be bulky, but she could fit it into her knapsack. Surely it'd be useful on the road, too, when she, Isao, and Hiroshi escaped Narashino.

"As *if*." Stepmother scowled. "Those—and the tapestries—are *mine*. Along with the crystal necklace, whenever it shows up. You heard the will."

"Mother's still looking for it," Reina said, opening up the box Mister Leo had handed her. It was made of the same reinforced paperboard as Grandmother's sewing box. She pulled out a heavy compass, with a flower etched in the bronze front. "Ah, look! I think that's rather nice of Grandmother to remember that time I wanted to explore the Walking Cliffs."

Reizo made a noise of disgust, tossing his emptied box onto the dresser. "Grandmother gave *me* her wristwatch, so I can look appropriate when I finally meet the Royal Advisor. At least I got something useful."

"At least my gift will guide me in the right direction!" Reina protested. "Who are *you* to say what I'll do?"

Stepmother clapped her hands. "All right, you three,

bring my tapestries downstairs. They need to go on display to sell."

Reina and Reizo were still bickering, but Alliana didn't listen; her eyes were glued to the embroidery box sitting on the low table. As she tentatively stepped toward it, her stepbrother pushed her out of the way.

"Why would she give you a stupid embroidery box— did she know that mending is all you're ever going to do in life?" Reizo snorted. He picked it up and tossed it into the air, the drawers loosening and spools of thread tumbling to the ground. The key to the attic spilled out, but that wasn't silver; her stepfamily didn't care about that. The boy surveyed the mess around him and snorted. "See? Useless."

"It's not useless!" Alliana cried.

Reizo kicked a round of ruby red thread; he didn't know it was a full four coppers. To Alliana, it was more than a thousand coppers. It was the faint red on Queen Natsumi's cheeks on the tapestries. It was the scarlet berries she'd helped Grandmother sew....It was a moment of laughter as Grandmother had pretended to gobble up the thread-and-fabric berries when Alliana's stomach had growled, and the pillowy slices of Baumkuchen Grandmother had dished out moments later.

Even if he had known these memories, he wouldn't have cared, because he never cared about the old woman, and he definitely didn't care about Alliana.

She stifled her cry as she collected the spools back

into the box. One of the drawers had broken into two, and her heart ached. She could make up a batch of the starchy paper glue, but it would never be the same.

"Gather my tapestries. *Now!*" Stepmother snapped. "Don't leave a single item here that belongs to me. Take everything down to my tearoom. I've been wanting new cushions."

Her stepsiblings began pulling the tapestries off the wall, grumbling, until their mother boxed their ears.

Alliana was too stunned to move. She'd thought that... that perhaps having something of Grandmother Mari's would feel like the old woman was back, just a little. But her heart still felt empty, as empty as the attic was getting as Reizo and Reina yanked down the glittering tapestries and exposed the bare boards.

Then Reizo tugged too hard, ripping the tapestry of Queen Natsumi. She cried out, pulling her stepbrother away, "Stop! Don't wreck them!"

"Go back to tending the chicken coop if you're not going to help," Reizo snarled, shaking her off.

Alliana felt like a shadowsnake, fangs flashing. "I don't have to stay."

Her stepfamily and even Mister Leo, from where he was simpering over Stepmother by the window, stopped and stared. A ripple of shock passed through her stepbrother's face, like a fish flopping out of water. "You—you *have* to—"

"Exactly," Stepmother seethed, taking her purple

ledger out of her dress pocket, snapping the pages in front of Alliana's nose. "You are in debt to me."

Alliana shook her head, the past five years seeping through her like the venom of a shadowsnake, acid in every word. "I will not work under you, not under these terms, not for another day. I am done."

Stepmother gaped.

"Your debt! You owe me—"

Alliana raised her head. "I will repay you, even if it means I have to send good coin back here, but there is no reason for me to stay."

Alliana gathered up one of the white pillows— Stepmother had a daybed full of soft blankets and thick cushions anyway—and Grandmother's broken embroidery box. "I stayed for Grandmother Mari. It is time for me to move on."

Stepmother spluttered. "I am your legal guardian! You will not be able to apprentice anywhere in the realm, not without my approval! The guards won't let you into the Farmlands Ball—"

"Apprenticeship or none, there is no reason for me to stay."

"I want you to stay," Reina piped up. "Grandmother Mari does, too."

Alliana spun around. "How do you—what—"

Reina held out a thin folded paper, a wax seal broken. "It fell out of the embroidery box. Grandmother

Mari wrote it to you. It was sealed but, well, I might've opened it?"

Alliana felt like the attic had collapsed around her, and she'd tumbled to the hard, dusty ground. *From Grandmother Mari…*

The letter. Grandmother Mari had finished it, finally.

Stepmother plucked it from Reina's hands, keeping it clear from the sleeve of her kimono; her fingers barely touched it, like it was repulsive, as she scanned the contents. "Indeed. This…this is for you." She let go of the thin piece of paper with a look of disgust, and the letter floated into Alliana's hands.

The woman seemed to vanish from Alliana's periphery to grab at more of Grandmother's stuff, or maybe she'd stomped off in one of her usual bad moods. Alliana didn't know, and honestly didn't care, because—

To my dear Alliana

The gentle, thin handwriting…the sun-soaked barley color of the envelope…the faint scent of straw, like the attic was woven into the very strands of the paper.

It was *the* letter from Grandmother Mari.

With trembling hands, Alliana traced her fingernails along the inky grooves of the words, as if she could find Grandmother in them. Slowly, slowly, she broke open the envelope.

Dearest Alliana—

I have written this many times. But there are sometimes not enough words to properly explain my thoughts. For, if you are reading this, it means I have passed on. But let us not dwell on that; I write this now, for you. For you to continue on, after I am long gone.

Do you remember how, so late in the night, you asked me what I dreamed of?

Alliana, I dream of my family. I dream of finding happiness for the ones I love. My daughter-in-law, my two dear grandchildren. I want you to take care of my family in every way you can. Because they need your help, and I know I can trust you to take this on, right?

With love,
Grandmother Mari

Alliana had heard an echo of these words directly from Grandmother Mari just before she'd collapsed: *It makes me happy to spend time with my daughter-in-law and my grandchildren.*

Still, this hadn't been what Alliana had hoped for. This wasn't what she'd wanted as Grandmother's last message.

She lowered the paper, and Reizo raised an eyebrow from where he was rolling up the tapestry of Kintarō, the metal of his wristwatch flashing in the weak light.

"You look like you're greedy for more than a moldy paper embroidery box and letter," he snorted. "Too bad. That's all you get."

Alliana's heart twisted. She hadn't cared for gold or heirlooms or crystal necklaces. But she'd never expected *this*.

She turned, rushing away from her stepfamily, her heart and mind whirling in confusion.

It makes me happy to spend time with my daughter-in-law and my grandchildren.

Take care of my family.... I can trust you to take this on, right?

CHAPTER SIX

A FLICKER OF LIGHT

Late in the night, Alliana stole out of the inn. As she passed by the rooms of the guests and her stepfamily, they snored peacefully. Her life felt like it had been ripped apart, but theirs continued on. Perhaps that was from the way the threads of Grandmother Mari's life had felt like they were sewn into hers, tightly woven together. Now, Alliana was missing a part of her that felt irrepairable.

At the crossroads, Alliana stared up at the wood signs creaking in the faint wind. *The path of dreams.*

As heartbroken as she was today, she couldn't truly leave Narashino. Not unless she left as a candidate for the Royal Academy. Grandmother Mari had supported that, at least, even though Alliana would never get the chance to go to the ball.

She looked over her shoulder toward the inn. It was

only a pinprick, and there was no one on the dusty road—
even the adventurers drew away from the abyss at night.
And, at least, Stepmother or her stepsiblings hadn't followed her; they were soundly asleep.

Grief colored her vision as Alliana stood alone in the
meadow where she and Grandmother Mari had had their
last conversation.

She needed to see this place for herself: the last place
she had seen Grandmother Mari standing and talking
and *alive*—

It was far too beautiful. Bright moonlight and the
shimmering white-clear barrier gleamed, illuminating the
thin trees swaying in the summer breeze. From the smattering of trees along the rocks, birds cooed sleepily to
one another and the shield hummed on the far end of the
meadow. On any other day, it would've been a wonderful
moment to spend alone. But today, she dropped down
into the tall grass, burying her head in arms, her chest
choking up with sobs. She fought to be strong, fought
to remember every detail about her father—the way his
voice sounded like the crackly fire at night and his tickly
whiskers when he kissed her forehead. Alliana tried to
hold on to the stories her father had shared of her mother,
the kindness she always showed each of the guests, inviting them into the inn as a home away from their own.
And she tried to sew memories of Grandmother Mari
into each beat of her heart—how she'd always have a

rice cracker or small treat to share with Alliana, how her smile would be so radiant upon seeing Alliana slip through the attic door.

"Father, Mother, Grandmother Mari," she whispered. "If you were here, everything would be different. I miss you. I miss you so much."

A hot tear trickled down her cheek as she fought down the urge to wail.

"Grandmother, I wanted to change things for you. I wanted you to have freedom, a room—no, a *house*, truly your own. I'm sorry, Grandmother."

Alliana lifted her face up to the sparkling stars, wondering if Grandmother Mari was looking down on her. Her heart ached for a sign as she searched the endless galaxies, glowing and burning bright, when all she could remember was the pallor of Grandmother's still face.

Utter silence.

Then a particularly hot breeze blazed against her skin. She spun around to stare at the shield and noticed a small tatter toward the bottom, where noise and light leaked through. In her haze of grief, she hadn't seen the dark shadows whizzing past, the flickers of orange-red light glowing. A roar rumbled the ground, muffled by the shield's spells; the nearby roosting birds took off in a clamor. From within the flock, the crystal pigeon let out a deep coo, and fluttered off toward the crossroads.

Against her better judgment tugging at her to stay

safe, Alliana pushed past the tall grasses and crept to a boulder next to the shield, ready to hide behind the rock.

It turned out that the rock was the *least* safe spot. Claw marks scored the shield, the ruined patchwork of spells fluttering like a torn curtain.

She'd heard tales of the endless black of the abyss, but it was a shock to her eyes. It was an ocean of thick ink, a world lost in night.

But she could see what was happening right at the edge.

Alliana had heard about fireworks. They'd been written about a few times in old newspapers that she'd collected from guestrooms. Or maybe this was an aerial form of the glowing lightfish that migrated past the Rivelle coast. She imagined that must look like this: brilliant streaks of fire blazing amidst utter darkness.

Then a trail of fireworks drew up, up, until it slammed against the barrier, and with a sheen of moonlight and the glow from the sparking patchwork of spells, Alliana gaped.

There was a colossal, angry shriek, then a returning challenge from a much smaller flying creature. The beasts were battling in bursts of flame and sparking fangs and claws. In the darkness, she couldn't make out their exact forms, but she could see that the larger beast was attacking the smaller flying creature, who had its back to Alliana and the barrier.

Alliana was about to hurry away from the gap—she didn't want to get scorched by a wayward pillar of flames—when she heard a high-pitched cry.

"*Cheep, cheep!*" She looked around, but the birds were all gone. It was a young, tiny creature that Alliana couldn't see, nor whose call she could recognize.

Then again—"*Cheep!*" The sound was coming from *within* the barrier.

The larger creature roared, sending its tail out to slam its opponent, and that was when lights sparked from the fight, illuminating a tiny, shivering bundle on the edge of the cliff. The gigantic challenger tried to fly past, but the smaller creature pushed back, fiercely guarding its young.

Perhaps the smaller creature had brought the little bundle here during the chase. Alliana was sure that the flying beasts—whatever these shadowy animals might be—didn't roost close to the barrier. Especially within sight of the abyss entrance—the adventurers would've noticed them the instant they'd started rappelling down to mine treasure, and tried to capture the wild beasts to secure a gold bounty instead.

Then the larger creature snapped out, and there was a shriek. The smaller beast tumbled down into the darkness. The predator let out a triumphant roar and flew toward the tiny bundle on the ledge.

There were vicious creatures—like shadowsnakes, or their far scarier cousins, nightdragons—but there were peaceful creatures, too, that simply had gotten stuck in the abyss when the rift first formed, hundreds of years ago, and had adapted to life in the darkness ever since. Perhaps the little one was a descendent of those. With that defenseless, sad cry, Alliana knew the small creature couldn't fend for itself.

But she couldn't get through the barrier, claw-slashed though it was. She hastily plucked a stem of grass and held it out. It sizzled immediately, smoking and crumbling into embers.

Through the gaps, she watched the larger creature approach. She could make out *two* long necks and massive heads the size of a stove; its eyes gleamed like coals.

This...this was a nightdragon. And, with a sinking feeling, Alliana realized that the small animal on the ledge was its prey.

"*Cheep, cheep!*" The helpless creature's cry grew shriller in the face of its predator.

Alliana should walk, no, *run* away. She should return to the inn, where it was safe. Where she could wait another year for the Farmlands Ball, and return to mourning Grandmother...

But before she knew it, she was using all her strength to haul a rock, and she tossed the small boulder onto the broken part of the shield.

The barrier sizzled at the rock, searing vibrant crimson, but the gap stretched—just big enough for Alliana to wiggle over the stone and get through. There wasn't much time before the spells burned through the rock, though.

Another shriek ripped through the air. The smaller dragon—for, from this close, Alliana could also see its scaly back and long wings—shot up in a burst of flame, shrieking at the two-headed nightdragon.

Alliana slid off the rock and into the abyss just as the two dragons collided, the vibrations rippling through the air. Unforgivingly freezing winds scraped at her like fingernails of ice.

Fear burned worse than the cold; sweat trickled down Alliana's forehead. The abyss was a desolate, lightless world, but she couldn't waste a second looking at anything other than the direct route to the tiny bundle, ten or so yards out to her left.

One step too far, and she'd tumble down into the abyss. The path was rocky and no more than a yard wide; she wanted to inch her way down, but there was no time.

Alliana tried to think of how she'd dodged the mop Stepmother *accidentally* dropped in her way as she was walking with two full trays of plates. Or when Reizo shoved his basket of dirty laundry at her, so she had to step around it extra quickly to avoid having it slam down on her feet.

Before she knew it, she was at the side of the tiny

creature, kneeling on the rocky ledge. She didn't have much time to study it, but she caught a glimpse of dark emerald hide, a flash of yellow eyes. It was no bigger than her two fists put together, huddled in the shadows.

"I'm going to take you with me, okay?" Alliana said. "To safety."

The creature, despite its tiny size, had a round belly, four short legs ending in claws, and smooth, hard skin as leathery as a shadowsnake. It couldn't be a nightdragon—Alliana didn't see its wings, nor had she ever heard of a teacup-sized dragon. And the lost, innocent way it gazed up at Alliana looked like anything but those vicious predators.

"Cheep?" It sniffed, lifting its muzzle up to prod Alliana's hand. And in the next second, the wild animal leaped into her arms.

Alliana couldn't waste a moment. She spun around, pebbles spraying down into the abyss, and hurried back, the warm weight of the creature held tight to her chest.

One yard, two. They were making it: The two night-dragons still battled to their left; the barrier was closer. She was halfway there, and—

"No, no," Alliana cried out.

The larger nightdragon slashed at the smaller nightdragon, and it let out a wounded whimper—and once again, tumbled down into the darkness. This time, Alliana feared, by how quickly it fell, it would not return.

The tiny creature in Alliana's arms squirmed, letting out a soul-piercing shriek.

They were only three yards away from the rip in the barrier, but the larger nightdragon soared toward them, sleek as a wood pigeon, yet a thousand times more deadly. Its hide was scarred with claw marks and old burns: markers of battles won.

The nightdragon swiveled its heads left and then right, its eyes not used to the brightness of the barrier.

Alliana dared not breathe. She clutched the little creature to her chest, begging it not to squirm, and she *ran*.

CHAPTER SEVEN

HATCHLING

Alliana had never run so fast; her lungs burned from the burst of speed. The nightdragon snapped, biting down on rock. The cliff crumbled behind her, and she cried out as she scrambled for footing.

This cannot be where my tale ends. Grandmother had wanted Alliana to fight on, even without her. She couldn't let her down.

She leaned forward, with one arm still tucked around the tiny creature, and grabbed at the shield with her right hand. Alliana let out a shriek as her skin burned from the pain, but that sacrifice gave her enough leverage to push herself up. She barreled down the last few yards; the shield had nearly burned through the entire rock, and it was closing up—

Alliana dove through the gap, but the opening had

shrunk; her left arm was going to graze against the scorching spells.

She braced herself for the pain but there was no time to think. She heard a sharp sizzle, and the next second she was tumbling out into the tall grasses, scrambling to lie low, out of the sight of the furious nightdragon. The enormous creature's two heads swirled back and forth, flames bursting against the shield, but it did not find its prey.

Alliana had her face pressed unceremoniously into a patch of shokyo leaves, the greens bitter and sharp. She had never welcomed a mouthful of dirt so much.

The little creature wiggled out from under her arm and pawed at her nose, and she slowly sat up. Beyond the barrier, the abyss was as dark as ever. The nightdragon was gone, probably to search elsewhere for its prey.

She took stock of herself. Unbelievably, like some sort of magic, she was safe. Where Alliana's arm should have been burned, her skin was intact. *How?* Perhaps the shield was magical enough to detect whether one belonged in Rivelle. But then it wouldn't have singed her before, or maybe—

"*Oh*," she whispered. A bright red, fresh wound seared the tiny creature's cheek. It was a singe mark that could only be from the magical shield. The little creature had tucked its snout around Alliana's arm to prevent her from getting hurt.

As she caught her breath, wiping the sweat off her forehead, she pulled out a tin of salve from her pocket and scooped up a bit of the tar-like beechwood ointment. It was a precious concoction, something that she regularly sold to adventurers for a whole gold coin—though Stepmother took nearly all of that as her "cut." But this tiny animal needed it just as much as any human; she couldn't let it be in pain.

Alliana hovered her hand close to the creature's cheek. She leaned in—just in case the gigantic nightdragon had particularly good hearing—and murmured gently, "I'm going to rub this on, okay? It's going to help you."

Yellow eyes studied her for a second, as if trying to decipher her words. Then, to her surprise, the creature stilled, turning its cheek toward her.

It jolted as she gently painted the cool ointment onto its cheek and let out a squeak as her fingertips brushed against its wound.

"Shh," Alliana murmured, glancing around. "How about I tell you a story?"

The creature blinked, crossing its front legs and pillowing its head on top, turned its head slightly to the side, and made a few squeaks that sounded strangely like, *I'm all ears!*

Alliana cleared her throat and whispered the beginning of a story. "A long, long time ago, before the rift cracked the land in two, splitting Rivelle from Constancia...Stay still! I can't remember the story and get this on you!"

Okay, okay!

A young, high-pitched voice echoed through Alliana's mind and she fell backward onto the grass staring in shock. When she glanced over her shoulder, the meadow was as empty as before. Not even a bird roosted in the trees.

Which only left...

Alliana turned back to the creature in front of her, staring up with wide, yellow eyes, its front legs still crossed but wiggling impatiently. *More more more storytime!*

"The—the ointment first," Alliana said, too shocked to recall the tale.

A few moments later, half the ointment from the tin was on the wriggly creature—some on its cheek, but most of it all over its face, because it seemed to like the feel of the greasy salve on its leathery skin. The creature wiggled and wiggled, shaking out its long spiked tail, and shifted, happily stretching out its long black wings.

Wings. Spiky tail. A leathery hide...

She frowned.

Alliana breathed in and spoke in the clear-as-crystal voice that she used when repeating Grandmother's most cherished stories. "A long, long time ago, before the rift cracked the land in two, splitting Rivelle from Constancia, dragons flew through the sky. The fiercest of them were the nightdragons, wild creatures that ruled over the rest, with their sleek, dark hide, their spiked tails that could swipe down an army, and fangs sharper than a thousand daggers....It is said that during those long-ago times, dragons could communicate with us, but that art has long since been lost...."

She stared between the hole in the shield, and then down at the creature now cheerily rolling around in her lap, smearing ointment everywhere.

"You're...you're a *nightdragon* hatchling," Alliana whispered.

The dragon cooed back with a flash of its tiny fangs. *Of course! That's why the Elders were fighting over me. The one that takes me under their wing claims me for their thunder. But* they *didn't win. I'm glad that bigger Elder didn't, he's not very nice.*

Panic swirled through Alliana. What was she supposed to do with a *nightdragon*? She didn't dare bring the hatchling home. If her stepfamily caught sight of the nightdragon babe, Stepmother and Reizo would drag him over to the Royal Advisor to claim the bounty. Being as legendary as they were, a nightdragon was worth a hefty lacquer chest stuffed with gold. She could just imagine her stepbrother declaring heroics over capturing a defenseless, tiny creature, and Stepmother using the coin to drape herself in more useless, clanking lacquer jewelry.

"What's your name?" she asked. "I'm Alliana."

I don't have a name, Alliana! the nightdragon cheerfully replied. *Nightdragons don't receive names until they choose one of their own. How'd you get your name?*

"My parents chose it for me. They thought it sounded pretty and had great meaning, because it's kind of like 'alliance.' Though, what kind of alliances they expect from me is yet to be seen, unless they count chickens—"

A shrill screech came from the entrance to the meadow. Alliana whirled around to see a cloud of dust in front of which Stepmother stomped, with Mister Leo close behind.

"You had better not be trying to escape, not with your mountain of debt!" the woman screeched.

Fear froze Alliana. Her debt was worrying, but the thought of the little nightdragon getting caught was even worse.

What is it? Who is that? The curious hatchling started crawling out of Alliana's hands.

She tried to think at it, *Stop! Wait!*

But, like the tales of old, the dragon seemed to be able to speak to her mind, but not to hear her speak to his. She didn't know how to talk to *minds*. Alliana grabbed at the nightdragon, but he slipped out, leathery hide sliding between her fingertips. She hurried in front, careful not to step on the nightdragon's long tail. Quickly, her heart in her throat, she called out, "I was just collecting fernleaf. But if you step too far into the meadow, you might crush it!"

Mister Leo's eyes popped open, and he pulled Stepmother back—not that the woman would ever willingly soil her gowns by trampling through the meadow's tall grasses.

"Get back here *now!*" Stepmother shouted, shaking her fist.

There wasn't much time. Alliana ignored the complaints of her stepmother—and Mister Leo's requests for the freshest fernleaf—as she bent down, under the guise of picking herbs, to speak quickly to the hatchling. "You *have* to hide. But you're not safe in the abyss—"

I'll be fine! The hatchling set his stout front legs on Alliana's knees and puffed up his chest. *I'm small enough to hide in spots the cruel dragon won't reach. Fast enough to fly. Stronger than he realizes!* Then he paused. *You're coming with me, right?*

Alliana's heart ached. "I cannot survive in the abyss, the same way you cannot stay out here, in Rivelle."

The nightdragon nuzzled her thumb, turned in a circle, and plopped down. *It's comfortable with you. You're nice. You helped me. You have tickly grease I can smear all over my snout. I want to stay with you.*

The nightdragon put his fangs around Alliana's thumb, and for a split second, she expected him to bite down. Instead he held her thumb ever so gently, as if holding on to her in any way he could.

"I will take care of you." The promise beat through Alliana's blood, tying itself deep into her soul. "I know what it is like to be alone, to be abandoned. So I'll be here for you."

But you're telling me to go.

"For now, for your safety. But every time I come back here, I'll leave food for you, right here." Alliana gestured at the crevice between the rock and the tatters in the shield. But the nightdragon stared at her, wanting something more. "I'll return as often as I can—but if someone is with me, *don't* come out, okay?" She shuddered. Reizo and Stepmother truly would sell the hatchling in an instant.

The nightdragon stared up at her, studying her to see if she really was telling the truth.

She brushed her free hand below the hatchling's cheek, careful not to touch his wound, and nodded. "I promise. I will return."

Then, finally, he let out a little squeak of happiness. *Promise! Promise!*

With that, the nightdragon slipped back into the abyss. Through the gap, Alliana could see his slender wings expanding, like a rippling mirror of the pitch-black sky. But before he disappeared into the darkness, the hatchling paused once, wings fluttering and his head craning over his shoulder, and Alliana felt like she was being truly looked at not just for who she was, but, most of all, who she could become.

Promise.

PART TWO
One Year Later

CHAPTER EIGHT

MOCHI

A *che. Ache, ache.* Every bone, every inch of skin ached. Last night, Alliana had barely caught an hour of sleep. She'd mended shirts until the first glimmers of dawn, falling asleep on her unfinished pile. And tonight—with all the cleaning she had to do before she could even start on her mending—was looking to be quite the same. Still, she folded her wet rag and began meticulously wiping down the tables crusted with Stepmother's root vegetable curry, which the woman had declared the best in the realm to all the guests.

Alliana was twelve years old now. Old enough to attend the Farmlands Ball and pretend she had a chance at becoming a princess. Old enough to apply as an apprentice for a guild—any guild would do, so long as it was far from Narashino—if only she didn't need her stepmother's permission. Her future glimmered just out of her reach; just a few more moons of this drudgery, and she'd have her chance to attend the ball.

Alliana tucked a flyaway strand back into her braid; her hair now reached beyond the bottom of her shoulder blades, though she braided it into a crown around her forehead. It helped to keep her hair out of her face, especially when she slipped out of the inn to hurry over to the hidden meadow and leave a square or two of mochi or a packet of natto for the little nightdragon. The treats always seemed to disappear by the next day, though she hadn't been able to meet him since the first time. Every time, she'd had to rush back to the inn to avoid Stepmother's increasing scrutiny; it seemed to get worse with each day that they got closer to the Farmlands Ball. And if she was there to collect herbs, Reizo or Reina always accompanied her. The nightdragon had made good on not popping up if she had company, but she swore that certain afternoons felt warmer than usual.

Alliana set the wire grill over the flickering embers of the dining room fireplace and placed a small, tough-as-a-rock mochi on top. The room was dark and usually empty—no one around to notice as she toasted the rice cake. This time, there was a traveler slumped over the table in the corner, her cloak wrapped around her, probably snoring after one mug too many of honey cider. Alliana returned to sweeping up the room, making sure to get every corner so Stepmother couldn't have a fit, her eyes occasionally drifting back to her dinner, waiting for it to be ready. She steered clear of the sleeping guest, though, to let her rest.

Reizo had laughed when the older woman had brought out Alliana's dinner—the plain block of mochi was a far cry from the thick curry and shiny white rice that the inn guests and her stepfamily gobbled down. But she'd learned her lesson from protests many times before, and only thanked Stepmother, patiently waiting for her stepfamily to go to sleep. Plus, Alliana had snuck in a pinch of an itching herb to Stepmother's sheets. The woman would sleep fine enough, but she'd wonder why her skin was all scratched up by her long nails when she woke.

Alliana knelt at the fireplace and wrapped a rag around her hand, removing the burning-hot grill. Reizo could laugh all he wanted; she wouldn't tell him that the heat puffed the rice cake up like a balloon, the inside melting sticky-soft and the outside toasted and crackly, like the rolls that Reizo waved in front of her face when her stomach growled. She'd get the last laugh tonight, and a delicious meal at that.

With a drizzle of shoyu, the salty seasoning that was all the rage around the realm, the puffed-up mochi was fit for a queen. Or, at least, fit for Alliana, the queen of dust and sooty fireplaces.

Alliana set down the miniature pitcher of shoyu, pinched the hot mochi on the corners, and lifted it up for a bite of the crackly yet soft treat and—

"Oh, curses!"

Alliana jumped at the sudden outburst, banging her knee on the molten-hot grill. The mochi plopped onto the hearthstone, instantly coated black with soot.

The traveler in the corner still had her head tucked on the table, but she continued muttering in her sleep. "If there are shadowsnakes, surely we can get rid of them all in one go! I wouldn't want to, but Hayato will be all for that, I suppose. Can't Taichi just tell us…"

The girl let out a loud snore. Alliana grimaced at her mochi, dusting off the majority of the charcoal. If she closed her eyes, maybe she wouldn't taste it—

Bleargh. The mochi was no longer smooth on the inside; it'd turned gritty, the traces of soot crunching between her teeth.

Alliana caught sight of the tapestry that hung next to the door, where Stepmother had pinned up Grandmother's last piece, the one of Queen Natsumi's story, all radiant whites and reds, with a sign reading *For sale, ten gold coins or similarly suitable offer.* Alliana never liked staying in the main room; she'd packed away those decadent, beautiful tales like an old jacket locked in a cedar box to keep out fluttering moths and nostalgia for days that would never come back.

Yet, if Grandmother Mari were here...Alliana knew what the old woman would do in an instant. She'd scrounge up one of her handmade drawstring bags and give away her whole stock of katori chrysanthemum, without a moment's hesitation.

Alliana rummaged through her pockets, her fingers brushing against a linen bag. She padded over, and with a piece of charcoal, she scribbled a note on a scrap of paper: *Sprinkle this katori chrysanthemum around you, and shadowsnakes will leave you alone. Just don't drink too much honey cider, as the sweet scent will attract them.*

Alliana placed the note and pouch down and frowned.

The girl had a thick black cloak wrapped around her—no different from the other travelers who came by the inn—but she was resting on a dark-colored hat crumpled under her head as a thin makeshift pillow. In the weak firelight, the hat looked pointy, almost like a witch's hat.

Witches in Narashino were rarer than castles spun of crystal. It was like saying fairy tales were real.

She glanced up at the tapestry, and Queen Natsumi's blazing eyes as she faced down the thieves seemed to meet her gaze instead.

Alliana rubbed her eyes. It'd just been a trick of the faint moonlight; the fading colors of the embroidery were as flat as before. It was almost daybreak, far past time to sleep.

At the door, Alliana took one more long look at the girl, now muttering something about the scent of bread. That girl couldn't be a witch. And if she truly had even a pinch of magic, she'd never come back the instant she realized what a sorry little town Narashino was: unfit for witches, and especially unfit for even *dreams* of fairy tales.

CHAPTER NINE

APPRENTICE NELALITHIMUS EVERGREEN

A few days later, Alliana was scattering a new layer of pine shavings through the walk-in chicken coop, with her favorite of the black-feathered chickens bobbing around her and clucking curiously at the basket of shavings, like she did every week as Alliana cleaned up the coop.

"Cute chicken. Does she have a name?"

Alliana bolted upright, knocking her forehead against one of the beams. "Wh-who's there?"

She stared at the figure in the entrance to the chicken coop. A girl in an all-black dress rested on her levitating broomstick, swinging her legs. Her inky black hair swirled around her shoulders, and the girl's rounded brown eyes sparkled with curiosity and mischief from under a pointed hat. She spun a wand in her fingertips, and it gave off little sparks of bronze light.

A witch was standing—no, *sitting on a broomstick*—in the chicken coop.

"Apprentice Nelalithimus Evergreen, at your service. Please call me Nela."

Alliana could only gape.

"So, the chicken?" the girl asked, smiling down as it clucked disapprovingly. "What's her name?"

No one had ever asked what the chickens' names were before. Nela pursed her lips, and Alliana felt a faint tug of panic. What if, by knowing the chicken's name, the witch cursed the bird and—

The witch took one look at Alliana's face and laughed. "I promise, I won't enchant her."

Alliana melted with relief; she didn't want to explain to Stepmother how the chickens had turned into water-rabbits or something like that. The rest of her stepfamily thought that they were, well, just chickens. They seemed to be more interested in clucking incessantly when she collected their eggs. But to Alliana, these surprisingly opinionated hens were her friends, just as much as Isao.

"Her name is Eggna," Alliana said, waiting for the witch's laugh.

But Nela only nodded. "Definitely an Eggna. It just feels *right*."

"Are all witches like you?" Alliana clapped her hand over her mouth. She hadn't meant to say that out loud.

Nela snorted. "As in, enjoying every magical moment instead of cackling over a cauldron or moping about the future they've seen in their crystal ball?"

"I'm not sure what exactly witches do....We *never* have anyone from your Guild in Narashino," Alliana blurted out.

Nela's forehead pinched. "Is it really that unusual? The boy at the diner kept looking at me funny, too, but I thought that was because I'd been shoveling bread slathered with that freshly churned butter into my mouth. Back at our camp, the wizard in charge of cooking isn't very good at making meals, you see. Magic like mine can't summon food out of the burnt sludge he makes, either."

"So your chef sent you here?"

"Hah!" Nela snorted. "Hayato's so proud that he won't let anyone else help, even if his cooking makes *him* gag. I just cast a navigation spell for the closest tasty bread, and my wand led me to this town." She waved a short, limber wand at Alliana, who tried to hide the urge to duck. What if the witch cursed her by mistake? How did wands even work?

Alliana must've been looking particularly curious, because the witch twirled her wand and said, "You're really looking at me like I'm the first witch you've ever met. Hasn't this place had *anyone* from the Guild of Magic?"

The bigger towns and cities of Rivelle Realm were able to scrape together enough coin to pay the fees for an appointed witch or wizard. "Narashino is barely a few buildings. There's no way one of your Guild members would be here. As far as I can remember, no witch or wizard has *ever* stopped by."

Nela whistled. "Wow. The Guild's supposed to watch over the entire realm, but I can't say I'm surprised."

"What kind of magic do you cast?" Alliana asked, eyeing the wand. Perhaps if she could get an idea, she'd know what kind of spells to stay on the watch for. After all, she'd heard from plenty of adventurers that the Guild of Magic charged sky-high prices for their charms.

"I've got an affinity for creation magic. So I'm good at making things out of thin air," Nela explained. To prove her point, a woven straw basket—perfect to carry the eggs, unlike the tattered basket Alliana was using— shimmered out of nowhere, dangling from Alliana's arm, solid as a copper coin. "All of us witches and wizards usually have an affinity for one of the main types of magic: There's creation magic like mine, knowledge, repair, scrying, and weather...but none of us are allowed to cast magic on you without your agreement, if that's what you're wondering. Magic manifests usually before five years old, too. So you likely don't have magic, if you're wondering that."

Alliana studied her new basket in awe, just as her stomach growled.

The witch grinned. "I know just what you need."

With a whirl, she spun her broomstick around and shot toward the inn, before Alliana could even splutter out a word. Moments later, Nela returned, pushing a warm, tiny roll into her hand.

Alliana was so hungry that she tore off a huge chunk and stuffed it into her mouth without a second thought. The sweet, airy bread melted on her tongue, and she sighed with relief. Then she paused. "Wait, this tastes like Isao's bread—"

"Isao was going to deliver a baker's dozen here, so I said I'd take it over for him."

Alliana felt her body chill. "Stepmother will know—"

"That grumpy stepbrother of yours counted the full thirteen when I dropped them off. You weren't anywhere in sight. Besides, you were hungry, right?" The witch studied her. "There shouldn't be anything wrong with grabbing a bite if you want to eat."

A strange flicker of confusion tugged at Alliana. *Is that really how things work outside the inn? Outside Narashino?*

But either way, it was too late. She'd demolished

the bread in a few hungry bites. Alliana licked the last crumbs off her fingers. "Thank you for the meal. What brings you here this time?"

The witch bowed dramatically, raising her hand out, like she wanted Alliana to take it. "You."

Alliana spluttered, the bread suddenly a cold lump in her stomach. *"Me?"*

"I'm in a bit of a pinch with a wild creature," Nela explained, pulling a wrinkled note and a very familiar linen bag out of her dress pocket. "And after what you gave me last time and what I've heard about you from the King of Bread, I have a feeling you're just the right person to help."

The King of Bread—Isao? Alliana groaned. The witch's adoration for his baked goods had certainly buttered him up and made him loose jawed.

But...her? Help a *witch*?

"How about a one-way ticket out of here?" Nela said, gesturing at her broomstick. "I've got something to show you at the abyss."

Alliana's eyes widened. *Out of here.* Away from the dust that coated everything. To a place where she could be more than the girl of dust and drudgery. "Well..."

The witch girl gleamed back at her. "Yes, it's time to unravel your own tale! Let's go, Alliana!"

It felt like she'd tried to clamber onto the broomstick and fallen straight to the ground instead. *Unravel your own tale, Alliana.* That was exactly what Grandmother Mari would have said.

Alliana bit her lip and shook her head. "I'm sorry," she said as politely as she could, trying to keep the sadness from sweeping into her words. "I can't."

Nela frowned. "Can't? Or don't want to? If you don't want to, that's completely okay. But I believe in the impossible. Adventures on broomsticks can be way more fun than you'd ever expect, which is totally fine. Ugh, fun? Who wants that.... But if you can't..." The witch looked around skeptically, not seeming to find the chicken coop particularly inspirational. Alliana couldn't disagree with that.

But she put her hand over the pocket on her tunic, where she'd tucked away Grandmother's final letter. The paper shifted ever so slightly under her fingertips; the year had worn it smooth as cloth.

"I must stay," Alliana said resolutely. "I have chores to finish." She hurriedly went to the chicken coop door, and pulled it closed. "Sorry!" she called, through the wood.

A muffled, "Next time!" from the witch didn't soothe her fast-beating heart. She sat down straight on the ground, Eggna clucking in circles around her, and the pine shavings sticking all over her clothes. But she didn't notice.

Away.

As she traced her finger along the edges of the magical basket, warmth swirled through her veins for the first
time in a very long time, a flicker so gentle that she'd
forgotten what this was.

Possibilities. A *dream.* A dream for something *more.*

Today's breakfast was—surprise, surprise—natto. As it
had been every morning for the past week.

Alliana unwrapped the crinkly straw, where she sat
alone at the kitchen table. The fermented boiled beans
stunk, so much that Stepmother could not bear to have it
in her sight. How the woman didn't notice her far stinkier
toes was a mystery. But Stepmother bought natto because
it was only a copper for a dozen packets, so that was
what she'd allotted Alliana to eat daily.

Her stepfamily and the rest of the guests were eating
freshly steamed rice and roasted mackerel in the main
room. Alliana had finally served them all; it wouldn't
be long before she had to fetch their mountains of dirty
plates. But for now, the gentle morning light drifted
through the kitchen window, and she could ignore the
long scribbled list of today's chores that Stepmother had
dumped in front of her before sashaying out to eat.

Footsteps padded through the door that led to the main
room, directly behind her. Alliana quickly pushed out of her
chair and started gathering up her dishes to bring over to the

sink, gulping down the last dregs of her barley tea. She called over her shoulder, "Just about to wash up and start on the chores."

"What chores?" asked a bright, cheery voice that was *definitely* not Stepmother or Reizo or Reina.

Alliana spun around and stared into the eyes of Nelalithimus Evergreen. The girl stood in the doorway, in long black socks that matched her inky black hair, dress, and hat, with a bright smile dancing in her kind eyes.

"W-witch!" Alliana spluttered on a mouthful of barley tea. She swallowed, trying to regain her composure. *Quick, quick…straight and tall; not above all, but see the truth…* "I mean…witch….er, *which*…way can I help you go?"

Nela plucked the dishes out of Alliana's hands and brought them over to the sink. She scooped up the goopy bar of soap, sudsing the dishes, but the bar popped out from between her fingertips, flying onto the window ledge. "Ugh, I'm no good at things like this…." The girl returned the soap to the sink and glared as if it was her archenemy. "Just a quick spell would take care of—"

"What is going on here?" Stepmother snapped, stepping between the two girls. Reizo and Reina followed in her wake. Reina absentmindedly drifted toward the window, chewing on a curl of yuzu rind she'd found somewhere, but Reizo stared at Nela suspiciously.

The girl studied the woman and Alliana's stepbrother, who were both staring daggers at her. "Is this a private area?" the witch said, glancing around in presumed surprise. "Why, my apologies. I should head back...." Alliana sucked in a breath as the witch unclasped the cloak pin and the fabric rippled, like the inky black depths of the abyss. She spun the pin with a twist of her wrist and then—

There was a puff of shimmering light, and the cloak...the cloak was *gone*. Instead, the girl was holding her broomstick; it was a knobby piece of wood that looked more like it was ready for the fire pile than a ride, but she clutched it gently, like it was worth more than a sack of gold coins.

"A *witch*?" Stepmother squawked.

"Apprentice Nelalithimus Evergreen. Technically not a Guild member since I haven't gone on my Novice quest, but that's soon enough," the girl said, sweeping into a bow. She didn't add the "at your service" phrase she'd greeted Alliana with. She popped back up, shot Alliana a mischievous smile. "Well, I must go."

Alliana's stepfamily stared as the girl sauntered out, broomstick in hand, disappearing into the shadows of the hallway.

The grandfather clock rang solemnly, calling out the noon hour, and Stepmother finally roused from her stupor. "What was a witch doing here?"

"She was just asking about the rates," Alliana blurted

out, unable to think of a better excuse. "I think she wanted to stay a night?"

Stepmother spun on her heels. "Why, she should've said! I'll find her." The woman gathered her dress in her hands and hurried out. "Reizo! Reina! Follow me! We must invite the witch to stay. Think of all the spells she can cast for us! Reizo, maybe she can enhance your intelligence!"

"I'm perfectly smart enough!" her stepbrother growled, following his mother.

"You can't ever seem to remember all of the realms," Reina said matter-of-factly, pulling another yuzu rind from her pocket. "Last week, you thought there were *three*. There's a reason it's called the *seven* realms."

Moments later, the shadows in the hallway shifted and Nela wandered back into the kitchen, spinning her wand. "What was that for?"

"Stepmother doesn't care for me associating with guests."

"That's not fair." Nela frowned, craning to look into the main room, as if she wanted to give the woman a piece of her mind. Or maybe even a curse? Alliana shuddered; Grandmother Mari would be appalled if her daughter-in-law or grandchildren turned into squawking chickens. And of course Stepmother wasn't fair; Alliana knew that. Nothing about working at this inn was fair, but it was the promise she'd made.

"Well, shall we?" The witch gestured at her broomstick.

"I...I..." Alliana inched back toward the table. "I've got so much to do and—"

"None of us witches and wizards can figure out these wild creatures," Nela said. "I'll pay you double what you make here at the inn, *and* it'll help the whole *realm*."

Alliana's heart whirled at that. *Help the whole realm*...In her mind's eye, she would travel the realm just like Queen Natsumi, helping the people who loved this land like Alliana did.

"I've got this whole list of chores," Alliana said, her throat aching with regret.

"It's not like they follow you around, do they?" the girl asked, a sparkle in her eye.

"No, they only check to see if I've done the work...."

Nela pulled her wand out of her pocket and spun it in her fingertips. "Then leave it to me."

"But—"

The witch snatched up the paper and scanned it. "Okay, let's do this." She rolled up her sleeves, brandished her wand, and chanted under her breath. "*Clean away and play today.* Hmm, the guest rooms...*All the rooms aglow, bright and clean as gingko*...As for this kitchen...*Polish the dishes, most simple of wishes*."

Alliana stared around her. The windows sparkled,

the pots and pans danced back to their racks, and the dishes clattered into their shelves one by one....

And on the paper, tidy check marks appeared next to the items in the most satisfying of ways. Minutes later, the witch handed back the list with a grin. "All good."

"You—did you just—" Alliana spluttered. "But—why don't witches and wizards do that for *everyone*?"

"It's a pretty big drain of magic, or else witches and wizards would do everyone's chores for a handful of coins. And I'm really supposed to save my powers for 'realm-saving' things, according to the Guild of Magic," Nela explained with a shrug, chomping down on a simple crusted roll. "*Ooh.* The dab of salted butter is perfect. I should ask Isao for his hand in marriage. It's *that* good."

"But—you shouldn't waste your magic on *me*."

"Waste?" Nela snorted. "We're doing a trade, aren't we? If I can get your help, it'll be better than any charm I can cast and save the realm *far* better than I could. Because no matter what spell I come up with, I can't get these strange creatures to leave. I think it's something to do with their resistance to magic, just like nightdragons."

Nightdragons. Alliana thought of the hatchling, a faint smile curving up her lips as she remembered the way the little creature had poked insistently until she'd petted its head. But...oh, *no.* If she didn't help Nela, the witches and wizards would use curses on the wild creatures. They didn't deserve that.

Alliana took one more look around the sparkling clean kitchen; she didn't doubt for a second that the guest rooms were just as pristine or that the laundry was already hanging out to dry. She turned to the witch, and her heart thudded, like it was about to leap out of her chest. "Can your broomstick really hold a passenger?"

CHAPTER TEN

GUARD HOUSE FIVE

Wind swirled around Alliana, teasing stray hairs out of her braid. Nela called over her shoulder, "Hold on tight!"

Alliana's knuckles were in a bone-white grip around the witch's waist; she was sitting sideways on the broomstick and should have been scared about tumbling off—

Then they burst out of the thick mist, shooting into pure blue sky.

A joyful laugh bubbled out of her; it felt like she'd become the sun, glowing with light. And, up here, there was no way that Stepmother could tear her down with her words, not from these impossible heights.

Rivelle Realm was spread out below, like one of Grandmother Mari's beautiful tapestries. From far above, the sun shone golden to where it met the robin's-egg blue sky. Northward, farmhouses were scattered amidst seas of green rice paddies. To the left, the deep, cavernous rift stretched east to west. From this distance, the Guild of Magic's shield was fully visible, a shimmering light that took the edge away from the pitch-black. There was darkness, yes, but in Rivelle, there was still so much light.

This, *this* was the world Alliana had always wanted to see. Her heartbeat pounded from the newness of everything.

"What's that?" Alliana asked. A dirt road turned to stone, leading up to a majestic castle. The swooping tile roof and the pure white walls gave it a sense of motion, like a bird stretching its wings out midflight. Even from afar, Alliana could tell that it was important.

Nela looked up from her navigation spell on the wood of her broomstick, a red arrow that was currently pointing straight east. "Oh, Advisor Miwa's estates."

"*The Royal Advisor* Kenzo Miwa?" Alliana tried not to gape, drinking in the sight of the castle. Reizo would throw the biggest fit if he knew Alliana had seen the location of the Farmlands Ball before him.

"Of course. He's quite nice, really, even though he's so very reclusive. His steward called on Master Yamane for a way to string up lights across the outside ballroom without causing any fires, so my master sent me in. It was easy enough to cast up the lighting, and Kyo—that's his

steward—gave me a gold piece. Which was a great payment for me, but for some reason that steward kept offering contomelon rolls so that I wouldn't leave—not that
I was going to try. Turns out the Royal Advisor wanted
to come out personally to thank me. That's rare with the
royals, honestly."

Before long, Nela was regaling Alliana with more
tales of her work as an Apprentice Witch, and Alliana,
to her own surprise, told the witch about how she'd lost
her parents, and about her almost-magical nights with
Grandmother Mari.

But all too soon, Nela called, "We're going to land!"

They began their descent toward the shield, zipping
into a set of clouds, thick and obscuring. Alliana let
out a surprised yelp as they suddenly lurched down, the
broomstick racing toward a tiny house perched amidst
rocks and sparse trees. A lantern flickered next to the
door, beckoning them.

They landed next to a tall, square building made
of white wood slats and propped onto four stilts. Nela
hopped off her broomstick, leaned it against the wall,
and hurried down the stairs toward the shield, beyond
the house, but Alliana wobbled on her feet. "Whoa, my
legs feel like a mound of jelly."

"You'll get used to flying by broomstick quickly," the
witch said, shooting a grin over her shoulder. Alliana met
her smile—she couldn't wait for the next ride.

Before Alliana descended the stairs, she peeked at the sign painted on the gray door:

GUARD HOUSE FIVE
OPEN ALL DAY, ALL YEAR*
RAIN, SHINE, OR NIGHTDRAGONS
*Exclusion: When compacted.

"Where are we?" Alliana asked. "What's Guard House Five?"

"The Royal Guard and the Guild of Magic often partner together to patrol the shield," Nela explained, waiting at the foot of the stairs. "It's 'cause the Guild gets paid four silvers straight from the Royal Guard for each week one of us is here. So our Master keeps sending us to line his own pocket; since we're under his 'supervision,' he takes it all."

Alliana had plenty of experience with that. Still, four silvers was more than she saw in ten moons. "Isn't that a lot?"

"Not enough for the Guild of Magic." Nela shook her head. "That's why they're sending low-level Apprentices like us. And it's also why there've been more breaks than ever in the shield."

"Why would they let that happen?" Alliana asked.

"Greed, mostly. That's what happens when leaders no longer care about the realm or its people the way they should."

Alliana's fists curled. How could people who *could* make a difference—unlike her—be so careless about the gifts and powers that they had?

"Anyway, enough of the Guild's awful policies. We won't be able to solve that today. What we're here for is over there." The witch pointed toward the shield.

As they got closer, Alliana realized someone was pacing next to the shimmering light. A boy broke off from the group and stomped over toward them.

"Get ready," Nela muttered under her breath. Alliana was about to ask what she meant when the boy stopped in front of them. He was just around their height and age, with clumps of dark brown, curled hair, and a sharpness to his face like a hawk.

"Nela!" He flicked his narrowed, hooded eyes at Alliana up and down, in the same disparaging way Stepmother and Reizo did. "Who is *this*?"

But Alliana wasn't going to pretend to be scared and back down. Grandmother Mari had asked her to take care of her stepfamily, and that didn't include this haughty boy.

"I am Alliana of Rivelle," she said, holding her head tall. "I am here to assist Apprentice Evergreen."

Nela leaned in, with a grin tugging on her lips. "Hear

that, Hayato? That means our business doesn't involve *you*, even if you are my fellow Apprentice."

Hayato spluttered. "Anything dealing with the abyss and a member of the Guild of Magic *is* my concern."

"That means it's my concern, too," said a new voice, cool as spring rain. A boy walked straight from Guard House Five, broomstick in hand, and nodded at Alliana. He was a bright-eyed wizard, maybe a year or two younger than her, with wavy black hair that fluttered over his eyes. This newcomer looked like a figure out of a portrait, except for the way the wind ruffled his clothes and hair—he wasn't a still life.

"Alliana of Rivelle?" the boy asked, flashing her a bright smile. "Apprentice Taichiro Suzuki, at your service. Please, call me Taichi."

"Oh. Yes." Then she said, "Wait, how'd you know my name?"

"Because you're the only non-magical person in kilometers, and Nela won't shut up about you," Hayato muttered.

Alliana crossed her arms. There was something about the way this Taichi boy seemed to *know* her, yet didn't want to reveal his cards. She'd been around too many people with their own agendas, and she wasn't going to let him be another tally in that list.

"I'm a scryer," Taichi said, answering a question she'd never vocalized.

"Did you just read my *mind*?"

He looked just like any other boy, albeit a slightly disheveled one. Scryers were legendary; she'd only heard of them in Grandmother's tales. No one she knew had ever met one.

Hayato spluttered. "You're not supposed to tell anyone! I'm going to tell Master Yamane!"

"Yeah, and I'll explain to him how Dorey was hanging around here the other day," Taichi shot back. "She's not even Apprenticed yet—you know that the Masters are concerned about her magic."

Hayato seemed to deflate and puff up his chest at the same time. "Dorey was happy to see me at work. I'm the best wizard she's ever seen! She learned lots from me."

Taichi rolled his eyes. "Yeah, yeah, and she wants to ask for your hand in marriage, we know. But you're also years away from being of age for that."

Hayato stuck his nose in the air. "You're jealous. No one would want *you*."

"Perhaps I don't want just *anyone*." Taichi grinned at Alliana, unfazed by Hayato's insult.

"Dorey isn't just anyone!"

Nela cut in. "So, Taichi, care to explain a bit more? Did you know that Alliana was going to help here?"

The boy glanced up at her from under his bangs; Alliana swore she'd seen little pups with less of a pout. "I'd never do *that*. I can't."

Alliana frowned. What did he mean? And *why* was he familiar?

The witch sighed and turned to Alliana. "You deserve an explanation. See the shield?" The girl waved at the hard-to-miss glowing light and winked at her when Hayato wasn't looking. *Play along.*

"Tell me more," Alliana said, and the witch grinned.

"Absolutely!" She clapped her hands together. "We're training to become Novices. But for Master Yamane to recommend us for the Novice quest, he's having us complete a set of three missions. I think it's mostly because he wants time with his precious books. Anyway, I was assigned to fix the shield from this point on"—she gestured from a spindly pine tree next to the shield and back toward the way they'd flown in—"to the abyss entrance near your town, Alliana. Hayato's a fast flier, so he's responsible for the area from the pine tree down toward the sea."

"Then are you both responsible for that gap?" Alliana pointed at a tear in the shield she'd just noticed. It was just about half her height of open air, the edges jagged.

"*Exactly!*" Nela said, just as Hayato snapped, "No!"

The witch explained, "He thinks that I'm trying to take the glory if I fix it, and might rank up before him. And I told him that he can't fix it then, either; we have to mend it together."

"It's not proper!" the boy said, puffing up his chest.

"I'm surprised he didn't just mend it while you were gone," Alliana said.

The wizard muttered, "I have more pride than that! Guild rules state that if two members are conflicted over a request, then they can appeal for proper advice."

"I got stuck as the mediator," Taichi explained. "Can't cheat a scryer."

"We don't need to fly all the way back to Okayama for *this*." Nela shook her head. "Plus, neither of our spells work."

Alliana hadn't heard of magic *not* working before. "What do you mean?"

Hayato sighed and gestured. *"Look."*

"We've got guests." Taichi led them to the shield. Through the gaping hole, silver-feathered birds shot in and out, trilling loudly.

"Rockcrows," Alliana gasped. "What are they doing here? And why are they so bright-colored? I'd read that they're supposed to be gray-black, in this one book someone left—I mean, that someone gave to me."

"I was right!" Hayato crowed. "It's not a plain rockcrow."

"Rockcrows are supposed to be in the forests of the North, not here," Nela responded. But the witch seemed to be stuck on what Alliana hadn't meant to say. *"Left?* Does your town school have no books of its own?"

"There is *no* school," Alliana replied. "And you *are*

right, Nela....Rockcrows don't belong here. Perhaps they're lost. What did you need me for, anyway?"

"It's a rockcrow," Hayato was grumbling under his breath. "I'm right, I'm right, I—"

"May *possibly* be right." Alliana stepped closer, and her jaw dropped as a rockcrow took one look at her and bared razor-like edges on its beak. It looked like the crow had met Stepmother's fancy serrated knife. "I've never heard of a rockcrow with a knife for a beak."

The witch and wizards silently gaped alongside her.

"Well," Taichi said finally, "even I wasn't expecting that."

Nela added, "So, um, can you help us? All our spells don't stop them from crossing back and forth between the abyss and Rivelle. And they keep attacking the guard house, so it can't move onward." She gestured at the building behind them, where the birds were flying up to the rooftop. "We need to close up the gap in the shield but...neither of us want to split up their flock."

"A non-magical shouldn't be helping!" Hayato protested, but Nela just waved him off.

Split up their flock...Alliana's heart dropped. If Grandmother Mari was trapped inside the abyss's shield and she was stuck outside, she'd break down any amount of spells to return to her side.

"I'll do what I can," Alliana said. The instant relief flashing over Nela and Taichi's faces surprised her. Was this, she wondered, what Queen Natsumi had felt when she'd set off on her adventures to help the realm? Well, it wasn't like everyone believed in Alliana. Hayato was still shaking his head, muttering under his breath.

There was no time to dally in fairy tales. Alliana studied the rockcrows and pulled out a small cloth bag from her pocket. "Let me try some katori chrysanthemum."

"Oh! More of that, perfect!" Nela said. "I'd used up all of mine."

"Those flower things?" Hayato looked unimpressed.

"Hopefully this works," Alliana replied. "I've never tried it with birds from the abyss."

There was a gap between the birds flying back and forth; now was the perfect chance. The white buds burst as she tossed them toward the shield, the long petals curling at their red tips, the musky-burnt scent wafting through the air. The rockcrows swerved, flying away from the barrier.

"It's working!" Nela cheered. "Now we can fix the shield—"

A high-pitched screech shattered the peace. Alliana spun around to see the rockcrows diving at a figure on the rooftop of the guard house.

"*Deflection for protection!*" Nela cried. A glossy, clear shield flashed into place between the guard and the angry rockcrow, and the man rushed back to the safety of the staircase. Still, the bird stayed, sweeping back toward a corner of the rooftop.

"Take me there, please?" Alliana asked.

Nela swirled her cloak. In an instant, it became her broomstick. "You don't need to ask twice."

The rooftop wasn't quite an ordinary set of round rooftops. Instead, a lush garden filled the four walls. Long boxes covered the ground, with bright vegetables and herbs reaching up toward the sun. Here and there, tall wood trellises rose with thick vines, heavy with fruit, sectioning off the garden.

The rockcrows weren't hungry; they weren't pecking at the yuzu tree or stealing the herb sprouts. Rather, the dozen or so creatures were tearing at everything in sight—including their own feathers—and piling it into a corner of the rooftop.

"They've lost their birdbrains," Nela said, shaking her head, as she nudged the broomstick to go closer.

"Wait, we shouldn't—"

The rockcrows turned, all together, and glared at Nela and Alliana.

"Go back, go back!" Alliana yelped, as the birds took flight, razor-beaks snapping as they dove straight toward them.

Nela pushed the broomstick down and they plummeted toward the ground, hurtling faster than they ever had flown before. The witch shouted, with a laugh, "Hold on tight!"

"A little late for that!" Alliana was already clutching onto the broomstick for dear life. She was sure she'd left her stomach somewhere midair and what felt like the rest of her body, too.

Nela managed to wrench the broomstick up; the tips of Alliana's boots bounced against the ground, and then they curved around the guard house, sharp around the corner.

"Do something!" Nela shouted at Taichi and Hayato, as they made another pass. The wizards were gaping at them leading the rockcrows in a merry chase. Even a few of the Royal Guards, in marigold cloth uniforms that marked their status, stood on the far end of the rooftop, their jaws swinging in the air.

The wizards looked at each other. Taichi shook his head. "My magic isn't good for this!"

"This is why we shouldn't have accepted help from a non-magical!" Hayato huffed, but pulled out his stout wand. With a snap, he shouted, *A protection for the witch and her friend, to bring this chase to an end.*"

All of a sudden, water swirled all around them, like they were in a rushing river, yet it was like they were in a bubble. Through the flowing streams around them, Alliana caught glimpses of the rockcrows circling in confusion. Nela and Alliana waited, their hearts pattering unsteadily, until the rockcrows finally returned to building their nest.

They landed, and the water evaporated into thin air.

"Clever spell," Nela said, but Hayato only frowned deeper.

"What were you two *thinking*?" he hissed. "Nela, if a non-magical gets hurt on our watch, Master Yamane and the whole Guild of Magic will put a mark against our names! I cannot have that—"

"You care too much for glory," Taichi cut in. Then he turned to Alliana. "You've got a plan, don't you?"

Alliana bit her lip, craning her neck to study the birds, who had returned to their strange patterns. She had an inkling of an idea, but she wasn't sure if it was any good.

"We've got to stop them from attacking the guard house," Nela said. "If the Royal Guards can't move, then the barrier won't get monitored."

"They're not attacking," Alliana blurted out.

"What?" Hayato said incredulously. "Does that *not* look like—"

"They're building a *nest*."

The witch and wizards stared at Alliana.

"Here?" Hayato said doubtfully.

She nodded. "The sparrows near me—" Alliana stopped herself. They didn't need to know about how she watched the birds fly free and wondered about the day that she might be able to do the same. "We need to make them a home. I think it should be in the abyss, the place they're used to. That's why they're trying to fly back inside, but they keep coming back here, where there are so many leaves and things like that to build up a cozy spot."

Hayato shook his head decisively. "I am not a bird. I am not going to build a nest."

"No one was asking *you*," Taichi shot back.

Alliana couldn't miss the way Hayato deflated.

"What do you need?" Nela asked. "A birdhouse?"

Alliana nodded. Hayato scoffed, muttering under his breath, "Of course, a birdhouse. Do you want a crown and a crystal palace while you're making your list?"

Taichi looked at the other wizard strangely. Then he said, "We *do* have magic."

"Would you really?" Alliana's heart leaped. The rockcrows were so intent on their goal of making a nest, but she could tell that they were confused by this bright, different world. There was a desperation to the way they dove for materials.

Nela spun her wand. With a shimmering glow, a tall, hive-shaped birdhouse appeared out of thin air, made of woven bamboo. Alliana tried picking it up. To her surprise, it was light and filled with downy cloth, soft as feathers. Nela—despite her humbleness—was *powerful*.

"Something like that?" Nela asked. "I tried to mimic what they're building up there."

"I think so, but maybe even more of this feathery cloth—"

The padding inside the nest doubled with another quick flick of Nela's wand. Hayato grumbled from behind them, "Show-off."

"That's perfect," Alliana said. "I'll figure out a way to attach it to the cliffside." She began carrying it toward the shield.

"I'll go with you!" Nela said cheerily, moving to help her.

"No. Way." Hayato crossed his arms. "No witch or wizard is allowed to cross the shield and go into the abyss. It goes against every rule in the Guild, it—"

Alliana stared fiercely at him. "Save your own hide. *I'll* go myself."

She strode to the opening in the shield with the nest in her arms, her blood boiling with fury. *It goes against every rule....* What *rule* was any good if it meant the harm of someone—or something?

"Wait, wait!" the witch called after her, and finally caught up, tugging at her arm.

"Please, don't stop me," Alliana said. "I will *not* let these rockcrows be torn from the only home they know, no matter what spell you try to cast on me. I'll do whatever it takes—"

"I'm going to help you."

Alliana nearly tripped over her own boots. Nela unclasped her cloak and gave it a quick spin of her wrist; the broomstick shimmered into place as the girl hopped on.

"What are you waiting for?" Nela asked, her feet hovering an inch from the ground.

"But—Hayato just said you're not supposed to...."

Behind them, the wizard was fuming. "The Guild *forbids* potential members like us from entering into the abyss unless it is a paid matter and—"

"Those rules and regulations will be the end of us," Taichi countered. "It doesn't take a scryer to see *that*."

Alliana spoke up. "Queen Natsumi recently instated a rule allowing anyone to help another in need. It was in the recent *Rivelle Times*." She'd found the newspaper lost under one of the dining tables, but that was something that the witches and wizards didn't need to know.

"That's too vague," Hayato complained. "I need—"

"Something in need?" the other boy growled, gesturing at the frantic, confused rockcrows.

Nela nodded her head. "Taichi's right. Who cares if this is paid or not? What rule is right if it means harm?"

Alliana added, thinking of how Stepmother was her legal guardian, for all that the woman never took care of her, "Just because a rule's been in place doesn't mean that it should *stay* there forever. Or that we should follow it blindly."

Hayato was too stunned to respond.

Alliana didn't waste another word; it wasn't like she could undo a law, no matter how unjust it was. For now, she'd simply have to bend it. She slid onto the broomstick and wrapped one arm around the witch, her heart blazing with determination. "Let's get these rockcrows home."

The flight back was surprisingly uneventful, though Alliana half expected the flock of rockcrows to come chasing after them. The birdhouse Nela made fit perfectly into the cliffs of the abyss; Alliana's heart had thumped, seeing how far she would've fallen almost one year ago, when she'd been facing the giant nightdragon. Though for the little hatchling's sake (and her own), she didn't dare breathe a word of *that* adventure, or the leftovers that always seemed to disappear within a day's time, behind that boulder in the hidden meadow, though she still hadn't been able to see the baby dragon. With a mixture of herbs—including the broad-leaved shiso, a rockcrow favorite—Alliana had managed to lure them back into the abyss and, with Nela flying her, straight into their new nest, which they'd entered immediately, cawing with happiness.

Nela and Alliana chatted more about Alliana's herb knowledge and Nela's parents back in the northern foothills of the Sakuya Mountains, who the witch seemed to miss very much.

"By the way," Nela said, as they soared closer to the

inn. "How did you know what the rockcrows needed? Taichi even tried to scry, but that didn't work."

"I...I simply studied their behavior. I've seen birds like that before, that's all." When Stepmother wanted to get her tea served directly to her, Alliana had to spend stretches of long afternoons standing idly in the corner of the tearoom, only moving to refill cups. It gave her plenty of time to stare out the window and watch the birds. Sometimes, the crystal pigeon fluttered by—on a few occasions, it even gave Reizo a stinky "gift" for trying to listen in—but it was usually the chittering sparrows. "It's nothing special."

"But that's the difference," Nela said simply. "You notice."

Alliana didn't know what to say. To her, it didn't feel like anything special.

Before long, they landed in the copse of trees on the far end of the chicken run; Alliana couldn't risk Stepmother or her stepsiblings seeing her with Nela. Her legs wobbled like before, but Nela was right: She was already getting used to the strangely weightless feeling of flying. Still, there was no need to get familiar with riding on a broomstick; it wasn't as if she would ever see the witch again.

"Farewell, Nela. It was nice to meet you."

"Farewell? I'm not a scryer like Taichi, but I have a feeling we're going to need your help again," Nela said.

"But you have *magic*," Alliana protested. Didn't a flick of their wands solve everything?

"I mean, you saw us today. Spells, surprisingly, aren't as foolproof as I used to think. While we're patrolling the barrier, we're going to need your expertise. So, until next time." Nela winked and kicked off. Gusts swirled as the witch shot up beyond the clouds, leaving Alliana staring up in shock long after she disappeared.

Alliana spluttered, "Next—time—?"

CHAPTER ELEVEN

CLAWS

Tea splattered down Alliana's front. The hot liquid seeped through her tunic and scalded her skin. She did her best to bite down her cry.

"You wretched girl!" Stepmother screamed. "How dare you mix up my tea! You know that I never want sugar in front of Mister Leo! How embarrassing! He tried my tea and nearly choked from how syrupy it was!"

It wasn't Alliana's fault that Stepmother preferred her tea with so much sugar that a spoon could almost stick up in it. She'd never heard of anyone other than Stepmother drinking sweetened tea, but apparently it was a tradition in Arcia, a realm to the far west.

"I hadn't known he'd be joining you." Alliana tried to reason with her stepmother, though she knew it was useless.

"Fool! Didn't you hear my request for five manjū? It's not as if I'd eat those all myself!"

Stepmother *often* gobbled up five, six, *ten* manjū on her own. But Alliana knew, no matter what she said, the woman would twist her words and make her feel stupid for even speaking up for herself. And like the hot water burning her skin, those words hurt more than she'd let the woman realize.

As the older woman raged at her, Alliana tried to remember the good in her days. Four full moons had passed since she'd first met Nela, and each morning she hoped her friend would appear. Sometimes, days would go by without a trace of the witch, and Alliana wondered then if she had made their adventures all up, like the tales on the tapestries. Not that she truly had time to wonder—Alliana had to return to working on Reizo's suit for the Regional Ball, and once she'd finished that, she reluctantly began on Reina's dress, all the while never getting the fabric to work on a gown of her own. Those days stretched on and on. Until another special morning, when she was eating her natto piled up on rice like usual, and a finger would tap her on the shoulder. Her heart zipped with a thrill each time she looked up and met the witch's grin with a smile of her own, slipping out for a new adventure. On days Nela didn't come, Alliana often found a magical paper bird twittering around the rafters of the attic, containing a message from the witch, sometimes with a sweet or two.

But it'd been three weeks since Nela's last note, and even longer since their escapades with Nela's witch and wizard friends. Alliana longed to be back in the Farmlands, where she, Nela, and Taichi had stuffed their bellies full of freshly picked contomelons after chasing off a herd of waterrabbits for a local farmer. She wanted to be laying out in the hidden meadow, sneaking a treat behind the boulder when the witch wasn't looking, and then laughing until she was crying as Nela almost fell off her broom trying to show off riding tricks. Those were stolen moments that felt like they'd been sewn in the tapestry of someone else's life—but were truly nothing but a distant dream. Even though she was taking care of the inn and her stepfamily for Grandmother, and she was bending to Stepmother's will, it felt like she was so close to breaking. *How could Stepmother call herself Alliana's guardian and treat her like this?*

She was about to burst out in a retort. Then—

Grandmother's letter crinkled against her chest. *Take care of my family.... I can trust you to take this on, right?*

She closed her mouth. She could last until the Farmlands Ball; she had to do that for Grandmother Mari. As her stepmother slammed her fist on her tea table, the mug fell to the ground and shattered into a million pieces. The woman screeched, "Get out of my sight!"

With that, Alliana spun on her heel and raced out the door.

At the crossroads, with one last longing glance at the marker that pointed east, toward the coast and the capital city, Alliana turned a sharp right to the abyss. Instead of following the main path to the abyss entrance, she slipped through the gap between the cliffs that led to the meadow. The rocks seemed particularly closer these days, but it was because she'd grown taller since the afternoons she used to race through the path, in front of her father.

The meadow was lush and green, filled with tall grass that now only stretched up to her waist. She loved it here; she felt a connection to this land more than she'd ever felt a connection to her stepfamily. Though they may not have ever loved her, by having this meadow all to herself, it felt like her father and Grandmother Mari were still with her, even just a little bit.

Stepmother hadn't wanted to see her. For once, she could slip away and have a moment to herself. Alliana searched her pockets, but she didn't have a single crumb to leave behind the boulder. Before she left, she would

pick some broad-leaved shiso and other herbs for at least
a small offering to her dragon friend.

She lay out on the grass, enjoying the fresh scent of
newly grown fernleaf and the music-like sparrows twittering. Even the crystal pigeon had fluttered to a branch
nearby, and was cooing to its bird friends.

Overhead, the pillowy clouds she'd seen earlier were
getting pushed eastward, toward the Constancia Sea,
by the same breeze that ruffled the tattered edges of her
hand-me-down tunic. She was used to that....

For some reason, though, the breeze was rather
warm, drifting across her face with the sweet scent of
roasted mallow root.

Her skin prickled as the cloud above her stayed. And
let out a grunt.

That was unusual.

Alliana sat up and looked straight into the yellow eyes
of a creature that towered over her. It stretched as tall as
the boulders around the meadow, with thick, green-black
hide and a swinging tail that could slam Alliana straight
into the barrier.

She yelped and fell on her rear end. The nightdragon
advanced, teeth flashing. Alliana was going to turn into
an ember, burned to bits.

The nightdragon arched his neck forward, dark scales
flashing under the sunlight. He fluttered his wings and

opened his mouth in a sharp-toothed grin. And, closer up, there was a familiar, faint white scar on his cheek.

"You?" Alliana yelped. "But...you've grown so much!"

Before, the hatchling had fit into her palms. Somehow, in just a year, he was already taller than her. But the dragon seemed unsure of his feet; he stumbled around a bit—leaving heavy-clawed imprints in the dirt that Alliana would have to sweep away to hide his traces—before plopping down on his spiky butt with a happy sigh.

Albeit a sigh with a puff of smoke at the end. *Friend.*

"H-how have you been?" Alliana asked. "Most of all, *how* did you get here?"

She peered around the dragon to look at the shield. And to answer her question, the nightdragon loped over to the boulder and the gap, low on the ground. It was a barely visible tear in the shield; the Guild members still hadn't noticed it as they flew over. Still, Alliana didn't understand how a dragon of *this* size could get through.

My door. The young dragon poked his head through the shield, wriggled a bit, and squirmed his way into the abyss side. There was a bit of a sizzling sound as the barrier stretched and stretched around the creature, but his thick hide now protected him, unlike when he had been a wee hatchling.

Through the faintly see-through patchwork of spells, the nightdragon flashed his sharp teeth in a grin.

"Well," Alliana said faintly. "I guess the shield isn't quite as dragon-proof as the witches and wizards thought. Maybe I should let them know—"

At that, the dragon jumped back through the tear immediately, eyes wide, and scurried in front of her, sitting on his back haunches with his front legs pressed together. *Please don't!*

"But..."

The dragon pushed his muzzle forward, rubbing his nose on her like he had when he was a little dragon hatchling, and she fell on her back from the force.

He eyed her with confusion, as if not sure why the girl had fallen, and hooked his neck around her back, setting her upright, his eyes still wide and pleading. *I missed you!*

Alliana's heart clenched up. This was a *nightdragon*. The most dangerous creature ever found in the realm. She'd *seen* the power of two nightdragons, battling it out. She wouldn't stand a chance against one. But there was a strange comfort from being in his company.

The nightdragon was warm to the touch, like the cups of tea she used to drink with Grandmother Mari. When he breathed out, there was that sweet, pure scent, like freshly roasted mochi, puffy and crisp at the edges. The way the dragon sat in front of her cheerfully on his spiky butt, like a dog in the body of a monstrously huge creature, was strangely reassuring.

"Nightdragons are supposed to be scary," Alliana

said. Back in the days when dragons still flew over Rivelle, nightdragons were named for how, when the creatures swooped down with their massive wings, they swathed the world in darkness, like night had instantly fallen. But, somehow, this bright-eyed hatchling didn't match what the legends warned her of.

She knew all too well that things often didn't match what they seemed on the surface, or what everyone else said about them. Stepmother dripped with sweet syrupy words for adventurers staying at the inn; they all thought her wonderful and so kind for taking in Alliana, a girl with no true relation to her. The way Stepmother dropped lies left and right about how useless and troublemaking Alliana was never helped, either. The guests never saw the thorns in the words she shot out at Alliana the moment their backs were turned, or how Stepmother took Alliana's meals away as a cruel punishment. Or Reizo, who could make his mother puff up with pride, but scald Alliana with his cruel, twisted pranks; just yesterday, she'd found her dinner of mochi and natto had been thrown into the fire.

This dragon wasn't like the cruel nightdragons of legend. He shifted forward with big wide eyes, as if he wanted to sit in her lap. Alliana cleared her mind, pushing away thoughts of her stepfamily. "You're like a pot of honey and butter."

Missed you. The nightdragon happily plopped his

head on her lap. It felt like one of those mornings that Stepmother had piled all of her dirty laundry on Alliana while she was sleeping—the nightdragon was *not* light—but he was comforting, unlike Stepmother's soiled handkerchiefs.

Alliana absentmindedly ran her hands along the dragon's muzzle, and the creature let out a content noise, puffing out his cheeks. "Do you have a name, little one?"

The dragon shook his head left to right. *No. I haven't found the right name, yet.*

"Can I try out a few?"

Yes. There was a brightness to the nightdragon's eyes. *Please!*

"Fireball?" Alliana tested out a few names. "Fried Potato? Rice Cracker? I'm just hungry, aren't I?"

The young dragon puffed up his cheeks again, and Alliana laughed. "Oh, I know! Can I call you Kabocha? You look like one of those green pumpkins that the general store sells, all puffy and plump and round. Maybe Kabo?"

The creature flared his emerald-rimmed nostrils and bared his fangs in a sharp smile. *Yes!*

"Kabo it is." Alliana scratched his soft, leathery back, under his flapping wings.

Alliana. Kabo looped around her, and it felt like she was protected in a fortress, like Queen Natsumi standing at the top spires of her stone castle. For a second, it felt like Stepmother was far below her, a hornet buzzing in the distance.

"I wish my father could've met you. Or Grandmother Mari, she would've sewn you into one of her tapestries."

Kabo shifted, flicking his spiky tail like a barn cat's. *What is a father?*

The question surprised her so much that she didn't feel the sting of pain she would have otherwise. Alliana paused, remembering the two nightdragons that had battled over Kabo when he'd been a tiny hatchling; hadn't one of them been his guardian? "Do you not have a family?"

What is a family?

At first, she didn't know how to explain that. Then, stiltedly, she told Kabo about how Isao had helped her the day before to get Stepmother off her case. The woman had been stomping around the inn, looking for Alliana to assign another list of chores. Isao, who had driven Mister Leo in the diner owner's new one-horse carriage, had sent the woman on a wild goose chase around the inn, while Alliana had slipped outside and peaceably eaten a rice ball in the shade of the chicken coop.

"He's like my brother," Alliana said finally. Even though Isao had a little brother of his own, their friendship felt like everything that Reizo and Reina should've been. "That's family."

Ah, a thunder.

Alliana mimed rain and clouds and zigzagging light-ning, then, "*Boom!* That kind of thunder?"

The dragon's laugh was like a creaky wheel rolling straight into Alliana's heart. She leaned closer, resting her head on his thick stomach. Despite the bumps, he was heated and there was a softness to him that felt better than her pillowcase stuffed with knobbly buckwheat hulls.

We choose who we spend our time with. My parents birthed me, but I am a free hatchling the moment I leave my egg. Those I care for the most become my thunder. You are my chosen thunder.

"Oh," Alliana murmured. "Like a chosen family?"

Family. The dragon seemed to roll that word around in his mind, trying to taste it for a sense of feeling. *Yes. Family, thunder. Your thunder is different from my thunder, but I hope that we are both part of each other's thunders.*

"Me, truly?"

After all, you found my name. Kabo. I like it. I wouldn't have let you even try if I hadn't felt you were part of my thunder.

Alliana couldn't speak. She simply nodded, her throat tight. Kabo was silent, but his neck wove around her, warm and reassuring. He understood.

They curled up like that, together. The bright sun chased away Stepmother's harsh words, and Kabo's gen-tle heat dried off Alliana's shirt.

*Why isn't your grandmother here? Or your—what
was it—father?*

"Grandmother Mari—she's not truly my grandmother. She's my stepsiblings' father's mother, but she
passed away a bit over a year ago. Before that, my mother
passed away, giving birth to me."

I'm sorry. Kabo snuggled closer, soothing the heart-
ache that swelled like she'd swallowed poisonberries.

"And my father...he never came back from his last
trip to the abyss."

Kabo sat up suddenly, and Alliana pitched forward,
barely catching herself from falling face-first into the
grasses. *I'll go look for him!*

"It's been six years." The truth tore at Alliana.
"There's no way anyone—nightdragons and abyss creatures excluded—could survive in the darkness that long."

Are you sure? What if he did survive?

Alliana shook her head. Slowly, haltingly, she told
Kabo about that horrifying day she had tried to forget.
But the feeling of her heart in her throat and the almost-
numb horror were etched into her mind like scars that
would never heal.

Alliana had run to the abyss the instant one of the
adventurers had returned with the news. Father's rope
had broken, they said. They called for him, lowered a
torch into the darkness, but—

Nothing.

None of them understood why he'd decided to rush down alone in the early hours of the morning. Alliana had been begging for a chance to go to the abyss with him. He'd always told her she was too young and that it was too dangerous. For him to go alone...

All the adventurers at the abyss had stayed at Last Stop Inn and had had their blisters healed by her father's salves or had warmed up by the fire with a mug of his warm tea. They all crawled up and down the rocky faces and poked through the tunnels to look. But the frayed rope was the obvious truth: Her father had fallen into the pits of the abyss, and he was never returning.

From that moment she'd heard the news, though, her memory got a little fuzzy. Reina had explained later that Alliana had snuck her way through the entrance to rappel down in search of her father. She'd actually managed to get down to the second platform—her father had apparently fallen somewhere in the darkness between the first platform and the second—when a pair of adventurers caught her, returning her to the inn. Stepmother had a traveling healer—the one time he'd been in Narashino in nearly a year—give her a sleeping draught to make her rest, for she'd been clawing her way out of the inn, trying to get back to the abyss.

Stepmother had arranged for another pair of young adventurers to search all the way down to the seventh platform, but she'd told Alliana that she'd have to pay her back for every copper it cost. She had said yes, even in her sleep-draught-induced haze, without a doubt. And that was how Alliana had begun the backbreaking chores of the inn. Stepmother soon let go of the cook Alliana had known since childhood and the maid who cleaned the room.

Just the chance of trying to get her father back would've been worth a lifetime of debt. But, as it turned out, it was fool's gold, and it'd left her without a copper to her name.

I would fly anywhere, do anything for my thunder, my chosen family, too.

It wasn't long before the Royal Advisor issued a declaration that Alliana's father had died in the abyss, even though there was no body—the Royal Advisor would never bother with sending his steward to look. One of the adventurers, taking pity on her, had told her that even bones didn't last long; it'd only take a few days before a creature gnawed through them.

I will look for him.

"He's gone." Those words ached, but she knew without doubt that it was true.

Kabo let out a soft, sad cry, shifting to wrap closer around Alliana. *It is not the same, but I am here for you.*

Her tears fell.

Her memories of Father and Grandmother Mari were the only real traces left of them. She didn't even have a recollection of her mother, though Father had said she'd sung to Alliana every day when Alliana had been growing in her stomach. But Alliana still had other members of her chosen family in her life, and more days, moons, years to make memories with them.

Nela had said, *I believe in the impossible.* And Alliana wasn't so sure of that yet—her dreams seemed beyond impossible these days: Get her father back? Attend the Royal Academy? Much less be free of Stepmother and the clutches of the inn? Some of these wishes were truly, absolutely impossible.

I am your chosen family, now. Kabo was firm. *And I will search for the rest of your thunder, too.*

Alliana's eyes burned with tears, but she pressed her forehead against the dragon's. "Thank you, Kabo."

CHAPTER TWELVE

THE ROYAL INVITE

Alliana was sweeping the main room when the front doorbell rang. It chimed through the chatter of the handful of inn guests devouring the fluffy soufflé pancakes she'd made for breakfast. Reizo was so busy stuffing his face that even he didn't have time for his usual barbs.

"Go," Stepmother said curtly, wiping crumbs off her lips and tossing the dirty cloth napkin at Alliana, her new enamel bangles clanking loudly. "If it's the diner boy delivering bread, remind him *again* that he isn't supposed to go through the front."

Alliana gingerly pinched the filthy cloth off her shoulder by the corner, holding it at arm's length until she could toss it in the hallway laundry basket, trying not to gag. As she hurried past the grandfather clock and to the

front door, she hungrily breathed in the aroma of the pancakes, almost tasting the thick brown sugar syrup on her
tongue. Stepmother had hovered around her the moment
after she'd decided the menu, just to ensure that Alliana
couldn't steal one. Her stomach growled. The thin gruel
this morning was nothing compared to the sweet and airy
confections that Isao had taught her how to make, but
perhaps her friend would have a treat for her. Alliana
tucked a few stray hairs back into her braid and pulled
open the door. "Isao, thank goodness—"

An older, dignified gentleman in a sharp sky-blue
uniform stood on the doorstep, his dark hair beginning
to speckle with lines of gray. Behind him, a horse nibbled
at the scarce grasses on the road leading up to the crossroads. The man gave a kind smile and swept into a bow.
"Hello, resident of Narashino. I am here to deliver this
message on behalf of the Royal Advisor."

"H-hello? Um, hello!" Alliana stammered, trying to
bob into a comparable bow.

Extending a gloved hand, the man proffered a thick
envelope stamped with a heavy blue seal. "For the three
of-age children in this household, according to the past
census. There are still three children, correct?"

"Yes—me, Reizo Enokida, and Reina Enokida."

"And your name?"

"Alliana. Alliana of Rivelle." She had no parents of
her own, not anymore.

Pity flickered in the man's eyes as he quietly pulled out a small notepad and a stick of charcoal. "Understood. We'll expect—"

"There will be two children in attendance." A claw descended on Alliana's shoulder.

Stepmother towered above Alliana; Reizo and Reina flanked her. Reizo snatched the envelope out of Alliana's hand and tore it open, pulling out three stiff parchment invitations, and Alliana caught a glimpse of gold-hued ink, her breath catching. *Her invitation to* the *ball.*

Her stepbrother growled, "I've been waiting for this. That stinking Royal Advisor took way too long to send the invite. Slow as molasses. He needs me to set him straight."

The man cleared his throat. "Ma'am, I see three of-age children here. Barring illness or their personal decision not to attend, we expect all three at the ball."

Hope glimmered in Alliana's heart. Including her?

"He's right, Alliana should go." Reina smiled widely, flashing the gap between her front teeth. "Duh, can't you count, Ma? Three. One, two, three."

Stepmother glowered. "Shush it, Reina!" To the man, she snapped, "I'm the head of the household, and I decide the matters of what happens to my charges."

The disappointment that Alliana had expected came back twofold, sharp as needles.

"Besides, who are you to say anything? You're just a

deliveryman." Reizo sniffed, his nose sticking up in the air. "Just Reina and I will go. We don't need *her*. It's not like the Royal Advisor will know the difference."

The man's mustache twitched. "I apologize. I should have properly introduced myself. I am Kyo Rydern, head steward to the Royal Advisor."

Reizo nearly turned purple. "That was a joke earlier, sir."

"That means *you* went to the Royal Academy," Reina said, goggling at him. "What was it like? You can choose different paths, right? Everyone talks about waiting on the queen, but you can also work for one of the Royal Advisors, or assist an inter-realm diplomat, even become a mayor of a town. If I go to the Academy, I can become whatever I want."

"I am indeed a graduate," Kyo said. "It's an admirable path, which is why I take this role of inviting eligible attendees very seriously. For *all* residents, regardless of their family status."

"Oh, but we're a very close family," Stepmother simpered, her hand snaking out to wrap around Alliana's shoulder. Her nails felt sharper than nightdragon claws, digging into her bones. "Why, Mistress Sakamaki, my mother-in-law whom I took care of, always said that Alliana was like one of her own grandchildren. They would spend their evenings telling fairy tales as they sewed tapestries."

Alliana's heart tightened. She'd always guessed that Stepmother had been jealous. After nights when she'd stayed up until dawn to help Grandmother Mari finish a stack of mending, Stepmother had been merciless with her list of chores.

"Which is why I *should* go," Alliana said, her voice light and clear as crystal.

Stepmother spluttered. Reizo's eyebrows knitted together more than ever, looking more and more like a unibrow with every second.

Alliana turned to Kyo and hope burned brighter than fire as the guard tilted his head in a decisive nod. "The Royal Advisor will expect all three of you."

Reizo opened his mouth to protest, but Stepmother quickly stepped in front of him, nervously clearing her throat. "Of course. We'll all be there."

"Good. Farewell until the Farmlands Ball." With that, the guard dipped into one final bow and turned back toward his horse.

Alliana stood in the doorway, her head spinning, like she was floating up to the clouds. She was truly going to the ball. *She*, Alliana of Rivelle, was going to meet the Royal Advisor and have a chance at attending the Royal Academy.

"Good luck finding something to wear." Her step-brother dangled the gold-stamped invitation in front of her with a grin. "*Proper attire required for entry.* You can read, right? Last time I checked, that"—he sent a pointed look down at her inn uniform, her ratty black skirt and faded top—"isn't enough to gain entrance at a ball. You're going to have to wait outside for us."

"But—"

Stepmother flashed a dangerous smile. "Your brilliant stepbrother is right. It's not like they'll have a spare gown for you to change into. And no one will want to meet you, least of all Royal Advisor Miwa. Besides, it's not like you have ambitions to attend the Royal Academy. That's too far above your position."

If Stepmother let her have some of the spare fabric from the recent dress Alliana had made her, that'd be enough to make a proper outfit to attend. "But I..."

It was too late. Stepmother had wrapped her arm around Reizo's shoulders and was walking with him back to the main room, down the hallway full of illustrations of her two children, without a second glance at her stepdaughter.

Quieter, Alliana said, "But I...I *do* want to attend."

Reina, who still had her head stuck out the door as she watched the guardsman trot off on his pony, turned around to pat her on the arm. "Good luck, then. I'd give you one of my gowns, since I have so many, but Ma would notice in a flash. Likely, she'd tear it off you at the dance and say you're a thief."

Reina knew the truth: Alliana would never be able to go to the ball.

Instead of following her stepfamily back into the house, Alliana hurried out the front, her eyes stinging. But, to her misfortune, she passed under the kitchen window, just as Reizo chucked out a chewed-up gingko nut.

She stifled her sob, the slimy mess dripping down her neck, cold and stinky.

"She'll never be allowed in with her usual rags." Reizo's voice floated out the window. The iron teapot clattered onto the tray; her stepbrother was mishandling the kitchen wares as usual, but he'd blame Alliana for any chips in the plating. "Wasn't that so clever of me, Ma?"

"You *are* a clever boy. You are so handsome and Reina is so gifted at conversation. As fitting for my darling children." A tin squeaked as Stepmother crunched down on a rice cracker. Alliana couldn't even remember what they tasted like anymore.

"And she's far from darling." Reizo's words felt like another kick to her stomach, pushing all the air out of her when she was already falling down. Alliana's eyes burned as Stepmother and Reizo swept off to the sitting room, to drink more tea and gobble up all the rice crackers, leaving nothing but crumbs to sweep up later.

But Alliana kept her head steady. Though Grandmother Mari had wanted Alliana to take care of Stepmother and her stepsiblings, the old woman had once urged her to go to the Regional Ball, for the chance to receive an invite to the Royal Academy.

This was the one chance she had to fulfill Grandmother Mari's wishes *and* finally follow the dreams she wanted.

She'd do anything for Royal Advisor Miwa and his scryer to pick her for the Royal Academy. The Farmlands Ball would be the last night she'd ever have to see her stepfamily. And then she'd leave, disappearing from Narashino like a ghost from one of Grandmother Mari's fairy tales.

PART THREE

CHAPTER THIRTEEN

CASTELLA CLOUDS

Wind rattled the windows, distracting Alliana. She pricked her thumb with the needle, scratching the skin next to an old sewing scar. "Ouch!"

The rosy evening had dipped into night rather quickly. Dark clouds, promising rain, had woven on the horizon, along with a whistling, icy breeze that felt like it'd come straight from the snowy slopes of the Sakuya Mountains. Even the most gallant of adventurers had turned in early, hoping for a brighter new day.

Alliana shifted where she sat on the faded gold-and-white pillows. Stepmother had taken them after the old woman passed away, but within a moon, she'd tossed them into the waste bin, her tearoom filled with a new set of costly, custom-ordered pillows. Alliana had snuck the old pillows up into her room, wiping off the stains and mending the tears. The pillows kept her company and softened the long nights, especially when she had to sew until the crack of dawn, like now.

She readjusted the yellow ribbon against the rippling, gaudy purple fabric of Reina's dress, fighting through her sleepy haze. She *had* to finish up this latest addition by dawn, or Stepmother would pile more chores upon her. And she couldn't miss out; any day now, surely, Nela would pop into the chicken coop as she was tossing out cracked corn, or Kabo would come back to meet her, like they'd promised each other.

But then she saw the tiny drop of blood on the canary-yellow ribbon, and her head throbbed. "Curses!"

She just as quickly clapped her hand over her mouth, glancing toward the attic door. Reizo, one floor down, would stomp up and extinguish the candle by dumping Alliana's precious barley tea over it, like he did the other night. Stepmother had already told her if she even had a *toe* out of line—even if Alliana somehow was able to patch together a dress out of scraps—she wouldn't be attending the ball.

She only had two weeks' time until the Farmlands Ball, and with her stepmother's constant demands, the alterations had taken over every spare minute. *Add a yellow ribbon here! Reina must positively glow! No, resew it a centimeter lower. Can't you see that gets in the way of her beauty?*

The countless ribbons and silk flowers (that Alliana had to craft by hand) looked like the current fashions in the capital city, according to the magazines that Stepmother had ordered in preparation for the ball...except it looked like those fashions had mutated from a cute hatchling to an eight-headed fire-breathing monster.

And Alliana still didn't have a dress.

The crystal pigeon chirped; then its wings fluttered away. Moments later, a sound came from the window. *Tap, tap.*

Alliana looked up. The flickering candlelight outlined two figures on the other side of the glass. Nela, of course. Only the witch would be floating outside on a broomstick. But who was with her? Perhaps Taichi?

The hinges squeaked loudly as she swung the windowpane open. Swirls of chilly midnight breeze tangled in her hair, whispering of adventures yet to be taken and cities to be explored, but she ignored its call. Instead, she looked between her two friends in surprise. "Isao! Nela!"

They grinned back; Isao, who was riding sidesaddle, gestured at the ground. "Come outside? We've got a surprise for you."

The weariness from hunching over Reina's dress washed away as Alliana stood and turned to hurry down the ladder.

"Wait." The witch's whisper was gentle as the breeze. "Come here. I have an idea."

Nela motioned for Alliana to crawl out of the window, even though there wasn't enough room for three on a broomstick. She shimmied through the frame; it was a tight fit. As soon as she stood out on the strip of flat roof tiles, Alliana rubbed her arms from the chill.

Deep in the nighttime hours, the inn hummed and creaked; guests snored and Reina babbled while asleep, her chatter drifting from the open window on the second story. This beautiful almost-quiet was one of Alliana's favorite times of the day.

"We should get a little further from that." Isao nodded toward Reina's window with a wry grin. "I'm pretty sure she's loud enough to wake the beasts in the abyss."

"Shall I meet you two downstairs?" Alliana asked.

"How about *upstairs*?" Nela asked, peeking over Alliana's shoulder. With a swirl of her wand, Grandmother Mari's white-and-gold cushions shot out of the attic—one sweeping Alliana straight off her feet.

"Oh!" The cushion carried Alliana upward; when she wobbled to the right, somehow the pillow shifted, ensuring she wouldn't fall.

Nela jumped off the broomstick and onto another of the awaiting hovering cushions, and Isao gingerly followed. Their makeshift seats brought them up, up, above the clouds, and into the deep sapphire nighttime sky, filled with golden stars.

"*Wow.*" Isao stared all around, round eyes full of wonder.

Nela giggled. "Haven't you seen the night sky before?"

But Alliana understood. She'd never seen it like this. Not so close it felt like she could pluck a star out and take a bite. Would it taste sweet and buttery like Isao's freshly baked loaves? Or was it cold and icy, tasty as jellylike blocks of anmitsu?

"*A rest for all here, a table that won't disappear. A light aglow just for us to know.*" Nela waved her wand, and clouds soft as spun sugar wove together and crystallized, forming into a table. Misty tendrils spun under Alliana's cushion to form a chair, and it felt like she was sitting on a throne fit for a queen. Above, little lights shone, like the witch had lit floating candles all around.

"We're lucky to know a witch," Isao said, shaking his head in awe.

The witch's cheeks turned surprisingly pink. "Oh, it's nothing, really. I'm just glad to be of service."

Isao pulled a small fabric-wrapped package from his pocket and untied the top knot. "I've been saving this for us."

He revealed a small tin filled with squares of cake as warm and golden as the stars, and Alliana beamed with delight. "Your castella!"

From far, far below, Eggna let out a sleepy squawk—
likely hungry as usual—but the chicken wasn't going to
get a slice of the delicate cake if Alliana had a say in it.

The three of them used tiny silver forks that Nela
had charmed out of thin air with a quick rhyme—"*A
way to eat a special treat*"—and plucked up tall, spongey
squares.

Warm honey sang with richness; the toasted-brown
top melted on Alliana's tongue with a trace of cara-
melized sugar. It was like Isao had pulled one of the
clouds around them, spun it with honey, and baked it
into a cake.

"Do you like it?" Isao looked nervously between the
two of them. "It's my first time making it in the tradi-
tional wooden cake pan. I finally tried building one of my
own...but it's probably not any good. I'll try again—"

The witch reached over the table and clutched his
hand. "Please, make me this cake every day for the rest
of my life. The way to my heart is through my stomach."

Isao stared at the witch, spluttering. Alliana covered
a giggle; she'd never seen easygoing Isao so in shock.

"I—I—of course I'd be happy to make it for you." A
scarlet blush was working its way up the baker's neck.

"Nela, you better ask for different cakes, or he really
will give you a castella every day for the rest of your life,"
Alliana warned.

The witch frowned, with a very serious look on her

face. "My favorite pastries are croissants, my favorite flavor is yuzu. Anything that has hints of either of those. Please. For the rest of my life."

Isao let out a happy, surprised laugh. "Any day, Nela."

Alliana joined them in laughter, her heart singing to be with her two friends. She wished every night could be like this. Despite the thick clouds drifting softly across the midnight-black sky, stars were scattered all over like Queen Natsumi had thrown her chest of diamonds into the world above—like a night that would never have an end, and only felt like the beginning of something so perfect.

But, like a star tumbling out of the sky, her happiness stuttered as she remembered that her life was far from magical. The throbbing pain from the earlier needle prick seemed to come back twofold. She rubbed at the spot, and the witch caught her thumb, examining the broken skin under her scar.

"Oof," Nela said, wincing. "May I?"

Alliana had barely finished nodding when the witch tapped her finger and said, "*Mend.*"

In a blink of an eye, her skin knitted together, faintly pink. If it weren't for her raised scar, she would've never been able to find it.

Isao blinked. "I thought you witches and wizards had to use rhymes for your magic."

Nela shrugged very casually. "True. But I've used that

spell for years and years, since when I first purposefully cast magic to heal a cut my father got from fishing. And after all the practice, I've shortened the enchantment. It's not a big deal."

Alliana guessed that the witch was being particularly modest; she didn't know too much about charms and curses and crafting magic, but everyone in Rivelle knew rhymes were used for spells by all in the Guild of Magic—except the most powerful. And, it seemed, their friend was one of them.

Nela cleared her throat, looking eager to change the subject. "I thought we'd surely be waking you. What were you doing up so late?"

"The ball is coming up, so I have to finish a dress," Alliana said. Isao sighed in solidarity. Mostly because Isao had no interest in being a prince in the realm, and just the thought of dressing up always made him itchy.

Nela looked between the two of them. "So that means you're making *your* attire, right?"

Isao snorted. "Not if Mistress Enokida has a word about it."

"What do you mean?"

"Well…" Alliana tried to search for a polite way to explain about her stepmother and her demands for Reina's dress.

"Those Enokidas." The normally mild-mannered Isao

shook his head with disgust. "Working for Mister Leo is tough enough, but the Enokidas are like a three-headed nightdragon."

"The king of dough says so?" Nela asked. "Then it must be true."

Alliana laughed at Isao's nickname. But then she protested—thinking of Kabo, her biggest (and fieriest) secret: "Surely nightdragons are better than my stepfamily."

At that, they all laughed.

"How about *I* finish the dress and then you can work on your own?" Nela asked.

Alliana brightened up and then just as quickly deflated, like the mochi that Reizo had stolen from her own hands earlier in the day. With a flash, the rice cake had crunched under his teeth and disappeared with a quick swallow. And she'd been left hungry.

"That's the problem. Stepmother demands alterations every day." Alliana sighed. "And each is more tiring than the last. The fabric would be all holes if I didn't spend time making the tiniest stitches possible. And if you made my dress now, I'm afraid Reizo might tear it up. But I've got plans to make my own dress, on my own terms."

Alliana would sew a dress out of thin air if she could. She would pull the moon down and weave the streaks of light into rippling silk, gentle on her skin. By spinning rays of sunrise, she'd sew red-orange cloth into a train as bright as fireblossoms. Stars from the sky would dot her hair, glimmering with light, like she was meant to wear a crown. And she'd have a pair of dancing slippers, soft as wisps from the clouds, as she swirled around the dance floor.

When she stepped into the Regional Ball, all eyes would turn to her. Some of the guests would murmur, *She's dressed as fine as the queen.* And the others nearby might say, *The girl looks like she could become the queen.*

But Alliana had no magic. She couldn't pull the sky down to wrap around her in a dress any more than she could convince Stepmother to buy her a premade dress sold at the general store. Despite what she'd told Nela, so her friend wouldn't worry, she still needed fabric.

Everything you need is right there, within reach. Sometimes, you have to look for what you're missing. But it's there. Take one step forward. Have faith in the future.

The voice was smooth as a summer day's light, as gentle as a breeze flowing along the tapestries. Alliana's heart thumped as she gazed between her two friends, who were teasing each other as they scarfed down the cake. Grandmother Mari wasn't here, not anymore. She knew that. Yet, as she scanned the otherwise empty clouds, remembering wonderful memories from the past, her eyes caught on something she'd missed. Something that had been here all along.

The white pillows, flecked with gold.

She *would* make her own dress. It would take every piece of fabric in the attic, and it'd be Grandmother Mari's last gift to her—but it'd be a dress.

Her heart pattered. With a simple design—she didn't need to look like a purple hornet like Reina—it wouldn't take long at all.

"You know, we can still put our plan in motion any day," Isao said brightly, drawing her attention away from drafting up a dress pattern.

"What's that?" Nela asked, and Isao began explaining it to her.

Their plan. The castles in the sky that they'd built of hopes and dreams, before Grandmother Mari had passed, and before Alliana had received that final letter. Still, she was getting closer to that dream, those hopes—*the path to her dreams*—as the Farmlands Ball drew near.

She felt the weight of the letter in her pocket. Even though it was as light as a feather, she could feel the corners poking through the thin cloth, rubbing against her skin, reminding her of the promise she'd made to Grandmother Mari.

Isao was busy telling Nela about a potential apprenticeship. "I was so close to getting a baker's internship, in this tiny town called Miyada, in the east of the realm. But they closed up their applications because the baker's cottage burned down in an accident, so they couldn't accept anyone new. They should be all built back up soon, though."

"That's a terrible pity," Nela sighed. "The next time I'm around that area, I'll fly over and place some charms on the baker's cottage to protect it against flames. Why, maybe you two will be there by then, and I can visit!"

Isao's eyes widened, as big as the pale moon above. "That would be wonderful! We really should go, Alliana!"

Alliana felt like she'd dropped a glass on the dining room floor, and all the inn's guests had turned to stare. "I...I..."

"Wouldn't it be nice," Isao sighed, taking in a lungful of clean, crisp air, "if we could travel all around the realm?"

"I'm sure we'd have lots of adventures." Alliana glanced at the horizon, where the barest rays of sunlight gilded the edges where the land met the sky. *I used to dream of that every day and night. In that strange time I call "before."* Alliana cleared her throat. "But I made a promise to stay here, at least until the Farmlands Ball."

"Still..." Nela glanced skeptically down at the inn; she'd

seen how Alliana was ordered around. "There's *more* you can be doing. You're so sharp at solving problems; you always seem to untangle an issue as easy as that mending you do. I know that when I bring you over to take a look at a wild beast who's trying to chase Hayato into the barrier, or if there's a group of adventurers all shouting at you for the best room in the inn, you'll know how to sort things out. That's special, Alliana. That's *rare*, even if you don't think it is. And there's so much more you can do... I mean, unless you want to stay."

Alliana, who had been following her words with a sense of sour dread, felt her stomach flip. "I'm...I'm happy here. As I am. As...as things are."

Nela raised an eyebrow. "I don't need to cast a spell to know that's a lie."

From the other side of the crystal and cloud table, Isao stared down, sad.

Alliana tried to say, with more feeling, "It's true. I need to be in Narashino, at least until the Farmlands Ball. I have a debt I owe."

Slowly, she told the witch about her father's death at the abyss, as painful as it was to explain. And how she'd felt alone, until Grandmother Mari had invited her up to her attic one night, and then it became her secret hideaway...all up until the old woman had passed away, and left the final letter. It was difficult to explain what the old woman meant to her—she had been quiet evenings and

warm cups of tea. Finger pricks from needles that immediately turned into gentle head pats and soft bandages.
All these things brought feelings that Alliana couldn't quite
put into words. And even though she never felt like she'd
be able to repay the old woman for taking care of her, she
was determined to take care of Stepmother and her stepsiblings for Grandmother Mari's memory.

"Your Grandmother Mari would be proud of you. I
wish I didn't agree with your choice...but I understand,"
the witch said, her fingers wrapping around Alliana's
hand and squeezing lightly.

And for once, Alliana felt her words were heard. She
wanted to revel in this moment, drinking in the moonlight
shining over them, the gentle breeze.... Alliana wanted to
capture this memory and live in it forever.

But the beauty of memory was no more than a looking glass into the past; the second after, time had already
turned and flowed on again. For Grandmother Mari was
gone, and Isao had to go back to the diner, and Nela would
have to leave again on another mission all too soon. And
Alliana would be alone with her worries, alone with her
piles of mending and a dress she had to make out of almost
nothing.

Something flickered in the sky behind Nela's shoulder, a streak of black across the early-morning golden yel-
lows and blues. Alliana squinted, trying to understand

what she was seeing. It was in the shape of a pigeon, yet flat and thin. "What *is* that?"

Isao turned. "Isn't it a bird? Did your crystal pigeon change colors?"

The witch sucked in a breath. "It's a summons."

"From the Guild of Magic?"

Nela frowned. "I'm not sure. But the black painted on the edges—that means the message is urgent."

The bird-letter swooped around them, and shot down into Nela's open hand. She tapped it once with her wand, muttering, "*Open*," and the paper unfolded. The witch's eyes zipped over the paper, widening as she read, her face turning paler and paler with every word.

"What's the matter?" Isao asked.

"I've got to go," she gasped out. "This message is from Hayato. There's been a break at the shield."

Alliana frowned. "But you fixed the barrier so easily last time after we got the rockcrows back inside."

Nela nodded distractedly. "I'm sure it's nothing major....I'll come back as soon as I can."

Isao brushed off his hands. "Can you get us back down?"

With a swish of Nela's wand, the clouds dispersed, and the cushions sunk, like leaves fluttering out of the sky, until Alliana's feet brushed against the rooftop again.

There, the witch unhooked her cloak and spun it into

the broomstick, kicking off instantly. "I won't forget our little chat. Our conversation isn't over!"

Alliana's heart pattered with tendrils of hope as Isao and Nela waved. Isao hurried home on foot; the witch disappeared into the pitch-black clouds, roiling thick and ominous over the horizon. Alliana waited and waited as she worked on Reina's dress, yet the witch did not return.

CHAPTER FOURTEEN

PARTINGS

The front door burst open, and adventurers swarmed through the entranceway of the inn. Alliana looked up from where she stood behind the register, calculating the sums after this morning's checkouts. The ball was tonight, and her mind couldn't seem to concentrate on the numbers. All she could think of was standing in front of the Royal Advisor in her dress made with Grandmother Mari's fabric, waiting for the scryer to decide her fate.

Would she be invited to the Royal Academy?

Or would Stepmother and her stepsiblings stop her, before she even had a chance to try?

"It's closed," groaned a freckled adventurer as they slumped down on the bench, pulling Alliana out of her thoughts. "I can't believe it."

"Is something the matter?" Alliana glanced between

the half dozen or so dusty travelers, shoulders heavy with knapsacks. They'd just left for the abyss a few hours ago; it was much too early for them to be back. Dirt still crusted their boots and powdered over their ratty clothes. They hadn't lingered at the entrance to the abyss, where most of them used the public baths to soak off the grime of the darkness.

A woman sliding off her boots explained, "That Guild of Magic, the Royal Guards…they closed the entrance to the abyss. Called up everyone at all the platform levels."

Alliana gaped. In all her years, that'd never happened before.

"I don't even get it!" a man with a thick mustache complained, tossing his knapsack onto the bench. "I was just about to get a lucky find, I know it!"

"That's what you say all the time, especially after you lose all your gold to me in hanafuda," his friend responded. "C'mon, they said there's a break in the shield. You heard the Royal Guards. They had to go with the Guild of Magic to take care of things, 'cause some creatures are escaping. All of that adds up to time for us to play some cards."

The man kept on whining. "Got nothing to do with my work. The guards don't mine the gold."

Alliana glanced out the entranceway window. There was something dark and tiny, flying high in the cloudy

sky. Was it a creature from the abyss? Or—better yet—
was Nela back, finally?

"Yeah, but if a nightdragon finds you and the Royal
Guards are gone, who's gonna save you from becoming
dragon fodder? Not me."

"Not much they can do about a nightdragon, anyway."

"Well, I'm not waiting around to find out."

The sliding front door rattled in the biting winds, cutting through the bickering. The adventurers grew silent,
and the man closest shivered. "I'm done with being outside, especially if there're creatures crawling about."

The group kicked off their boots and lumbered into
the main room to gather around the tables. More likely
than not, they'd spend the rest of the day betting on
rounds of hanafuda, wagering gold flakes and chips of
gems they'd mined on the striking red-and-white playing
cards, as they filled their bellies with salty rice crackers.

Alliana would drop by to take their drink orders
later. Her eyes stayed trained on the dot outside as it shot
closer. It was too small to be a witch and her broomstick.
The skin on her neck prickled.

Reina was sitting on the front steps, interrogating
another set of adventurers before they could make it in.
"I've heard the abyss has been particularly windy these
past few days. Is it true that one of the adventurer's ropes

got eaten by a shadowsnake? And is it true that a night-dragon has escaped?"

Alliana didn't stay to hear the rest of her stepsister's interrogation. She couldn't risk drawing Reina's attention to whatever flew above. Quickly, she hurried through the hallway, her thoughts skittering as fast as her socked feet. There wasn't enough time to make it to her bedroom. Stepmother's bedroom and adjoining tearoom overlooked the back and the chicken coop; the woman was lounging with her morning tea as usual, and she'd notice if Alliana ran out.

She burst into the empty kitchen and threw open the shutters. This room faced the side of the house, and she craned her neck out the window, just as something small shot inside.

The bird-letter swooped around her and landed in her hand. Her shoulders eased with relief when she caught a glimpse of her name written in Nela's elegant cursive on the wing; then the bird unfolded into a flat piece of paper. The witch was safe. She'd just been busy—that was all. Then Alliana started reading the letter, and her shoulders hunched up again.

Alliana—

This letter is for your eyes only. Don't let anyone see—especially those who might spread rumors.

The break in the shield wasn't as tiny as Hayato had made it out to be. Hayato was "fixing" the rip (he was showing off to Dorey again) when one of his spells misfired and let out a bang with sparks and smoke. When everything cleared, there was an enormous rip in the barrier, almost the size of a full farmhouse. And creatures were crawling out. Shadowsnakes worse than nightmares, scuttlerats, beetles with pincers the size of my arms . . . I got there well after his too-late call for help . . . but there were still monsters breaking through.

Hayato and I have collected most of the escaped creatures—Taichi's stuck with family duties, so he can't help. But one beast—or beasts, we're not sure which—still eludes us.

When we search—whether by broomstick or spells—we can't find the culprit, but the lands are burning. It's sudden. The sky will be clear one moment; then smoke rolls in and the fields burst into flames. We're protecting the farmers and not a soul has been hurt—yet. But what do you—

"What's that?"

Alliana spun around, clutching the note behind her.

Reina stood in the doorframe. Alliana's heart pattered. Then there were heavy footsteps clomping down the hallway.

"What's what?" Stepmother strode into the kitchen, her beady eyes scanning the kitchen and landing square on Alliana, who had her hands behind her back.

"Nothing."

"Show me your hands."

Alliana slowly uncurled her fists in front of her. Two bare, empty palms faced up.

"Empty your pockets."

She turned her pockets inside out. They were nothing more than bare linen, raggedy from wear.

Stepmother growled, yanking at her pockets until the fabric ripped. "I *know* you had something! You liar. It *was* you who stole that roll the other day, wasn't it?" The older woman's angry gaze cut to her daughter, prodding for answers. The girl chewed on her bottom lip, the gap between her teeth flashing.

"I didn't see anything," Reina said finally. "I just wanted her to make me a new cup of barley tea before the carriage arrives."

Stepmother frowned. "Make me one, too. Now. It's not like you'll be going to the ball; you don't need to spend the time I do to get ready."

Alliana felt the woman's eyes follow her every move, but she had nothing to hide now. The stove sizzled as the flames overtook the letter. The last bits turned into molten sparks, flying up and out of the chimney, filled with words unread.

CHAPTER FIFTEEN

THE FARMLANDS BALL

W hy, hello, Royal Advisor Miwa." Reizo simpered over his reflection in the mirror of Stepmother's tearoom. The glass was cut in the eight-point shape that was all the popularity in Okayama, but the mirror was chipped at the edges, not unlike his mother's patience, which was wearing quite thin.

"Reizo!" Stepmother snapped, and then gestured at her daughter, too. "Let's *go!*"

Alliana stepped aside from where she was helping her stepsister adjust her bows. Reina was asking, "Can't you make it look like I have purple hornet wings?"

One thing was certain for tonight: Reina's dress *would* catch the Royal Advisor's eye. Along with everyone else set to be at the Farmlands Ball. Everyone... except Alliana.

Reizo stopped in front of her, snickering. "I hope you'll have fun here. Maybe have your own dance with your favorite chickens."

Alliana let out a sniffle, and just as quickly clapped her hands over her face, turning away, as if she couldn't *bear* the sight of Reizo, all suited up in his orange suit and ready to slobber over the feet of the Royal Advisor. "I—I couldn't make a dress!" Alliana cried out, with another fake sob. "I didn't have any fabric, and I—oh, can't I *please* borrow one of Reina's dresses? Or maybe yours, Stepmother?"

Never mind that Reina's dresses were much too short, and Stepmother's dresses would be like swimming in an abyss of fabric.

The woman leaned in, her vinegar breath instantly overwhelming. "Oh, I forgot to mention. Mister Leo installed these beautiful locks on the dressers." She pointedly dangled a bronze key in front of Alliana's nose, and just as quickly pocketed it.

Alliana wouldn't be caught *ever* in her stepmother's awful dresses. Besides, her stepfamily would notice her from a kilometer away if she wore a bright purple-and-orange dress like what her stepmother was traipsing around in now. Between the three of them, in their overly attention-getting outfits, they'd stand out like beacons amongst the guests.

"We must go, we can't be late," Mister Leo called

from the doorway, anxiously wringing his hat. "Or else we'll spend all night waiting in line to meet the scryer and Royal Advisor and have no time to explore." For the past moon, he'd been waxing on and on about all the free honey cider he'd be able to drink there.

He offered the crook of his elbow to Mistress Enokida, who took it with one last glance at Alliana.

"I had better hear that all the guests were fed, or *you* won't be fed," the woman snapped. "Don't you dare cause a speck of trouble."

Alliana pretended to nod earnestly. *Trouble? What was that?*

"Have fun here." Reizo smirked, like he thought he was so much better than Alliana. "I'll bring a souvenir. How about a used toothpick from one of gourmet food stands at the ball? It'll be a gift from servant to servant."

Alliana had been endlessly patient throughout all of her stepfamily's dithering in front of the mirror, but at this, her blood boiled. She almost snapped her head up and shot back a retort, but barely reeled it in.

Reizo didn't see how it was *her* work, as their servant, that kept the inn running. That it was Isao's days filled with cooking meals at the diner or relaying messages at the abyss that kept most of Narashino fed and informed. Or Nela flying back and forth, doing the minor jobs that her Master Wizard wouldn't bother with. Workers like her and her friends were the blood and backbone of

Rivelle Realm, no matter how much her stepfamily would try to pretend she didn't exist.

Alliana forced her head down into a deep bow, just like any other day.

Reizo let out a loud, ugly snort and swept past, dragging a protesting Reina behind him. "Ugh! Let Alliana go instead of me! I realized my true calling: I want to study the unicorn village across the sea!"

Alliana stood on the front step of the inn, watching her stepfamily ride off in Mister Leo's rented carriage. She was the picture of desolation: lost and alone, a tiny figure behind them, so desperate to be included.

Until they disappeared in clouds of dust.

And then the front door slid back open with a rattle, and she turned around with a grin.

A figure stepped out of the darkness, and a little shadow followed.

"Ready to go?" Isao asked, holding something out to her.

"Are you sure you don't want to join me?" Alliana asked.

Her friend shook his head with a smile. "Nah, that's not the place for the likes of me. I'm happier here."

"Isao is gonna be a baker." Hiroshi held the other end with one hand, sucking his thumb with the other. "And you're gonna be a beautiful princess!"

"I'm not a princess." *Yet.*

Alliana gently took the white-and-gold dress from them. She'd sewn it up as quickly as she could, and little Hiroshi had helped hide it in the tiniest crawl space underneath their living quarters in the diner.

"But..." Isao took one last glance at where Mister Leo's carriage had rattled away. No one else remotely near Narashino would be heading over to the Farmlands Ball. And it'd take a full day to walk. "How will you get there?"

She winked. "I'll worry about that part."

Before Isao could say another word, Alliana stole out into the falling night.

CHAPTER SIXTEEN

THE ESTATES OF ROYAL ADVISOR KENZO MIWA

This was it. As guests frolicked at the Royal Advisor's beautiful estates, kilometers and kilometers away, this was what Alliana's plan had come down to: staring at the barrier.

She was surrounded by the same tall grasses, the same curling fernleaf, the gentle wind that haunted her dreams. She felt Grandmother Mari's presence all around. Perhaps Grandmother Mari wasn't standing next to her anymore, but she felt her touch in every part of her surroundings, like the old woman had illuminated the world in a way that Alliana had thought she'd long forgotten.

Excitement sparked through her. Tonight, this adventure felt like the start of something new.

That is—if anything would happen.

Well, she had to try. Alliana cleared her throat. "Kabo! *Kabo!*"

From one of the trees, the crystal pigeon squawked loudly, wings fluttering.

Alliana inched closer to the barrier. The gap that the nightdragon hatchling had slipped through last time had been mended, probably by someone from the Guild, but...

She closed her eyes, training her hearing.

There was the softly swishing grass, the whirling wind that flowed around her...

Alliana swallowed, though her throat was dry from shouting. What if she never made it to the Farmlands Ball? All her bravado in front of Isao...the dress she'd tried so hard to make...it'd all become nothing.

Her feet felt heavy as she turned around, looking at the meadow, like Kabo might pop up in the grasses, munching a mouthful of fernleaf, about to trot over and deposit the half-eaten herb in her lap, to help her "collect" a basketful.

She glanced one more time, over her shoulder, but he was nowhere to be seen. Perhaps, like Grandmother Mari, Kabo was also never coming back.

Then a terrifying shriek echoed through the meadow, making the hairs stand on the back of Alliana's neck.

She whirled around.

From beyond the barrier, a dark shadow rose, and terror filled Alliana's heart. It was too big to be Kabo.

The wild creature roared, and Alliana could see its wings, its clawed leg that rose up, and *slash*—!

The shield shattered, and the beast flew through, its hide sparking as it flew into Rivelle Realm, sharp nails glittering as it slid to a stop.

Alliana stared up at the fierce beast who was as large as the trees lining the meadow. The creature—with a familiar scar on his cheek—stared back down at her and gave a sharp, fanged smile.

"Kabo!" She rushed forward. "You grow so fast!"

Alliana. The dragon swooped his head down, and she wrapped her arms around his neck and pressed her forehead into his steady, warm hide. *I have missed you, as I always do.*

For a moment, she rested there, her breath evening out. Kabo snuggled closer, sensing her worries. *What is it, my thunder?*

"I have to go to a castle over there." Alliana pointed to where she and Nela had passed by the Royal Advisor's estates before. "Would you be able to help me?" She glanced up at the night sky. "I don't have a lot of time."

The nightdragon looked behind him, at the abyss. *I have a—what do you call it—gift?—for you, but it will have to wait. Let us go.*

Alliana took a step backward, staring deeply at her friend. "There's one catch. I can't let you be noticed by anyone else."

Are you ashamed of me, Alliana?

"*Never*," she whispered, flinging her arms around Kabo. "But...but...the rest of the realm is scared of nightdragons. And, well, I'm starting to realize that fear is like a nightmare pushing people in the wrong direction, away from hope and joy. If I let you fly out in the open, there's a chance that they'd trap you—because you're a young nightdragon—and the Guild of Magic or even the hunters' guild might try to capture you as their own. There will be a day that I will truly make it safe for you to fly over Rivelle's skies—I promise. I'll find a way to change their fear into belief. As for today...Nela wrote to me—beasts escaped the abyss, and they're getting captured and sent back in—or *removed*. I can't let that happen to you."

The nightdragon blinked solemnly. *I would burn down all that try. Though, I suppose, that would cause trouble for you, my thunder.*

Alliana bit her lip. "I'm sorry. I'm asking too much—"

There was a sudden thump as Kabo moved forward, surprisingly graceful despite his towering height, and his neck swooped under her as he lifted her up onto his back. *Never. I will fly to this castle—I will fly to realms beyond this one, if it is for you.*

Alliana clenched onto the thick grooves of his leathery hide as Kabo kicked off, soaring up into the clouds.

Royal Advisor Miwa's estates were beyond magnificent. Surely even Queen Natsumi's stone castle in the capital couldn't be more beautiful than this. Alliana made her way along the path in awe; she could barely believe she was in the Farmlands for all that it felt like she was in a different realm. The sprawling lands were elegantly dotted with manicured juniper trees, orderly stretches of grass, and low rocks. Either the Royal Advisor had an army of landscapers or he was a very generous patron to the Guild of Magic. Even the dirt road, which Alliana walked alongside, turned into gray pavement: something she'd never seen up close.

But that wasn't all. From above, the grandiose castle ruled on top of the hill, with sloping white roofs and shining windows rimmed with sheets of gold.

Alliana glanced back over her shoulder, where Kabo was happily rolling in the dirt, scratching his back on a particularly jagged-looking rock. He poked his head up around the evergreen tree, sensing her gaze. *Go on, Alliana. I will stay hidden. I am, after all, a* night*dragon. And I can blaze anyone to embers if they* do *notice me.*

She nearly tripped over the edge of her ball gown, which she'd hastily changed into moments before. "Kabo!"

The nightdragon flashed his sharp fangs before going back to rolling on his back.

He likely meant it as a joke. Hopefully.

But true to his word, the nightdragon had melted into

the shadows. Alliana was likely the last to arrive at the ball, so the nightdragon would be safe there. The cloud cover overhead was low enough that it'd been easy for them to land, but she'd have to leave early so they could safely fly away.

The gentle sounds of stringed instruments coaxed her forward, drifting out from beyond the walls of hedges.

She started to turn for one last look eastward, back where Narashino was, but stopped herself. Keeping her eyes steady, Alliana strode up the sloped path, up to the Royal Advisor's estates.

Her dress fluttered behind her, like wings lifting her higher. She didn't have to look down to see the creamy white silk, bright against her tanned skin, laced with an edging of gold along the bodice. Alliana knew the dress just as well as she felt Grandmother Mari's presence, in the letter that she still carried in her pocket, and in the fabric that Grandmother Mari had once sewn.

Even though she was going against Stepmother's bidding, Alliana knew that this was still following Grandmother's wishes. Grandmother Mari had wanted her to go to the Regional Ball, to test her luck and fate for the Royal Academy.

If tonight worked out, Alliana would go beyond the shadow of the inn, beyond the dusty crossroads. Beyond the reach of her stepfamily. And it would all start tonight, with her dress, and her first—but hopefully not last—ball.

CHAPTER SEVENTEEN

SMOKE AND MIRRORS

Guests danced under the mesmerizing starry sky like figures leaping out of Grandmother Mari's tapestries. The Farmlands Ball felt like a tale so beautiful that Alliana hoped it would never end.

Partygoers milled around as she stood at the edge of a mossy dance floor. This region's annual ball was held on the side of the Royal Advisor's castle, and it was absolutely enchanting. Bright lights twinkled above, like the Guild of Magic had pulled down the stars from the sky, and the air was perfumed with scents from the tables lining the rectangular dance floor. A small orchestra serenaded guests with elegant music that wrapped luxuriously around Alliana, like trills of silk with a steady beat of thick velvet.

"Wait for me!" a girl called, laughing as she brushed

past Alliana to follow her friends to a stand for roasted fish, her ribboned hair streaming behind her.

Ah, that was the difference. Alliana had come alone, whereas everyone else had friends and family to chatter with. Thankfully, though, with a crowd this large, she'd be able to stay out of sight of Mister Leo and her stepfamily.

When Alliana had approached the Royal Advisor's castle, stablehands were taking care of the horses, but no one batted an eye at the lonely girl walking up by herself. She kept a wary eye out, but it seemed like there were more people here than there could be in the capital city, and the handful of dutiful servants at the door greeted her, but to her relief, simply explained that the festivities would be taking place outside, so the Royal Advisor's house was strictly off-limits—which wasn't a surprise given how notoriously private the man was. Then they'd waved her through, and that was that.

From deep within the Royal Advisor's walls, a clock rang, deep and solemn. Eight o'clock. Between waiting for her stepfamily to leave and searching for Kabo, Alliana had arrived so late that it was getting close to the end of the scrying.

She needed to meet the Royal Advisor. And hope that she was invited to the Royal Academy. If not—she'd have to rush back to the inn, fast.

Alliana hurried through the crowd, until she approached

a line snaking out of a courtyard. There, others waited for their chance to see if they'd get to attend the Royal Academy. So far, Alliana had overheard, no one had been selected by the scryer. That wasn't too unusual, though, given that no one from the Farmlands had been chosen in more than fifty years.

Then she ducked. From behind the Baumkuchen oven, she peeked out.

Loitering next to the line was an all-too-familiar face.

Mister Leo glugged down a tankard next to the honey cider stand and wiped his mouth clean, puffing his chest out as he boasted something to the guest next to him. If Mister Leo was here, Stepmother, Reizo, and Reina were likely near. And indeed, when she glanced around, she found her stepfamily shoveling mounds of rice rolls into their faces a few stands down.

Alliana grabbed a slice of the Baumkuchen, keeping her head ducked as she pretended to be enchanted by the cake—which wasn't too difficult given how airy and buttery-sweet it was—and slipped through the crowd until she was well hidden. She'd have a little longer until she could approach the Royal Advisor and his scryer.

Finally, Stepmother, who had been busy stuffing her face at the roasted squab stand, dragged her children over to meet with Mister Leo, and the four of them disappeared in the crowd, heading to the far end of the dance floor, probably for some of the famed steamed buns on the far end.

Alliana sighed with relief.

"Last call for meeting Royal Advisor Kenzo Miwa!" a guard called from the side of the dance floor, cupping her hand around her mouth to shout. Down the way, a few other guards were doing the same, but only a handful of dancers broke away to join the line. It seemed nearly all the guests had tested their luck already.

"Last call!" the guard shouted. Then, with a nod to her comrades, the guards made their way back to the Royal Advisor's courtyard.

Alliana took one more glance at where Stepmother and her stepfamily were pushing through the crowds, and hurried to the end of the line.

The Royal Advisor and his scryer were meeting the constituents of the Farmlands in a smooth rock-filled courtyard to the side of the dancers. Nearly fifty or so children Alliana's age waited in line. A few were with parents or guardians, but most laughed and chatted within gaggles of friends, in frothy dresses, rippling kimonos, and smart suits.

Alliana stood on her tiptoes to see the front, and her heart pattered with a thrill. The Royal Advisor was dressed in opulent black robes that shimmered in a shade deep as the night sky. He was seated at the top of a small dais. At the bottom, a rather messy-looking man, unshaven and with rumpled robes that he kept tripping over, muttered to himself. An attendant in a black cloak kept trying to help him, but the wizard kept dropping his book.

Transfixed, she watched as the wizard nodded at a girl who was twisting her hands as she tiptoed closer in her deep purple dress and golden dance slippers.

"Name?" the man barked.

"Alvina Ichaso, sir."

"And you want to attend the Royal Academy?"

The girl was nearly breathless. "More than anything, sir."

Alliana looked down, clutching the folds of her dress. This girl wanted it just as much as her, it seemed. How was Alliana any different?

I want to fight for something I truly believe in. I want to change the realm.

But didn't all the others standing in line want the same? How could the scryer tell who would truly deserve a spot in the Royal Academy?

The Master Wizard made a disgruntled noise. "You and the rest of the realm want to attend the Royal Academy more than anything. It's far from a stroll in the park."

The girl shuddered, but the man wasn't waiting for her response. With a hasty tap of his wand on the book that the attendant held open, gold sparks flickered on the paper.

The girl brightened hopefully. "Is it—please—"

Then the man held up his book. Gilded letters shimmered: *Declined*.

"But it's all I've ever wanted!" The girl burst into a wail. Her friends led her away, all of whom, judging by their tear-streaked faces, had already been rejected.

Someone in one of the groups in front of Alliana whispered, "That's his power."

"Reading books?" his friend whispered back. There was a silence, then: "*What?* That's what it looked like!"

"He's scrying, you pot of potatoes. The Master Wizard casts his scrying magic on a blank page and some sort of pictures or words show up."

"That sounds easy."

"Says you, a non-magical. Also, scrying hundreds of us?" The boy shook his head. "That's like trying to create an epic tale on the spot. There's a reason why he looks so exhausted."

Then there were clattering noises as a new group approached.

"I can't believe we're one of the last in line!" a girl complained from behind Alliana, getting louder and louder. "It's all your fault that you wanted to spend all our time stuffing your face!"

"That was only proper!" a boy shot back, boots

slapping against the rocks. "If I'm to be selected by the Royal Advisor and his scryer, I need to know the type of food and service I'm going to receive at the Royal Academy! This is an *investment* in my future."

That voice was too, too familiar.

"The only investment you should've made was in some soap to wash up your greasy face." Then there was a very recognizable giggle. *Reina.*

Alliana froze as the footsteps stopped behind her, and she kept facing forward, not daring to move a centimeter to the side.

A glance at the curtained windows to her left confirmed her deepest fears. In the reflection of the glass, she could see that Stepmother, Reina, and Reizo had lined up after her; Mister Leo was glugging down another mug of honey cider not too far behind. If she took a step back, she'd knock into Reina's hornet wings.

When she went up to meet the Royal Advisor and his scryer, they'd see her right away.

She had to leave the line. Perhaps she could circle back and join after her stepsiblings got their reading.

Another group was heading back to the main ball area, passing by only a meter away from her. Alliana slipped out of line, ignoring the strange looks they gave her, and hurried to the other side of them, her heart pounding in her chest.

There—she was steps away from the cover of the

Baumkuchen oven, she could almost taste the buttery sweet cake, she—

"You!" Stepmother's voice shouted, sharp as a pickax. Alliana darted forward, shielding her face, but she was stuck. Stepmother was advancing on one side; the backs of the stalls were on the other. There was nowhere to go—

"Come with me, please." An arm slipped over Alliana's shoulder, and someone quickly shielded her from Stepmother's dagger-sharp gaze as they circled around the older woman and toward the castle. Before she knew it, the guards opened up the sliding doors, and she was deposited into the Royal Advisor's quarters—where no guest was allowed to go—and the mysterious figure had returned outside.

She spun around, trying to make sense of where she was. It was an enormous main room, with curtained glass windows that stretched up high to the ceiling. This area alone was enough to fit almost all of the outdoor dancing floor, but instead, the tatami floor was filled with opulent cushions and low tables here and there.

Through the crack in the sliding door, Stepmother's angry voice rose above the gentle music and chatter. "I know her! She's an intruder! Alliana isn't supposed to be—"

"Who's Alliana? That's my friend Misaki." Alliana's mysterious savior had a voice smooth as a rolling river. She still couldn't figure out who he was.

"Misaki? Who's that?" Reizo said.

"Um, who are *you*?" Reina cut in. "Are you...there's no way."

"Misaki?" Stepmother coughed. "I suppose there's no way that stupid girl would know the Royal Advisor's heir....I must've been mistaken."

"Remember that time you thought a moth was a butterfly?" Reina piped up helpfully. "You let it linger around your room for days, even though Alliana tried to tell you it was a wood-eating type. And then you were all surprised when your dresser broke into two."

Then another figure stepped close to Alliana's stepfamily, the overhead enchanted lights illuminating him perfectly. Alliana could recognize *this* person anywhere. Royal Advisor Miwa put a hand on the mysterious interloper's shoulder. "Nephew, are these your friends?"

The boy's voice was cool. "Anything but."

Royal Advisor Miwa smoothly turned to Stepmother and said, ever so politely, "By that, he must mean that we're not acquainted yet. I must retire to my private room to respond to a message from the capital, but I look forward to meeting your two young charges after I return."

The Royal Advisor and his nephew swept past Alliana's stepfamily, still gaping in awe, and made their way to the doorway—straight to where Alliana was hiding. The guards jumped forward to open the sliding doors, and Alliana stepped into the shadows, out of the sight of her stepfamily, as the Royal Advisor and his companion entered. Before anyone outside could peer in, the guards slid the doors shut.

The Royal Advisor turned to her, eyes quizzical. But Alliana's thoughts were buzzing with questions, for next to Royal Advisor Miwa, Taichi, the scrying Apprentice Wizard, stared back.

"You—you're the *heir* of the Royal Advisor?" Alliana whispered.

CHAPTER EIGHTEEN

A NIGHT OF LIGHT AND FIRE

Bright lights flashed on throughout the room, and the Royal Advisor dropped his serenity like a mask. He tossed off his elegant robe, and half a dozen waitstaff hurried forward, catching it midair.

"Taichi." The man pressed his hand to his forehead. "We have a messenger coming in. I need you for this; the preliminary note they sent doesn't sound promising."

The wizard shot a glance at Alliana. "Sorry, there's been an urgent message from the Guild—"

"Apologies, I should have introduced myself." The Royal Advisor turned to her and bowed. Alliana couldn't believe her eyes. If Reizo caught wind of this, maybe he'd be nice to her for once.

"Kenzo Miwa, at your service," the man said. His

hair was tied back, and he was beyond elegant; his long cheekbones and thick eyebrows made him look like he had been painted into existence with a brush, delicate yet strong.

"It's a pleasure to meet you, Royal Advisor Miwa." Alliana dipped into a deep bow. Then she sucked in a breath. Would he still be polite when he knew she wasn't anyone important? "I'm…I'm Alliana…of Rivelle. From Narashino, at the edge of the abyss."

She was naught but a commoner—an orphaned commoner.

But that was who she truly was.

Her throat felt stuck as she trained her eyes on the ground, waiting for a response, waiting for the Royal Advisor to flick a hand, and then the guards would cart her away.

"Ah!" The man let out a noise of surprise, and Alliana looked up in confusion. The guards still waited at the doors, though they eyed Alliana slightly differently.

"That's why my team couldn't find a trace of an Alliana within the capital city," the Royal Advisor said with a quiet laugh. "Very well, then."

"Uncle!" Taichi groaned. "This is why I never bring any friends back—"

"Well, you can't tell me all about your new friend and not expect me to check on her background," his uncle responded. The way he looked down at Taichi was warmer than a hug, even if the wizard's ears were all pink. Alliana's heart ached.

Then the Royal Advisor cleared his throat. "Right, right. We can't get distracted. Taichi, the message I got from the capital was grim. Would you scry?"

"What about Master Yamane?"

The Royal Advisor shook his head, and waved his hand at a figure collapsed on a pile of cushions, who'd slunk in through a side door. "He's drained. I always tell the Guild of Magic to send more, but you all never have enough scryers to encompass the Regional Balls. Or perhaps our gold isn't good enough. We still need him to check the rest of the attendees; we must pretend all is normal."

Taichi bit his lip and nodded. Without a word, a servant brought over a tall, thin table and a cool gray stone basin, filled to the brim with water.

"The Guild makes a big fuss over small issues, just to collect more gold. I'll see if it's really something." Taichi spun his wand; a bronze glow burned like it'd become a torch. *"A glimpse of the future, the world yet to come. A hint to be revealed, before it's set and done."*

The water began swirling as thick mist skittered across the surface. The boy breathed heavily, his face paling from the drain of magic.

Clouds parted, still swirling at the edges, and Alliana

gasped. Below, she could see miniature trees and stone gardens and *fire*. Impossibly, flames danced across the surface of what Alliana had been sure was water, but the flames leaped and roared, consuming everything in their path.

And, impossibly...it was the Royal Advisor's estate. How? And why?

"No." Royal Advisor Miwa could barely speak. "If this is our fate...Taichi! Scry for a way to stop this!"

The miniature world flickered, and Alliana worriedly looked up. Beads of sweat trickled down the sides of Taichi's forehead. "It's...it's slipping from me—"

All of a sudden, from the tiny, flickering clouds, a creature burst out, lunging. It was too real, with fangs that flashed and fire that plumed over the walls of the manor, burning it into clouds of ash—

Advisor Miwa shouted out, stumbling backward, and Taichi caught him. The vision disappeared in a burst of light, burning Alliana's eyes. When she could see again, the water was still, as if nothing had ever occurred.

But the heavy silence hung over the room. Even the Master Wizard, sitting on the other chair, was starkly out of words.

Finally, Royal Advisor Miwa croaked out, "A night-dragon. Is it—"

Taichi nodded. "This scrying felt *real*. It's happening soon. If not now, time is soon to trickle away."

Guards brought over a seat for Royal Advisor Miwa, but he waved it aside. "Master Yamane, can you protect us?"

The man shook his head. "I can do a few more scryings for the Academy, but I'm at my limits already. I'd be a candle in the wind against a *nightdragon*."

The Royal Advisor paled. A steward—the man who'd come by the inn to invite Alliana—stepped forward, with a small piece of paper, folded in the shape of a bird. "If you approve this request, sir, we will send it to the Guild of Magic."

"They'll bleed me dry for this," Royal Advisor Miwa growled, but he pulled a seal from his robe and stamped it, the red ink bright against the pale letter. "But let them take each last coin. They can have that on their conscience, and maybe that'll finally make the queen crack down on them. Until we get help, Ryo, invite all the ball's attendees inside to explore my estate. Allow the guests into the rooms, wherever they want to go, to keep them busy."

If everyone was going to be in here, in closer quarters, Alliana had to leave before she bumped into her stepfamily.

As the Master Wizard charmed the bird-letter to fly off, one of the guards cleared her throat. "Sir—a request for clarification. You've never—"

"No life is worth my privacy. The spells on this building may protect us all enough. At least until the Guild of Magic sends help." Then the Royal Advisor added, "Don't breathe a word of what we just saw. We can't have them panic, or worse, try to return to their homes."

Taichi slumped onto the chair that the Royal Advisor had rejected. "This...this was more corporeal," the wizard whispered, aghast. His eyes met Alliana's, and his voice cracked. "That...that means it's almost *certain* to happen."

Alliana couldn't breathe. A nightdragon...But it *wasn't* Kabo. There was no scar on this dragon's cheek; she'd seen that much in the scrying.

"I'll fight it." Taichi looked up to meet his uncle's eyes.

The man leaned down, gripping Taichi's shoulders. "I lost your parents. I can't dare to lose you, too. Stay safe, please."

Alliana gazed at the two of them. "How about—how about...can you cast protection spells from the inside?"

Taichi's forehead wrinkled as he seemed to have warring thoughts, but, finally, he nodded. "I'm not good at nonscrying magic, but I might be able to cast something like the barrier—though a thousand times weaker. No one will be able to get in—but that means we need everyone within these walls before the nightdragon nears."

The Royal Advisor let out a deep breath of relief. "I will invite the crowd inside. You can start your spell from here. Stay safe, dear nephew." With that, the Royal Advisor swept through the door, followed by his guards.

Taichi was looking rather pale. "I'm not sure my protection spell is enough." He stared at the basin of water. "I'm not strong enough to fight off *that*."

Alliana's heart burned.

My thunder.

"Taichi." Alliana tugged on his sleeve. "Can you wait to finish the spell until I get out?"

The wizard looked up, eyes widening. "That's too dangerous."

"I think I may be the only one who can stop the dragon."

Taichi stared.

"I know it's impossible to believe—"

"It's impossible to believe...." He shook his head and said hoarsely, "But I believe you. I have a feeling...you might be the answer."

"What?"

Taichi's gaze turned inward yet also far away, as if he was recalling a vision. "Alliana, your future is yet to be decided. But those talents you hide, where you come from, and those who choose to walk—or fly—alongside you... You are irreplaceable, though you may not realize the magnitude of that yet." He finally met her eyes. "I can sense that for certain."

Those talents you hide...Those who fly alongside you... Alliana had a feeling he wasn't talking about her skills mending adventurers' ripped skirts and trousers, or witches on broomsticks. Did he know about how she and Kabo could speak to each other? But what did that have to do with her future? Surely she wouldn't become someone of note—not her, Alliana, a girl of dust and nothing. "You're certain because of what you scried?"

He shook his head. "No. Because I believe in you, just that."

Oddly, without magic, his words felt more real.

Then he added, "I still don't want you to go."

Alliana's spine stiffened.

"Is..." Taichi muttered, as if not realizing he was speaking out loud. "Is that why I couldn't see? Because it's a decision *I* have to make?"

"What do you mean?"

"Before my uncle interrupted my scrying, I felt the sands of the future slipping through my fingers," he said. "Even if he hadn't interrupted, I wouldn't have been able to see much else...."

Alliana put her hand on his arm, and his eyes drew up to meet hers.

"I don't want you to get hurt," Taichi whispered.

"Let me make this choice."

The boy's eyes were shadowed as he turned to look out the glass window. Alliana *would* be safe inside.

But nothing would be safe if Kabo was hurt. Nothing was safe if the realm burned.

Alliana could not hide, not from this.

Then he breathed out, nodded. "You're right. It's not my choice to make."

Again, this sensation was strange. Was this what Kabo had meant? That a true friend, that true family wasn't tied by blood or marriage or laws or a choice not her own? Even if they didn't agree—like Taichi clearly didn't—they would still support her in this decision she had made all on her own.

"Are you sure?" Taichi asked. "If you stay, Master Yamane can scry your future, see if you're eligible for the Royal Academy. After tonight, the Guild of Magic is not permitted to scry on behalf of the Royal Academy for another full year. Enrollment will be closed."

Alliana froze. The deep longing that filled her heart burst forth, tugging her toward that future.

Cast into shadows on the curtains, the partygoers swirled around in their delicate frocks or devoured spun-sugar confections. She would be safe here. Just for one night, she could pretend to be part of the many and stay at Taichi's side.

But outside—beyond the walls of the Royal Advisor's estate—there was the *more*, the everything she'd longed to see, to know.

That was the realm she needed to protect.

Alliana's eyes blazed as they met his. "I'm ready to do whatever I can to save the realm. If it means I cannot have my chance at the Royal Academy, I will make peace with that. I must go."

The sliding doors opened, and a smooth voice cut in. "But you're not going alone."

Taichi and Alliana spun around.

"Cast the protection charms, Taichi. I'll stick with Alliana and make sure she's safe." With a flick of Apprentice Nelalithimus Evergreen's wand, the doors slid shut behind her. As the witch stepped closer, Alliana realized her dress was singed and torn at the edges, and she was pale with exhaustion. Nevertheless, Nela held her chin up bravely. "Alliana and I will fix this."

CHAPTER NINETEEN

ASHES AND DUST

The wind carried the smoke tinged with an edge of bitterness, as if Alliana could taste the nervousness stiffening her bones. As Alliana and Nela touched down, on the rocky road that led away from the Royal Advisor's estate, the witch asked, "Where—or to whom—am I taking you? Why *here*?"

Alliana swallowed. "It's . . ."

Then, beyond the orchard of plum trees, a dark shadow rose.

Nela backed up, her wand pointed out. "Alliana," she hissed, low and steady. "Get behind me, fast. If this—"

"Don't cast anything!" Alliana cried out.

Nela's jaw dropped. "No, you can't seriously mean—"

The shadows seemed to jump as the creature leaped forward, spreading its wings and shooting across the distance between them, landing squarely in front of Alliana. *No. I will protect you.*

Nela screamed, stumbling backward, half-uttered spells lighting and extinguishing in frantic sparks.

"Please!" Alliana pleaded. "Don't hurt Kabo!"

The witch was too stunned to even utter another spell.

"When I sent a letter for help since you're skilled at working with creatures..." Nela studied the nightdragon cozily wrapped around Alliana. "This... wasn't what I was expecting."

The dragon snuffled loudly. *You weren't what I was expecting, either. I'm here to see* Alliana, *not a witch.* He gave a shudder, showing exactly what he thought of magic.

"Do you hear him?" Alliana asked, peeking out from under Kabo's head.

"Hear what?" Nela's eyes widened. "You hear the nightdragon? Like, *speaking?*"

Alliana swallowed and nodded.

"Well," the witch said faintly. "I'm not surprised that you'd want to keep your dragon friend hidden, but you'll definitely want to keep *that* skill hidden, too. I haven't heard of anyone being able to talk to dragons in *ages.* Pleased to meet you—"

"Kabo," Alliana said. "Kabo, meet Nela. Nela's one of my best friends, and the brightest witch I know. Kabo is... well, I think you can tell."

"I thought we were trying to get a nightdragon *out* of Rivelle, not double our nightdragon population?" Then Nela's eyes widened again. "*Oh.* You want him to *help.*"

Alliana nodded. Kabo was truly their only chance at protecting Rivelle from the intruding nightdragon. As she'd had to make the choice between her own safety and the safety of the Farmlands, one of her favorite stories came to mind, clear as day, settling in her bones, true and solid.

"Sometimes, you have to fight fire with water. But other times..." Grandmother Mari's voice dipped. "It was a terrible fire that plagued the Sakuya Mountains, igniting the thick brush in a flash, spreading and spreading, threatening to swallow whole all the villages in the foothills."

"But Queen Natsumi saved the towns!" Alliana chirped, looking up from her sewing. Her toes curled with delight; this was her favorite part.

"Yes." Grandmother nodded gravely. "Though she was just a princess at the Royal Academy then."

Alliana sighed wistfully, thinking of the Royal Academy in the capital city. Oh, if only she could see that beautiful school in person! Why, Narashino's school had shuttered years ago—a few moons after the last big gold deposit had been discovered.

"Why don't you finish this story?" The old woman's eyes sparkled. With the tapestries, it was as if the stories

were written on the walls surrounding them. But Alliana knew the little twists and turns that the cloth and thread didn't show; she memorized each word of Grandmother Mari's tales and repeated them as she cleaned, as she followed Stepmother's bidding, as Reizo taunted her. No matter what, Alliana believed three things: She'd always be able to climb the ladder up to Grandmother's attic, the stories would stay tucked in her heart for all of time, and one day she'd leave this dusty town and enter the Royal Academy.

Alliana cleared her throat, trying to mimic Grandmother Mari's steady, soothing voice. "So, on that terrible day of burning, hungry fire, Queen Natsumi—well, Princess Natsumi, then—decided to fight fire with fire. She asked the witches and wizards to burn a circle around the growing fires, a thousand meters of scorched land. It hurt her heart to see the realm she loved being reduced to cinders, but she had to stop all the realm from being burned." Alliana shivered at the thought of the beautiful land burning. She'd never been to the Sakuya Mountains, but she imagined the stately peaks, teeming with wildlife, yet on the brink of burning with flames.

"And then?" Grandmother Mari prompted her.

Alliana straightened her shoulders. "Then, when that fire, with its ferocious hunger, tried to gobble away at Rivelle, it met the stretch that the witches and wizards had burned down already. There was nothing for the fire to eat, so it could only stop. And, finally, the Guild of Magic could use their magic to pour water, and the fire was extinguished once and for all. And the townspeople cheered for Princess Natsumi's quick thinking. For, thanks to her idea of fighting fire with fire, the beautiful little towns had been saved."

Alliana breathed in deep. Kabo turned his head toward her, and she placed her hands on his cheeks.

"We will fight fire with fire," Alliana said. "Or, in this case, we need a nightdragon to help us with another nightdragon—I hope."

The nightdragon turned his head to the side, curious. *Another? Do you have a new nightdragon friend and you didn't tell me?*

"There's a gigantic nightdragon in the Farmlands," Alliana explained.

Oh, so me? Kabo flexed his wings.

"Burning down the Farmlands."

He folded his wings. *So, not me.*

Alliana swallowed. "It's going to burn down *everything* if we don't stop it. This is the realm's harvest, the food all the cities need to survive."

The nightdragon turned his neck to look out across the fields of sunset-purple rice stalks, shimmering in the wind. For a moment, it felt like Alliana had his sharpened senses: She could taste the coppery-burnt air, feel the deep coldness of the dirt as he dug his claws in. And she could almost see how he saw her, as something more than she'd ever seen herself. Trust woven in with respect—in his eyes, she looked taller, older, and more *regal*, somehow. *What do you need from me?*

Nela glanced over. When Alliana nodded, Nela said, "The Guild's witches' and wizards' spells don't work on a nightdragon of that size, and they aren't able to guide it back to the abyss."

Kabo grunted. *How come* that *nightdragon gets to fly out of the abyss, and not me?*

"It was a mistake," Alliana explained. "Someday, someday, I *will* change things so dragons can roam freely. But this dragon...it's burning down farmlands."

I'll remember that promise, Alliana. Us dragons, we have memories better than those flappy things you like sticking your noses into. What were they called—looks? Ah, yes, books. Then Kabo nudged her nose with his rather warm one. *Tell me what's making your forehead pinch, my thunder.*

"Would you—would you be able to help?" Alliana felt like she was asking for the impossible. What if Kabo said no? What if he refused to fight one of his own kind? What if—

Kabo crooked his neck to look Alliana straight in the eyes. *I can feel your connection to the land, Alliana. It is a part of you, too, like it is for me. That is why I can speak with you. And also why I must protect this realm.*

With that, the dragon decisively shifted his head into a nod. *For my thunder, for you, Alliana, yes.*

"Let's go!" cried the witch. "Onto my broomstick!"

But Kabo had other ideas for Alliana. With a firm shake of his head, he knelt slightly, with a delicacy fit for serving a queen. *Stay with me. I'll protect you.*

Nela's eyes widened. With a twirl of her wand, the witch summoned up a thick strap of leather that landed softly in Alliana's hands. "See if the dragon—see if Kabo will let you put that on."

Kabo turned, eyeing the straps dubiously.

"It'll keep Alliana on safe," Nela added.

In a flash, Kabo slipped his snout through the harness and shifted so the straps rested in Alliana's fingertips; in another fluid motion, his neck lifted her off the ground and onto his back. *Hold on.*

The nightdragon spread his wide black-green wings and shot into the sky—with Alliana holding on for dear life.

CHAPTER TWENTY

EMBERS ANEW

Smoky gusts whirled around Alliana as she and Kabo soared through the sky. Nela flew by their side, using the charm etched onto her broomstick to guide them toward the nightdragon.

Seconds after they'd kicked off, the rumbling sound of deep thunder shook the sky.

"What is that?" Alliana cried out, pointing at a sharp crack of fire, piercing through the smoke like fiery lightning.

Kabo let out a low growl. *This may be more than what I can handle.*

A dark shadow passed overhead, then—

"Watch out!" Nela cried.

The sky burned with fire, raining on them. The witch shouted a spell, and a clear barrier flashed into existence

over their heads. Rounds of flame shot down, like fiery
sleet, sparking on the dry leaves of the plum orchard
on the edge of the Royal Advisor's grounds. Kabo spun
around to track the new dragon's path, letting out a cry,
but his noise was washed out with another far deeper
roar.

They had found the nightdragon.

A breeze pushed away the thick smoke for just a
moment. From the ring of burnt trees, bright rays of
spells shot up into the sky, and the enormous nightdragon
snapped at the light, dipping down menacingly toward a
small figure zipping around the trees on a broomstick.

"Hayato!" Nela gasped. "Oh, he's going to get burned
to a crisp."

"Nela!" Alliana pulled up on the harness, and Kabo
batted his wings, keeping them afloat. "We can't let anyone see Kabo! They'll think he's attacking, too!"

"But—how can we manage that?"

Alliana frantically thought of ideas. "Oh! Nela, what
if you pretend you cast him out of thin air? And Kabo
and I will try to bring the dragon further up into the sky,
so they don't see me, and bring it back to the abyss!"

"But—can you face the nightdragon alone?" Then
Nela glanced at Kabo, who was glaring at her.

She is never alone.

Nela couldn't hear his words, but she seemed to com-
prehend the nightdragon's glare. "You're right, Kabo."

Then Alliana drooped. "But there's still a chance we might be seen.... And if someone sees *me*, they'll know an ordinary servant girl can't magic up a dragon out of thin air. This plan won't work."

"I'll go low and stay hidden. I can help Taichi with the protection spells without being seen. But for you..." Nela spun her wand, and bright light glimmered down in a gentle shower, like crystal snow. When Alliana looked down, a cloak similar to the witch's own—the emerald color so deep it was almost black—fluttered from her shoulders.

"For tonight, don't go as you. Go as me." The witch grinned. "Now fly, fast."

"Stay safe!" Alliana waved her friend away to hide, even as her heart continued to pound. *I must show her I believe in this plan, just like Queen Natsumi did when she fought fire with fire.*

She *had* to believe in this plan. After all, the realm depended on it.

Nela dipped down on her broomstick, instantly getting swallowed by the thick clouds.

Alliana adjusted the hood of the cloak; it seemed that Nela had used some sort of charm. Even with the smoky gusts that battered at the fabric, the hood stayed put, hiding her face from view. "Kabo, can you communicate with the nightdragon and persuade it to return?"

Of course. But you must stay in the protections of the witch girl. Her dear friend quickly let out a loud roar, and before Alliana could even shout, they dropped through the clouds, back down to the ground.

He dipped, tunneling through the smoke to a part of the Royal Advisor's estates, away from the Guild of Magic members. *Alliana, stay safe. No flying.*

"Wait, don't drop me off!" She wrapped her hands tight around the harness.

Kabo's wings churned air as he slowed, looking at her one more time.

"I believe in you," Alliana repeated. She wrapped the harness tighter around her hand. "And I'm going to stick with you through this. I cannot ask this of you and not fight by your side."

It is not safe.

"Do you believe in me?"

I believe in you, too. With that, Kabo shot upward, twisting through the sky, his wings pulling in close as he neared the beast.

The nightdragon stretched longer than the Royal Advisor's main room; if the creature had laid on the ground, Alliana might've mistaken him for the Sakuya mountain range. But the beast was no slumbering mountain. As he flew low over the plum orchard, his spiked tail lashed out, dragging burning trees to catch others on fire, sending the blaze higher and higher into the smoky sky.

But Kabo did not hesitate—for if he did, the other dragon would easily overpower him.

With a shriek, Kabo slammed against the bigger night-dragon, jolting Alliana nearly off his back. She gripped tighter to the harness, too winded to even scream.

The nightdragon roared, turning to glare at the spells shooting up from Hayato—no more than annoyances bouncing off his hide—and then at the young dragon flying around him. *Hatchling! How dare you test me, Ryuji, most ancient of the nightdragons.*

I am Kabo! Protector of my thunder! Kabo's cry sounded like mewling in comparison.

You cannot expect protection from a human thunder. They will betray you. Ryuji drew up to his full height; Alliana was sure he was *taller* than the Sakuya Mountains. Kabo, even though he'd grown beyond twice Alliana's height, was truly a tiny newborn compared to a full-grown nightdragon.

Sweat trickled down her neck. In that moment, the dark yellow eyes of the scarred, older nightdragon studied Kabo and then her. Alliana gulped, wondering, *Do nightdragons eat humans?*

The nightdragon bared fangs as tall as Alliana. She didn't have time to ask Kabo—

Because in the next second, the enormous nightdragon shot toward them. *Begone! Let me have my revenge on these human traitors.*

They have done no wrong! The abyss was formed hundreds of years ago! Kabo narrowly dodged and swirled to the right, turning sideways and knocking the air out of Alliana's lungs.

Then the nightdragon flew closer, and Kabo pounded his wings.

"Fly, fly!" Alliana urged him. "We've got to keep moving!"

The nightdragon swept in, just a mere yard away from shearing Kabo's neck. Again he pulled up into a corkscrew, but the larger nightdragon buffeted its wings, and the sudden change in air sent Kabo off-balance. In that instant, Ryuji shot forward, slamming his entire body into the smaller dragon, with a shriek that vibrated Alliana's bones and shook her skull—but it seemed to have a worse effect on Kabo.

Her dear friend cried out in pain and then—*Alliana!*

"Kabo?" Her shout turned into a scream as he tumbled out of the sky, his head tucked in, eyes closed. They fell, plummeting toward the earth. "No, *Kabo*!"

CHAPTER TWENTY-ONE

FLAMES AND FURY

They fell out of the sky, the scream stolen from Alliana's lungs. Their bodies hurtled down so fast, no longer carried by Kabo's wings, that Alliana felt like the rocky courtyard was coming up to slam into them.

Just when they were about to hit the ground, the thin layer of air between them and the rocks burst with shimmering lace-thin light—a net—that strained under their weight, taking the worst edges off their fall. *Nela's magic.* But Kabo still slammed hard into the ground, and Alliana crumpled, the wind knocked out of her chest, with the momentum sending her tumbling off Kabo.

Sharp rocks scratched at her hands and face, but she scrambled to her feet, despite the sting of pain.

"Kabo!" she cried, rushing to his side. The night-dragon's breaths were labored. Now, more than ever, she wished for magic. She had never longed so deeply for a charm to heal the nightdragon's wounds.

Then she glanced over to the side of the meadow. In the Royal Advisor's gardens, only a handful of feet away, was a white-red flower that she recognized so well.

Katori chrysanthemum.

The thin petals were closed in a ball, with a few green leaves wrapped tightly around it. It was as if the flower knew how valuable it was, and wanted to keep itself safe.

Overhead, Ryuji swooped threateningly, but she raced to the edge, plucking a blossom off, ignoring the thorns that scratched at her skin. Alliana skidded back to a stop in front of Kabo, pushing it in front of the nightdragon's nose like a proper lady's vial of smelling salts.

Screams echoed around Alliana, and for a second, she thought it was Nela. But when she looked up, a gasp caught in her throat.

They had landed directly in front of the long windows of the Royal Advisor's main room. Guests shouted over one another, swarming to the glass with eyes wide and mouths gaping to stare at the nightdragon nearly at their feet, and the cloaked figure who had fallen off.

But that wasn't what drew Alliana's attention.

In the reflection, behind Alliana and Kabo, the giant nightdragon flapped his wings, a wicked look flashing in his eyes. *The end is near.*

Alliana was so close she could almost count Ryuji's

teeth, glinting like a mouthful of dancing daggers. He reared his head back, to strike down.

"Stop!" Alliana stood in front of Kabo, steady as could be. She held out what looked to be a witch's wand, short and stout.

A witch? This human thinks—

"This human *knows* this nightdragon should not be hurt!" Alliana shouted back, holding up the wand threateningly. "I will protect him with my life!"

Ryuji batted his wings back in surprise. *You understand me.*

Tears pricked at Alliana's eyes. "I do. Please, I'll do anything if you'll leave Kabo alone. He was trying to help me."

Under her breath, she begged, "Please, katori, *please.*" But behind her, Kabo was silent and still.

Ryuji buffeted his wings, sending dust and dirt flying into Alliana's face. From her side, she caught a slight movement in the bushes, and a pair of familiar dark eyes peered out from a cloak identical to hers. Nela.

Alliana shook her head ever so slightly. She couldn't risk Nela spooking the nightdragon with a spell, and having him fly off to rampage through the rest of the Farmlands. Besides, the Guild's magic didn't seem to work so well on nightdragons.

From behind her, Kabo gave a snuffling cry. She spun around, her heart in her throat, and the stick she'd picked up next to the katori chrysanthemum clattered to the rocks.

"Stay with me!" Alliana cried out. "Please, don't be hurt."

Her dear nightdragon friend shifted on his side, still silent, eyes still closed.

"I've lost Grandmother Mari," she whispered. "I can't lose you, too."

From behind, the sharp-hearing nightdragon shifted forward, his words laced with a snarl. *It looks like your weak nightdragon is already gone. I tested him, the way I test other young nightdragons. If they fail, they are lost forever. If they survive, they'll be part of my thunder. It looks like this one didn't survive.*

Flames began to glow from deep within Ryuji's throat, his teeth sharp. *I will give him an honorable nightdragon's death.*

"He is my thunder!" Alliana shouted. "I will not let you get to him!"

But she had no spell to cast. Nela's magic couldn't outwit a nightdragon's powers. In her last moments, she dashed to Kabo, wrapping her arms tight around his body, her forehead pressed to his thick hide, expecting the burning flames to consume her.

Then—

It'll take more than that, honorable Ryuji. I will not leave my Alliana.

Kabo scooped her off the ground, and they hurtled up into the sky, the breath stolen from her lungs. Tears sparkled like crystals as Alliana hugged Kabo. "You're safe! Oh, you're safe!"

He was stronger than I expected.

"Don't leave me like that!" Alliana cried. The terror of seeing Kabo so closed off, so empty—it'd been like seeing Grandmother Mari, frozen and laid out on the bed.

At her cry, the nightdragon let out a matching roar, and his wings billowed out. *I'll stay with you, Alliana. Promise. So long as I have wings, so long as I can roar, I will fly to you.*

They flew up, up, up, beyond the smoke, beyond the clouds, so high up that she thought they might reach the sun.

And Alliana's heart soared.

Kabo let out a shriek, echoing through the sky, and Alliana felt his wordless cry in her bones. The nightdragon let out a pillar of flames, a fierce emblem of his life, his will.

The other nightdragon circled below, letting out another shriek, like a cat whose prey had escaped.

Kabo roared, *I will not be defeated by you, Ryuji!*

The other nightdragon snapped back, *You should be lucky your human stalled for you! I would've burned you to a crisp!*

For that, Kabo swooped down and nipped at Ryuji's

back. The larger dragon couldn't turn in time, but instead sent his tail swiping at Kabo.

Then Ryuji spat a fireball at him; Kabo neatly ducked, turning as Alliana held on to the harness with clenched hands.

They were *fighting.*

Alliana wouldn't let the realm be burned down, not if she could help it.

Kabo danced through the sky, nimble and sharp, out of reach of the older nightdragon's claws and fangs.

Alliana kept an eye on the older nightdragon's movements. "He's coming to the right!" she shouted. "C'mon, let's lead him back to the barrier!"

Kabo roared and shrieked and shot through the sky. Together, they were so much stronger. Together, they breathed and burned and felt the salty sweat of the battle....

Together, they fought.

The enormous nightdragon roared with frustration, snapping around at the sky, certain Kabo was just about to swoop down.

"He's coming up behind us, on the left!" Alliana cried, and Kabo shot forward, out of the older nightdragon's grasp, snapping back.

Meter by meter, they lured the nightdragon away from Rivelle's farmlands and back toward the abyss.

Kabo beat his wings as fast as he could as Ryuji shot

toward them, and Alliana kept an eye on his coordinates through the smoky haze.

"From the right!"

"Flying above us!"

Just before Ryuji bit into Kabo, the younger night-dragon darted forward. *You can't catch me!*

Each time, they flew further and further, and hope swelled in Alliana's heart.

Again, Kabo flew out of reach.

But Ryuji swooped down sharply, his wings fast as streaks of lightning. Terrifying fear froze her breath in her lungs. He was right above them, and his claws raked out over Kabo's wings—

"You promised he'd be part of your thunder!" Alliana shouted.

Ryuji's jaws snapped with an ear-piercing screech as he swerved off to the side, sending Kabo and Alliana—holding on for dear life—spinning in the other direction.

When Kabo pulled back up, batting his wings furiously, the older nightdragon watched them, studying the girl and the small nightdragon. His eyes were sharp, yet the anger in his eyes had melted.

I do ever so hate when little ones are right.

Kabo crooked his head. *Ryuji, Alliana is part of my thunder. I wouldn't let a weak human in. She's as smart as any nightdragon.*

Without warning, Kabo darted forward and knocked

his head against the older nightdragon's. But instead of tearing Alliana off Kabo's back, the older nightdragon *laughed*.

It was a deep and rich laugh, like the river at the bottom of the abyss, bubbling and strong, rumored to be full of riches and treasures.

Very well, then.

Kabo turned, soaring toward the abyss, and Ryuji buffeted his wings, following close behind. When the older nightdragon snapped at Kabo's tail, Kabo only flicked it, tapping Ryuji straight on the cheek.

Alliana was sure that Ryuji would roar, or maybe even shoot billowing flames to burn them into a crisp, but instead, the older nightdragon flew in a loop around them, snorting out puffs of smoke.

She gasped. The dragons were *playing*.

Kabo looked over his shoulder at Alliana and, to her surprise, *winked*.

She breathed out in relief—even though she was feeling a little green at the edges—and grinned, as Kabo led the bigger nightdragon on a chase back south through the realm, swirling through the sky.

Alliana spotted a small dot flying below them, and her heartbeat spiked with fear. *Hayato?*

Then the outline of a familiar pointy witch's hat materialized through the haze.

"Nela!" she called.

Her friend burst through the thick clouds, leaning low against her broomstick to fly fast.

"Hayato's following us!" she shouted.

Alliana breathed in the cold, sharp air. "Oh, no." She couldn't let Kabo get caught by the wizard. The instant he saw the small nightdragon, Hayato would use all his powers to enchant him to fly straight into the money-greedy hands of the Guild.

Kabo stretched out his wings, sensing her spiking fear. *No wizard can ever match my flying skills. That's why none of them have caught me before, and it'll never happen.*

Still, even if Kabo could outfly most wizards, Hayato was one of the fastest fliers in the realm.

"I'll cast a few spells that'll slow him," Nela shouted, her wand already sparking at the tip. "Go on, I'll meet you at the meadow!"

The wind stuck her hair to her sweaty skin. Alliana leaned down, pressing her hands on Kabo's thick hide. "Fly fast, Kabo!"

The nightdragon tilted his wings. *Me? Get caught? Never.*

We can do this, Alliana thought grimly. *We* must *do this.*

Together, the girl and dragon soared through the air, their hearts pattering in sync, the dangerous, enormous nightdragon tailing close behind.

The clouds were starting to thin out; the smoke hadn't traveled over this way yet.

Alliana spotted the crossroads, the faded signs pointing to four different directions. Thanks to Kabo, she'd been able to travel in an utterly new direction today. Still, she craned her neck to look eastward. Even perched up high on the nightdragon, she couldn't see what lay on the path leading to the capital.

Kabo dipped down and her stomach lurched, pulling her attention away. *Especially* with a nightdragon, it wasn't as if she could go down that path.

But if she could see the crossroads—

"There!" Alliana leaned forward, pointing at the shield. A few minutes' ride away, she could see the meadow.

From behind them, the trailing nightdragon let out a loud roar. *Finally! Home.*

Kabo began the descent down to the meadow, but the gigantic nightdragon soared past, sending them tilting to the side. Without hesitation, Ryuji burst through the shield, sparks flying where his hide scraped against the patchwork of spells, and dove into his familiar territory. But not without one last warning for Alliana. *Stay safe, dragon-talker. If others hear of your powers, you will be in danger. Not just from your fellow humans, but other dragons, too. I will keep your secret for now, thunder of my thunder.*

With one last flash of his tail, Ryuji disappeared.

As Nela and Kabo drifted slowly down to the meadow, all was quiet.

And, finally, the realm was at peace.

Alliana slid off the moment Kabo's claws landed amongst the tall grasses; her knees shook, but she needed to feel solid dirt below her. Moments later, Nela landed next to them, swirling her broomstick back into a cloak, and pinning it around her neck, against the evening chill; she seemed just as wobbly. "You—you two did it."

"We did it," Alliana said hoarsely.

"I don't think many have faced down a nightdragon and survived," Nela replied. Kabo sent her a pointed look and the witch added, "Present company excepted. You're right, Kabo. Not all nightdragons are frightening."

Kabo opened his mouth in a fanged smile, and Nela laughed. "Okay, you're still strong and frightening. But, you're also a friend. Because a friend of Alliana's is a friend of mine, too."

The nightdragon's eyes lit up at that. *Friend.*

Nela shot back a quick smile, but then she glanced over her shoulder, at the sky. "My wind spells only did so much. Hayato's still following us."

"Oh." Alliana locked eyes with Kabo, her heart wrenching.

The nightdragon shook his head vehemently. *No. I still haven't been able to give you your gift.*

"You don't need to give me—"

In an instant, the nightdragon loped to the tattered shield and reached with his long neck to pluck a rock from the inside of the barrier.

He nudged at her fingers. When she opened her palm, he deposited the slightly soggy rock into her hand. *This. I found this for you. You should look at it.*

"Thank you, Kabo."

I promised. I promise.

Alliana frowned. "What promise?"

This smelled like you, just a little bit.

A strange prickle ran down her spine as she turned the stone over in her hands.

But it wasn't a rock. It was the torn-up remnants of a notebook. The black leather jacket was crumbling from age; the papers were slightly damp and smelled of mildew. But when she lifted up the cover, she saw the familiar title: *Travel Tales of the Abyss.*

Her father's notebook. In the corner, there was even her handwriting in faded ink: *With Alliana's help!*

She'd forgotten all about that, how she'd scribbled that line and mussed the otherwise pristine first page. But her father set her in his lap and read it out, his chin thick with whiskers that tickled her cheek, his arms wrapped warmly around her. *It's now perfect*, he'd said.

"Oh." Alliana couldn't breathe. "*Oh, Kabo.*"

The nightdragon looked utterly pleased with himself, and flicked his tail to and fro.

"What is it?" Nela asked.

"My father's notebook. He had it when he went on his last trip to the abyss."

Quietly, the witch stepped closer to Alliana, deep within Kabo's protection, and gave her friend a hug. "I'm sorry," she whispered.

A paper fluttered out from the journal, landing at their feet. It was pressed flat from years of being stuck in the notebook, but smaller than the dog-eared pages.

> Alliana has snuck out of the inn. Mister Leo mentioned someone saw a small figure go down to the third platform. I worry she may be trying to rappel into the abyss to go after you.
>
> Fusako

"He was looking for me. *Stepmother* sent him looking for me." Alliana's whisper felt like a scream raking at her throat. "I never went into the abyss when I was younger—the first time was when I met Kabo."

The witch's forehead furrowed. "Perhaps your stepmother was mistaken?"

Alliana's throat ached. "I've never heard of anything like this from her or anyone, that he'd thought I was in the abyss." Alliana looked up at Kabo. "Was there anything else? Any sign"—her voice broke—"of him?"

Kabo let out a mournful noise. *I am sorry. This is all I found. It was deep inside the abyss, a long flight down. Much further than the platforms and tunnels that your people travel through. I believe a shadowsnake or another creature brought it there.*

She absorbed the words, pain and sorrow battering against her heart. "Thank you for letting me know."

It felt like she was six years old and reliving her father's death all over again. *Why* did everyone she love always leave?

Alliana drank in the sight of Father's sketches of plants and recipes for remedies. She'd tried to remember all that she could and experiment to figure out what she didn't, but seeing the pages was like flipping through her memories once more. All the rainy days when she and Father would let the cook and maid take care of the inn, and the two of them would sit out in the meadow, picking the dewdrop berries until their cheeks were tinted blue. The fruits were icy cold and delicious, freshly budding from the flowers that had burst into bloom in the rain. Though the skies poured with rain, she'd never felt so warm and cozy inside.

But now was not the time for misty recollections. Alliana tucked the paper and small notebook into her chest pocket, next to Grandmother Mari's letter. "Hayato will be here any minute now."

I don't want to go. Not when you look more and more tired than the last time I saw you. Not when my gift hurts you.

"It heals me more than anything." Alliana wrapped her arms around Kabo, her head still reeling from the feel of the black leather notepad clutched in her hands, the gentle curves of her father's handwriting—a sight for sore eyes. "I'll let you know when I'm in need, okay? I *promise*. But you have to go. I can't let you get caught."

No, no, no. The nightdragon shook his head with a huff, steam hissing out of his nostrils. He was *not* happy with the idea of leaving Alliana.

"I think I have the perfect charm," Nela said, stepping forward.

Kabo swirled around Alliana, wrapping his body protectively around her. Alliana peeked out from behind his scaly neck. "We'll take whatever you have."

The witch waved her wand around the two of them. *"A connection beyond barriers, a connection beyond what we see; let friendship tie you together, no matter where you may be."*

Glittering dust flowed through the air, fluttering like snow around Alliana and Kabo, and the nightdragon snapped his mouth to and fro, trying to capture the glowing sparks.

When the magic faded, Alliana blinked in surprise. "Oh!"

The nightdragon had an emerald cord tied around his scaly leg; a similar cord of soft, braided twine dangled from Alliana's neck, complete with a droplet of gold shaped like a fireblossom.

"In times of need, just give it a tug," Nela explained. "It's just one way I want to thank you both, for everything you've done to help the realm. Go on, try it out."

Alliana hesitantly pulled at the string. A split second later, she felt a tickle on her neck; the necklace warmed, and a tiny threadlike white arrow appeared on the pendant, pointing straight ahead at Kabo.

"This is *wonderful*," Alliana breathed out. She hugged the nightdragon, putting their keepsakes side by side. "Isn't this amazing? No matter what, when I'm back at the meadow, I'll be able to let you know I'm here."

Kabo stared deep into her eyes. *But why would you ever leave?* And then he started tugging on the bracelet with his teeth, again and again.

Alliana and Nela burst into laughter. "Only when you're truly in need, Kabo," Alliana said, squeezing him close. The warmth from her necklace felt like it had enveloped her heart. "Whenever that time comes, I'll find you. I promise."

The nightdragon snuggled closer, his scaly neck resting gently on her shoulder, assuring his promise in return.

Then Kabo broke off, letting out a deep growl at a pinprick in the horizon. Nela spun around. "Oh, *no*! Hayato caught up."

Alliana's skin prickled with foreboding. "Kabo, get back to the abyss. Quick!"

The nightdragon let out a whine, but Alliana threw her arms around him again, in one last squeeze. "Go on. I have my necklace; you have your bracelet. We'll never be apart, not when we absolutely need each other."

Promise. I'll see you soon. He pressed his forehead against hers, for the briefest moment, before breaking away. The nightdragon loped to the hole in the shield, stepping through with ease, even as the barrier sparked against his skin. Nela waved her wand with a quick chant, mending the hole, but Alliana couldn't concentrate on the words. All she could focus on was Kabo, her dear friend, disappearing into the dark beyond. With one last glance over his shoulder, he spread his wings and dove into the abyss. A swirl of dust—whirling around Alliana and her burning, stinging eyes—was his last trace.

CHAPTER TWENTY-TWO

CASTLES OF AIR

A few minutes later, Hayato landed in the meadow, his beady eyes sweeping the fernleaf and the tall grasses. Alliana hated how he looked around at her sacred place like it was nothing special. Nela leaned on a boulder casually, using her wand to siphon dust off her cloak. Alliana was behind the boulder, with space to peek through the vines tangling over the rock.

"Where did the nightdragon go?" he snapped.

The witch gestured toward the patched-up shield. "I guided it through."

His forehead furrowed, showing his skepticism that the nightdragon had just daintily followed the witch through the sky, instead of burning her into a crisp.

Alliana could hardly believe it, either. But what else

could explain that the nightdragon was finally gone from Rivelle Realm?

Nela tossed a blossom at Hayato. The wizard fumbled it in his hands, and frowned at the red-tipped flower.

"Katori chrysanthemum," Nela explained. "It's a deterrent."

"That's right. This is same thing Alliana tried for the rockcrows." Hayato's eyes widened. "That's brilliant. Where is she, anyway?"

The witch shook her head. "Her stepfamily wouldn't let her come out to the Farmlands Ball. She stayed home at the inn."

The wizard frowned. "Then who was the rider on that other nightdragon, if that wasn't Alliana? That wasn't you. And Taichi didn't know who it was."

"A friend," Nela said crisply. "None of anyone's business."

"The Royal Advisor's looking for the figure in the cloak," Hayato said. "He wants to offer a reward. Three gold coins, I heard."

Alliana muffed her gasp. *Three* gold coins? But— *no.* She couldn't reveal herself; then there'd be questions about where the *other* nightdragon had come from, and she wasn't ready to answer those questions.

"Well, Royal Advisor Miwa will be looking for a while. My lips are sealed," Nela said. Then she added quickly, as if the thought had just occurred to her, "Um, the area of the shield that the nightdragon first came through...isn't that still broken?"

Hayato jolted up. "Curses!"

"Master Yamane was already grouchy when I last saw him," Nela said. "Leave it sitting any longer and he'll be ready to burn you down like a nightdragon."

The wizard growled under his breath, tossing the katori chrysanthemum back. Nela caught it with an innocent, wide-eyed look on her face. "Or—are you running out of magic? I can go fix it."

"I'm *fine*," the wizard snarled. He glanced at the shield one last time, shaking his head, before leaping back onto his broomstick. "If you see Master Yamane, *don't* mention the gap is still open."

"Sure, sure." Nela waved. "But you better fly fast."

With a curt farewell, the wizard soared away in a huff.

Alliana stumbled out from her hiding spot and breathed out with delight. "Oh, you convinced him!"

"Only with your help." Nela pushed off the boulder, and they lay out in the grasses of the meadow, relief melting their bodies as their fingers tangled with the sweet-scented grasses and earthy undergrowth.

"We saved the realm," Nela said, her voice brimming with joy. "*You* did it."

"We did, together," Alliana said loyally. But it was

true—without the witch, she would've never made it back safely.

"You heard Hayato, though. Are you sure you don't want that reward?"

Alliana shook her head. "And get questions about Kabo? No. He's worth more than all the gold in the realm."

The witch squeezed her hand. "And you're worth all the gold in the realm to me."

Together, they stared up at the sky that had faded from its brilliant red to a deep blue. Like the rich fabric of Grandmother Mari's tapestries, stars glittered with whispers of galaxies swirling around them.

This, this precious, beautiful moment, was perfection. It wasn't about fancy balls or trying to impress a Royal Advisor who probably had more interest in her night-dragon than her. It wasn't about a list of chores or debts owed. During the long days, with hours that stretched on and on as Alliana drudged her way through taking care of the inn, time seemed meaningless. But now, in this moment with Nela, it felt like everything else had faded away. With the right company, the only time that mattered was now.

Time. *Time...*

"I've got to get back," Alliana gasped, sitting up. Already, the ticking hands of the future were moving onward all too fast.

"Want me to take you back to the Farmlands Ball?" Nela offered. "Why, the queen herself should be inviting you to the Royal Academy! I'm sure I can figure out some way to explain away why you disappeared."

For a moment, Alliana was sorely tempted. She imagined hopping off Nela's broomstick and sweeping up the stairs, to the shock and furor of Stepmother. Alliana would bow deeply in front of Royal Advisor Miwa, as the scryer announced, *Yes, this girl deserves an invite to the Royal Academy.*

But—she'd build up a crystal castle of dreams, only to find out that fate foretold she wouldn't be invited to the Royal Academy after all. Fairy-tale endings didn't exist, not for Alliana. The most she could hope for was to return to the inn without Stepmother knowing she had gone, and work off her debt until next year's ball.

So, despite the castles of crystal spinning around in her heart, full of impossible dreams, Alliana shook her head. "It's almost midnight. The scryers are only allowed to cast magic for the Royal Academy on the day of the ball, nothing further. Plus, I need to return to the inn before my stepfamily does; I'm already cutting it close as is."

Nela grinned. "You've got the fastest-flying witch in the realm at your side. We'll get there in no time."

"Fine, but the last one to the broomstick is a stinky natto," Alliana called over her shoulder, as she scrambled to where the witch had left her broomstick. Nela burst into laughter as they raced under the twinkling night sky.

The inn was dark and silent, and Alliana had never been so glad to see the ramshackle chicken coop. From inside, Eggna gave a sleepy cluck as Alliana got off the broomstick. She and Nela had, against all odds, managed to save the realm and make it back before her stepfamily returned in Mister Leo's rented carriage, gloating about the ball. Tomorrow, she'd have to listen to story after story about the decadent food or meeting the Royal Advisor up close, or perhaps Reizo would brag about his incomparable courage in the face of the nightdragon, but hopefully they wouldn't remember any chance encounters with a girl who looked peculiarly like Alliana.

Nela nodded toward the inn. "Are you sure you'll be all right?"

Alliana reached out to squeeze the witch's hand. "Of course. See you soon?" The witch's eyes dropped to the ground, and Alliana felt her heart stutter. "What is it?"

"I...that's what I meant to tell you," Nela said. "I'm getting summoned to the Guild's chambers. I'll have to go off on my Novice quest soon."

"You'll be able to finish that in a jiffy," Alliana said loyally. "You'll earn your Novice rank in no time."

"It's a moon in a new town," Nela explained.

Oh. A whole moon. For some reason, Alliana's eyes were burning. After the witch officially became part of the Guild of Magic, she'd be flying off on quest after quest, traveling around the realm more than ever, and Alliana...

Alliana would be stuck here.

She quickly blinked back her traitor tears and brightly smiled. "You'll be a proper witch in no time."

Nela frowned, peering close. "Are you all right? Maybe it's the moonlight—"

"Some dust just flew into my eye." Alliana laughed, waving her friend away. "But to hear you're going to be an official Guild member soon—that's thrilling." She smiled as bright as she could, pushing the dire loneliness far deep inside her, to that same dusty place where she'd stored Grandmother Mari's dear stories, to where she'd locked up all hopes and dreams of escaping this middle-of-nowhere town.

Nela nodded eagerly. "There's so much I want to do. There's so much I want to change! The Guild of Magic is far too self-serving—we should be using our gifts to do good!"

Then the grandfather clock tolled, deep and steady, and Alliana glanced over at the inn. "I have to go."

"But—"

"I'll miss you terribly. You'll write to me, won't you?"

As soon as Nela promised, Alliana quickly embraced

her in a deep hug and hurried off, leaving the witch in the copse of trees before she could get out another word.

The pigeon squawked as she slipped through the side door, but she barely noticed it in her haste.

Perhaps it was her deep sorrow over Nela's departure, or maybe she just was too weary after the long day...

But she didn't notice how strangely dark the attic was until she'd stepped inside, and the door clicked shut behind her. And when she'd reached out to where she normally stored her candle, on the low table next to the door, her fingers swept against bare wood. Perhaps she'd moved it in her haste to depart, perhaps—

Hiss. A spark of a matchstick, then the room flared with light.

And, as horrible as any nightmare, Stepmother lounged in the rocking chair, her eyes glued on Alliana.

"Well," she said. "*Welcome* back."

CHAPTER TWENTY-THREE

THE STRIKE OF MIDNIGHT

Alliana stumbled back, searching for the door, when a pair of hands roughly pushed her forward, into the middle of the room.

Reizo.

"You are *not* getting away," her stepbrother snarled. "Not on my life."

She searched for an escape as her eyes adjusted to the light, inching toward the window, but—

Sitting below it, in her ball gown, Reina looked exactly like a rotted contomelon, her dress drooping. Her eyes darted to her mother; she bit her lip as she shook her head sadly.

No, even with Reina out of the way, Alliana couldn't get through the boarded-up window. Thick panels had been crudely hammered all over it.

She felt the warm hum of her necklace. Maybe she could signal Kabo somehow. She glanced down—and then realized her necklace had fallen out of her blouse.

"What's this?" Stepmother snapped, yanking Alliana's necklace to eye the gold pendant and the faintly lit arrow. "I never gave anything like this to you."

"It's just a gift from a guest, a thank-you for checking them out so quickly," Alliana lied, her heart pattering.

"It's flickering!" Reizo leaned in close, his thick, unwashed scent making Alliana gag. "I bet it's some magical thing."

Stepmother's nostrils flared and before Alliana could protest—

Snap!

"No!" Alliana cried out.

Stepmother dangled the pendant from her fingertips. "Magic, hmm? Maybe the general store will resell this. I'm sure the adventurers would be interested."

Alliana despaired as the glowing arrow faded away in front of her eyes.

Kabo.

Stepmother tucked the torn necklace into her pocket, patting it down with a satisfied smile. "Thank you for this *gift*, Alliana."

"I never would've given that to you," Alliana shot back.

"You owe us your life," Reizo snarled. "Without us,

you would've been without a copper to your name, all alone. You *owe* us."

Stepmother's lips parted, her teeth sharp. "Which reminds me, I saw a most peculiar figure at the ball. Someone who looked like you, even though you were never supposed to be there. Then, after that person disappeared, a figure flew in on a *nightdragon* of all things. Just when I thought it was a witch or a wizard from the Guild of Magic, Royal Advisor Miwa sent out a request to find out just who that person was." Her eyes dragged down to Alliana's clothes. "There was only one description: an emerald cloak."

Alliana's heart jumped to her throat, and the weight of the thick cloth felt more like an anchor dragging her down. In her haste to return, she'd forgotten to take it off.

With sudden motion, Reizo yanked it off her neck, leaving a searing cloth-burn, and draped it around his shoulders. It went down to his thin calves, clearly far too short. "Thank you. I'll use this to collect the reward. A few gold pieces will go far for gingko nuts."

"Let Reina wear it," Stepmother snapped, grabbing it away from her son.

"No, I want the cloak!" Reizo tried swiping it back, but his mother slapped his hand.

"It's mine!" Alliana cried, but her stepbrother shoved her. She stumbled back, eyes stinging.

"I won't tolerate this," the woman said, putting her greasy hands all over Alliana's precious cloak as she inspected every centimeter. "I will not have my stepdaughter take the glory of my family. You—*you*. You think I didn't notice how your father fawned over you, instead of me? *Me*, his rightful wife. A girl like you must understand your station. A girl like you must respect everything, *everything* I have done for you."

Alliana's father *had* cared for Stepmother; he'd never have gotten married otherwise. But Stepmother, who had *always* put herself first, hadn't seen it possible that he could care for anyone more than her. The woman's jealousy, her desperate need for attention, had driven coldness into her heart, where there could have been joy and gentle care.

"That's not true—"

"Oh, Alliana. You can feel it in your bones, can't you? You are meant to be here, nothing more than that. You will not be able to rise above being a servant, not an orphan girl like you." Stepmother shook her head sadly. "Even Mistress Sakamaki—for all that you called her *Grandmother*, wishing she was your own—didn't ever see you as true family. She only pitied you. That's why she gave you her embroidery box, so you could continue working here, and repay what I am due."

The words burned at her. She'd read Grandmother's letter countless times, knowing that all the old woman had wanted for Alliana's future was to take care of her daughter-in-law and grandchildren, a family that would never consider Alliana as part of their own. She didn't belong here, but truth be told, she didn't belong anywhere.

No matter which way she turned, her stepfamily stared down, cold and unforgiving. Reminding her that she had to rely on them. Reminding her of her proper place. Reminding her of how much she owed them...

"You can't take my cloak from me, not if *I* was the one who helped the realm!" Alliana said, blurting out the truth. She'd resigned herself to working at the inn until the next Farmlands Ball—as tough as that would be— but it'd mean she'd be able to continue fulfilling Grandmother Mari's wishes.

Reizo snorted. "You think anyone is going to believe *that*? Believe *you*?"

Stepmother let out a shrill laugh that sent shivers down Alliana's spine. "Knowing you, it's likely that you let *in* the nightdragon after all the time you spend near the abyss, collecting herbs."

"I'm telling the truth. Ask the Guild of Magic—"

"The Guild," Reizo repeated, flatly. "Those money-grubbing little witches and wizards? Your tales are as stupid as Granny's."

Alliana's little corner of her heart, warm with Grandmother Mari's stories and memories of adventures with

Nela, felt like someone was trying to break in and grind everything to dust.

"*Her stories were never stupid,*" Alliana shot back. The letter crinkled in her pocket. Even through the fire and smoke, Grandmother's precious words, her precious request, stayed close to her heart, no matter how ungrateful the Enokidas acted. "Grandmother Mari cared so much for you, and this is how you treat her memory—"

A hand snaked out, skin cold and nails sharp. Stepmother clenched Alliana's chin, forcing her eyes up. "Say that again."

"I wish I wasn't stuck here," Alliana said, her words sharp yet true. "I wish I wasn't stuck in the middle of nowhere with you. Everything I've seen of the realm is far better than this."

"You—" seethed Stepmother. "You thankless wench. After all that I've done for you! I'll show you who you really are. How about this—you are *not* allowed to see anyone. Anyone, at all. I don't care if it's an inn guest, the Royal Advisor, or the queen. You may not step out of this attic. Soon, you'll see that everyone else will forget about you. You are unnecessary, unneeded, and most of all, *unwanted*. You will sew for me, and *barely* earn your keep, as usual. In time, you'll learn proper gratitude for me, the one person who keeps you fed and clothed. This is a *necessary* lesson."

Stepmother grabbed her daughter by the wrist. "I am not spending another minute in this cramped, awful attic. Let's go. Reizo, grab the key."

"Wait—" Panic rose in Alliana's chest as Stepmother shooed Reizo and Reina out, holding the emerald cloak like a trophy.

"Remember this: You, Alliana, are no one, and will become nothing." The older woman sashayed down the ladder, her lips curved in a sharp smile. "Perhaps even I'll forget you, too."

With that, the door slammed shut and the lock clicked, sending Alliana into darkness.

Late the next day, the door swung open. Alliana looked up from where she leaned against the wall, her fingers sore and aching from tugging at the lock on the door, trying to pry it off, and then at the window, neither to any success. Instead, she gathered a cloth and grabbed a needle, pretending as if she'd worked on mending.

"Mother told the witch that you don't want to see her." Reizo's voice grated against her ears.

Alliana jabbed her finger on her needle. "What?"

"I bet you're mad the witch got you in trouble, right?" her stepbrother continued, eyes glinting. "At least, that's what Mother told her. 'Alliana is feeling terribly today. She doesn't want to see you anymore.'"

Alliana no longer felt the pain of the needle prick. The falseness of the lie washed over her, overwhelming her senses. *Surely Nela wouldn't believe that—*

"The girl looked *really* sad," Reizo said. "Stepmother explained that you were honoring your Grandmother Mari's final wishes to only spend time with your family."

"*Oh.*" Alliana's heart sunk with sadness. Nela knew how much Grandmother Mari meant to her, and the old woman's request. With Stepmother's perfect excuse, Nela wouldn't think twice about it being a lie.

Then there was another knock. Alliana's eyes slid toward the doorway, but Reizo shifted in front of it. There was no way Alliana could dart past.

"Your friend stopped by." Reina poked her head inside.

"Nela came back?"

"Not the witch," Reina said. "The boy who works at the diner. The baker boy."

Isao.

Alliana clasped her stepsister's hands. "Is he here? Oh, please, isn't there some way for me to see him?" *Perhaps he could get a message out to Nela to come save me—*

Reina shook her head. "He left."

"Stepmother chased him away?"

"No, he didn't want to stay."

Reizo leaned on the doorframe, a cold smile dancing

across his lips. "He just came with a message, so you'd know where he'd gone."

"*Gone?*"

"He's heading somewhere on the eastern edges of Rivelle to be a baker's apprentice." Again, that smug smile from Reizo. "A few adventurers were traveling that way, so your friend and his brother went with them."

Joy filled her heart. Isao was finally going to his apprenticeship in Miyada.

Then it sunk in.

And Reizo could tell the moment of her realization; he grinned, sharp and mocking, and tossed a piece of cloth in front of her.

It was Grandmother Mari's unfinished tapestry, the one of Queen Natsumi's birth. It was the last piece Alliana and Grandmother Mari had worked on together.

"If you want to eat, here's your ticket to your next meal," Reizo snarled. "Finish this, and we'll give you something to eat."

"It'll take a full week *if* I don't sleep—"

"Good luck with that." Reizo snorted as he pulled Reina out of the attic and locked the door.

With that final click, Alliana stared numbly at the unfinished tapestry in front of her. At the reminder that Grandmother Mari was gone, that Nela wasn't returning with her magic, that she had no way to find Kabo, that Isao had finally left this dusty town—and her—behind.

Then she scrambled to pat through her pockets. The remains of her father's words. She still had that—

Her pockets were nearly empty. In her rush to return to the inn, she must've dropped the notebook. All she had was a pocketful of dust, dry and crumbling between her fingers—and Stepmother's note to him. Alliana tossed it into the corner of the attic, her heart aching. She was without the necklace, without her father's notebook, without her dear friends.

Alliana slumped against the wall, under the boarded-up window. With the panels that her stepbrother had hammered in, she couldn't see the outside world anymore.

She was truly, completely alone.

PART FOUR

CHAPTER TWENTY-FOUR

The Longest Night

The darkness surrounded Alliana. She was swimming in an infinite sea of black, as if Narashino, the dusty town it was, had sunken into the abyss—though perhaps it was just her future—and she would be stuck here, lost in the rift.

Her fingers met the wall and she searched upward, until she hit the thick boards plastered over the window. Perhaps she could pull off some of the wood and crawl out.

Alliana tried to pry off the boards, this time with her sore hands wrapped in cloth. She pulled at one end, her muscles burning to raise up the wood.

"Please, please," she whispered, digging in her heels. She adjusted her fingers for a better grip and then—"*Ouch!*"

A thick splinter had woven through the cloth, burying

into Alliana's index finger. Hissing from the pain, she yanked it out. With nothing but sewing needles, there was no way she could break out of the attic.

Alliana slumped against the wall, her head aching, her eyes burning. As she pulled her knees up to her chest, the letter crinkled in her pocket. From outside, she could hear the faint cooing of the pigeon and Eggna's answering call.

Like she had so many times before, Alliana pulled out the letter, tracing her fingers against the imprints of the old woman's final words, wishing she had Grandmother Mari at her side instead.

Her head spun, trying to think of ways to get out of the attic. Away from Stepmother's grasp.

There might've been a time, while Grandmother Mari was still alive, when the old woman could have convinced Stepmother to allow Alliana to apprentice elsewhere. But that chance was long gone.

Isao had forgotten about her. He'd moved on to his apprenticeship—he'd even moved across the realm.

Nela was going on her Novice quest. In that moon, the witch would forget about her, too. Anyway, after what Stepmother had said, Nela surely would think Alliana was serious about never seeing her again.

She was alone.

Alliana pounded her hands against the boards and let

out a sob. "I am more than a girl of dust. I am not going to be forgotten. This is not where my story ends."

Her voice was nothing more than a whisper, stifled by the dust that was coating everything, her heart feeling drier and brittler with every breath.

A tear spilled over. One, then another, until her cheeks were wet. But she wasn't like Stepmother. She wouldn't hide behind acidic smiles and cold words.

Those tears—they were *not* a sign of weakness. They showed she cared.

She cared. She cared about Nela, she cared about Isao. She cared about Grandmother Mari. And that love for her friends, the family she had chosen—Alliana would never, *ever* consider that a weakness.

Maybe the only memories she would have of the people she loved—long after they left her—were the dusty memories in her heart. But she would cherish those memories fiercely, because she didn't have a copper to her name, but those memories—they were worth more than gold, more than any gem.

She slammed her fist against the boards once more, and one panel shifted slightly with a creak. It let in a bit of moonlight, shining down on the unfinished tapestry that had fallen to the floor.

Alliana gathered the cloth into her arms, her tears blending with the thread. The faint letters that Grandmother had been sewing in, the faint smudges of charcoal to out-line the thread... The old woman hadn't even been able to trace out the entire line. It only said, "*Unravel your—*" And that was where it ended.

Then Alliana took in a stuttered, confused breath.

The loop at the bottom of the *y*. Grandmother Mari's handwriting had always been simple, yet with faint echoes of elegance that Alliana loved. They hadn't had many books nor parchment, but Alliana didn't need that—Grandmother had sewn her stories into tapestries, and what words she did write were charcoal dust, soon to be spun into flaxen gold floss and ebony thread. She knew Grandmother's pieces like there were exact replicas tucked into that dusty corner of her heart.

Alliana pulled Grandmother Mari's letter out of her pocket, her hands trembling as she smoothed out the creases. She laid the parchment alongside the tapestry, her heart pounding as her eyes strained in the near dark-ness, flickering from the charcoal-and-thread embroidery to the splotchy ink on parchment....

And the characters were similar, but for an eye like Alliana's, an eye that had spent years carefully noticing the differences between the rice piled high in the shiny porcelain bowl for Reina and the crack on the bowl for hers. The times she'd noticed Stepmother's thin, barely perceptible frown of disapproval whenever she looked toward Alliana's way, words heavy with lies and slick as oil...

Alliana *saw*. She felt the truth, deep in her bones, ringing true in her heart.

It wasn't magic, by any means, but perhaps Nela and Taichi were right. Maybe not all things required a wand and an enchantment.

Alliana studied the letter and tapestry, her throat feeling tight and strange.

Every time she had looked at the letter, tears had blurred her sight. She had been too caught in the words of Grandmother's letter to see it as a whole.

In Grandmother Mari's letter, the *y*'s had short and abrupt loops at the bottoms. It was like when Alliana messed up a stitch, never making it quite as smooth as Grandmother Mari's, and the old woman would smile and say, "Room to grow, my dear, room to grow."

But, in this case, Alliana had an inkling that it hadn't been about room to grow, but rather a careless mistake.

She reached out, searching along the floorboards until her fingertips met paper, and she pressed Stepmother's note alongside Grandmother's letter.

Alliana had remembered Grandmother's handwriting to be gentle and delicate, like the old woman was brushing ink spun of clouds onto paper.

The thickness of the ink on the two letters—*they were a match*. And the *y*...the *y* was nearly identical, too.

What if...

Alliana looked between the two letters and the tapestry one more time.

What if Grandmother Mari's letter had never been written by her after all?

CHAPTER TWENTY-FIVE

WITH THE FURY OF A NIGHTDRAGON

Fire burned in Alliana's heart.

She turned back toward the boarded-up window. The hefty weight of betrayal flickered in her mind, red-hot as flames, as she slid the letter back into her pocket. Instead of providing the reassurance she usually felt from its presence, the letter felt odd, like a stitch out of place.

What if Alliana's so-called promise to Grandmother Mari was because of Stepmother? Reina wouldn't bother with forging a letter. Reizo despised Alliana's very existence and clearly saw no reason to keep her around except to tease her.... If—if Stepmother had *falsified* Grandmother Mari's letter... what would the old woman think now? Of Alliana being stuck here, in this dusty town?

The path was clear in her mind, no longer tangled up in responsibilities and burdens. The door was locked from the outside, so she had to go out the window, boarded up and all. She hurried to the window, running her hands over the planks; nothing had changed. There was no leeway. The boards were nailed firmly on.

Alliana spun around, fumbling through the dark. Grandmother Mari's embroidery box sat on the side crate. She yanked open the top drawer and ran her fingers along the packets of needles till—

There it was. The seam ripper, like two thick needles spread out into a Y shape. Grandmother Mari's tool wasn't dainty and shiny like the ones in the embroidery catalogues, and before, she'd always thought about getting the old woman a new one to match the current fashion, but Alliana had never been able to scrape together enough coin.

"*You can use this to undo things,*" *Grandmother Mari had said.*

Alliana had studied the rusty blades. "Does it still work?"

"*I know you think it's terribly ugly, and true, it's quite rusted. But it does its job well. Sometimes, you've got to look beyond the appearance of a thing to find its true value.*"

It was as if the old woman knew the path Alliana would take someday.

Alliana gripped the copper handle, and with her other hand, she felt for the small head of the nail, the cold bump in the splintery wood.

There it was.

She held her breath as she carefully pried away the nail, metal scraping against metal as she aligned the seam ripper and pulled up.

Screech!

It was a horrible sound, like she'd scratched her fingernails along the metal. She swallowed, pausing, and listening to the inn.

Silence...

Reizo hadn't woken from his slumber, thankfully.

More quietly this time, she worked the seam ripper up, pulling the nail up bit by bit until, finally, it was loose enough to wiggle. She wrapped the cloth around her hand and yanked it up.

The board slid down, and her heart jumped to her throat as she grabbed it before it clunked against the wall....

And then she looked at the tiny gap between the other boards that were still plastered all over the window.

There wasn't much to see, yet determination pounded anew in her body.

A sliver of moonlight and dark blue-black sky.

An escape.

The world outside was so close, yet just out of reach.

Alliana set her jaw, her eyes glued on the world. She *would* get out of here. She would find the truth, one plank at a time.

She pried away another board. Two. Three.

It would be nearly impossible to pull off enough boards by daylight.

But she would try. Because she wasn't a nobody. Because she was tired of being trapped as the servant to someone else's demands, someone she realized she had never respected. True, Stepmother had given her food. A roof. But each gift was barbed with expectations. It was never given with love, without requirements. It was a cleverly decided trade, and it was never because Stepmother had cared about her, not like Nela, not like Isao, not like Kabo, and never like Grandmother Mari.

Anger fueled her, and she pulled off the next board roughly—

And came face-to-face with a floating eye.

She stifled a shriek. The wood clattered to the attic floor, but Alliana didn't hear it.

Because a pair of familiar brown eyes grinned from the other side. "Long time no see."

"*Nela?*" she gasped. "How—*how?*"

With a spin of her wand, the witch broke off the rest of the planks, sending them lurching to the ground in a pluming cloud of dust. Nela slipped inside, clambering off her broomstick and giving Alliana a big hug. "C'mon, hand me your stuff," Nela said, glancing worriedly at the wood lying around them. "Yikes, that was loud."

Alliana scrambled to grab the embroidery box and shove it in a cloth bag. "How are you here?"

"Isao and his brother came to find me."

Alliana took in a sharp breath. "Isao? But...he went off to his apprenticeship."

"He realized that your stepfamily was keeping you locked in the attic, and if you were to escape, you'd need to leave fast." The witch gestured at her broomstick. "So he and his brother came to find me. One escape route, at your bidding."

Tears welled in her eyes, and Alliana didn't try to hide them. She threw her arms around her friend and let out a sob of relief. "Thank you, Isao and Hiroshi. Thank you, Nela."

"I would've come earlier, but he had trouble getting into the Royal Advisor's castle; I was there explaining a few things to Royal Advisor Miwa. I'm sorry I took so long."

Alliana shook her head wordlessly. Now was better than never.

Nela grabbed Alliana's bag and stuffed it into her knapsack. "Let's get out of here."

Suddenly, the door flew open.

"You will *not* be leaving!" a voice screeched.

Stepmother stood in the doorway, eyes burning with anger as she stared down Alliana and Nela.

CHAPTER TWENTY-SIX

A GIRL OF DRAGONS

From behind the older woman, a figure charged forward, shoving Alliana. She fell backward, hitting hard against the floor. Her stepbrother towered above her, lurching toward the witch. Nela darted nimbly out of Reizo's reach and pointed her wand at him. "Don't you come a step closer!"

But instead of reaching toward her, Reizo's hand snaked out to the side, lightning fast, and grabbed the broomstick, lifting it up above his knee.

"No!" Alliana and Nela cried out in unison.

Alliana stumbled back onto her feet, trying to get to her stepbrother in time but—

Reizo brought the broom down; the handle cracked in two with a horrifying *snap!*

Even Nela was wordless with shock as she gaped at

her trusty broomstick, the wood shriveling and turning a burnt-out gray. Breaking the handle seemed to drain all the magic from it.

Nela let out a horrified, mournful cry as she yanked the remains of her broomstick from Reizo's grasp, cradling it in her arms. "Oh, no. No, no, no."

Alliana despaired for her friend's loss—and for what had been their ticket out. "How could you?"

"You're not leaving," Reizo snarled. "You owe us."

"I owe you nothing," Alliana seethed.

Stepmother grabbed one of Alliana's wide sleeves, yanking her back. "You have *nowhere* else to go. After all I have done to take care of you, to feed you—"

Alliana yanked her shirt out of the woman's grip. "*No.* That's your story for me, not mine. I do not belong here; you cannot keep me trapped a moment longer."

"You must stay!" Stepmother screeched. Then her eyes narrowed, clever and insidious, as she ran her fingers along her clinking enamel bracelets. "Without a proper home, without a guardian, the Royal Advisor will *never* invite you to the Farmlands Ball again."

"That chance has long since passed," Alliana shot back, feeling the sting of the truth. All Stepmother wanted was for Alliana to work for free, so that the woman could use all her money on her jewelry and extravagances. "The next Regional Ball won't be for another full year. I'll find a new guardian by—"

"You won't find work elsewhere," Stepmother snapped. "You underestimate how kind I am as your guardian: feeding you, taking care of you. You miserable, wretched girl. How stupid, to think you can rise above your station, with your debt to pay. You will never do more in life than sweeping after dust. *I will make sure of it.*"

Stepmother's furious words burned like fire, twisting and breaking Alliana's spirit as they always did, time and time again. Reminding Alliana of her little worth, how there was nowhere else she belonged, how she should remember to be grateful to the one person who had taken care of her all these years.

But those were lies.

Alliana had Nela, who stood next to her, fury alighting her face—her wand sparking and ready to cast a spell if Alliana asked. She had Isao and Hiroshi, who had traveled far to find the witch. There was Kabo, who would battle against bigger, more frightening nightdragons for her sake.

"I may be a girl of dust," Alliana hissed out, her throat burning with every word, "but that is not all that you'll find of me."

I am not so alone as you thought. There is more to me than what you know, and I will travel far, no matter what you say I can do.

"Just like how *you* have more than one facet; you simper at guests and turn around to spit out poisonous words about their cleanliness or who they are."

Stepmother gaped. "I don't...I..."

"You do." Reina nodded firmly. "That's true, you were just talking about how boring Mister Leo is the other day, but when he's around, you pretend like he's the best thing ever."

Alliana raised an eyebrow at the older woman, who was still searching for words. "So?"

"You owe me! You are a nobody, a complete and pathetic orphan. I took care of you—"

"Do you call this taking care of me?" Alliana lifted up her sleeves to show the gaps in the cloth. She put her hand to her belly. "What about the endless grumbles in my stomach, the porridge that was more water than rice? How is that taking care of me?"

From next to her, Nela growled, a jagged, heartbroken note woven into her voice. "Alliana, you should've told me earlier."

"Stop your lies!"

Stepmother lunged forward, but Nela swung her wand down. *"Pure as crystal, bright as light; may this shield protect and deflect!"*

A clear wall shimmered between them and Alliana's stepfamily. Reizo roared and pounded on it. "What is this?"

"My way to ensure that you *never* hurt Alliana ever again," Nela shot back.

Stepmother snarled, pacing back and forth on the

other side of the crystal wall. "Fine, I'll tell you the truth from here, Alliana. You're greedy. I know you always stole things, anyway. So a little less dinner is only fair after all that you took from me."

"Yeah, you stole that roll!" Reizo snapped. "I counted thirteen, and then the next moment I looked, there were only twelve! I told Ma—"

"Tasty bread. It went to a good home." Nela grinned.

"You!" Stepmother cried. "I'll file a complaint with the Royal Advisor. This will go on your record! The Guild of Magic will hear about this, too!"

"Try me," Nela said brazenly. "But you'll have to answer questions about your son, who broke my magical broomstick."

"As if you haven't stolen from *me*?" Alliana added, incredulous. "My missing embroidery kit, my dinners, the handful of coppers I managed to save up that disappeared from under my mattress—"

"None of it was yours!" Stepmother shrieked. "You *owe* me for all I've done for you!"

"What about what *you* said I owe you?" Alliana echoed. "How about six years ago, when you said you'd paid an adventurer to search for Father? I wrote a letter to every patron who signed our guestbook during the moon of my father's accident. None of them had ever mentioned such a deal."

Stepmother spluttered. "That's not possible."

"*Something* does not add up," Alliana said. "And the truth will come out."

"I have asked the Royal Advisor to look into Alliana's father's death," Nela added, and Alliana's eyes widened. "In fact, I have just come from the Royal Advisor's estates, and the Royal Guard will be here shortly."

Alliana's heart pounded. "You used to work at the general store, Stepmother. You knew how to get into the storeroom. Father had just purchased his rope that morning and headed straight to the abyss."

Stepmother paled.

"And then when he was on the first platform, he got a message, didn't he?"

"I don't know what you're talking about," Stepmother snapped.

Alliana pulled out a small piece of paper from her pocket, and read it out.

Alliana has snuck out of the inn. Mister Leo has mentioned someone saw a small figure go down to the third platform. I worry she may be trying to rappel into the abyss to go after you.
    Fusako

"With a note like this, my father would have immediately rushed to rappel down, without a partner to watch his rope," Alliana said. She knew this was true; her father had loved her with all his heart and would have moved the Sakuya Mountains for her sake. "He would have been so worried, so concerned that he wouldn't be checking his *newly* purchased rope."

Reizo and Reina stared at their mother, as if beginning to truly see who she was for the first time.

"She's lying!" Stepmother shrieked. "I can't believe your gall. And how *dare* you put up a wall in my own house, witch!"

Alliana's voice was sharp as a dagger. "How dare *you* send my father to his death."

Stepmother gaped, but Reizo sneered. "You are such a *dumb* girl!"

"Call *Alliana*—she has a *name*—dumb one more time, and I'll turn you into a *dumb* toad," Nela snapped. She spun her wand in her hand. "It'd match your insides."

"A toad!" Reina echoed. "I'd feel bad for toads everywhere—even the stinkiest of all toads are far more likeable than *him*!"

"I've read the rules of your Guild," Reizo shot back, and Nela's eyes widened with surprise. It seemed the studying he'd done to prepare to meet with the Royal Advisor hadn't been in vain. "You witches and wizards can't cast spells on another person, not without their approval. And there's no way I'd give a witch like you a chance to curse me."

Nela glanced at Alliana worriedly; her trick wouldn't work.

But Alliana knew, now, that she had the strength. With friends like Isao and Nela and Kabo, she was *never* alone, no matter if they were next to her or supporting her from afar.

Alliana raised her chin, regal as Queen Natsumi. "I may be a girl of dust, but that's not all there is to me. Remember this: I am a girl of dust *and* dragons, and I will *not* let myself be treated like this a moment longer."

Reizo let out a loud scoff. "A girl of dragons? What, dragons made of dust?"

"Um, dearest brother," Reina said, tugging his sleeve. "Those shadows in the clouds..."

"I will never forget how you treated me," Alliana responded. "And I will never let this be forgotten."

And, as she finished speaking, she stepped backward—through the broken wall. She should have fallen—she should have tumbled straight out of the sky....

She'd spent years falling onto her knees, cleaning the inn until her skin burned raw. Alliana had years and years of falling and breaking and cracking....

But she was not broken. The memories of these past years, hard as they were, as tough as every day had been going through them...it had put her soul in a constant, burning fire, and she fought and fought, each day, until her heart shone brighter and stronger than crystal.

So she took a step backward, into empty sky, tugging Nela with her, and Stepmother let out a gasp despite herself—

And Kabo soared up, hovering with his great, emerald-black wings, and let out a roar as Alliana stood steady on his back, Nela at her side.

Stepmother screeched. "Reina! Reizo! Get over here! Protect me!"

Reizo was already scrambling toward the stairs, too shocked to hear his mother's demands.

"A-a-a *nightdragon*?" Reina's eyes were wide with glee. "But—*how*?"

Alliana gave her stepsister a sharp smile. "Grandmother Mari always said that crystal pigeons carrying wishes were harbingers of destiny. Especially when enchanted into a nightdragon."

Reina inched *closer*; she looked like she was ready to crawl out the window. "Can I pet it?"

"Get back here!" Stepmother screeched, catching her daughter by the collar and dragging her backward to the stairs. Then she pointed her finger straight at Alliana. "You owe me for all the years I've taken care of you, for—"

"I owe you nothing." Alliana's voice was strong and steady, filled with the assurance she'd hidden away all these years. She was no longer her stepmother's maid. She was no longer tied to the inn; her parents were long gone, and so was Grandmother Mari. And Alliana knew that the old woman would want this for her, too.

Alliana raised her eyes to meet Stepmother's, and uttered a promise that boiled with her blood and rang out as clear as crystal. "You may wash your hands clean of me when I leave, but I will not be forgotten. Mark my words: I will *not* let people in the realm be treated like this. There will be a day when no orphan will be allowed to go hungry, and people like you will be punished for your actions. *Mark my words.*"

Stepmother tossed her head in the air. "I doubt it—"

I don't. Kabo opened his mouth with a roar. A plume of fire tunneled toward Stepmother—

"*Water all around, a fire that will slowly spread; until remorse, it'll have no end,*" Nela called, with a swirl of her wand. Her bronze magic blazed through the sky, glimmering around the fire.

Stepmother turned from side to side, screeching at the flickering walls of fire, held in place by Nela's magic.

"Oops, my wand slipped. But I didn't cast a curse *on* you, don't worry." The witch flashed a tart smile. "In a minute or two, this fire will cover every centimeter of the inn. I'm afraid there's no way to get out until the Royal Guard comes and collects you. Polishing up your ways of saying 'sorry' might be a good way to start."

Stepmother spluttered. "I—no—wait—I'm sorry—"

" 'Sorry' was missing from your actions *years* ago," Alliana said. "If there was ever a hint of true love in your actions, this would have never happened. Father would still be here, at my side. If you truly loved me, I would have stayed. But my life—nor my family's—is not yours to toy with, not with your fake help and cold lies and cruel words. This is not where my story ends."

And with that, Stepmother was silenced completely, eyes wide and mouth gaping, relying on her children to keep her upright.

Alliana raised her chin and gave them one last smile— as strong and true as Queen Natsumi might—but even stronger, because, for once, this smile was real, and most of all, this smile was her own.

For Alliana! With one last roar from Kabo, they shot into the sky. Her heart pattered faster and faster, with disbelief, as the clouds swirled misty and cool and strange against her skin.

Below, in gaps between the clouds, a legion of guards marched with the morning sun glinting off the crests on their metal helmets, to surround the inn. It seemed, after all this time, Stepmother's sordid past would finally be put to justice.

Nela was watching her curiously. "Are you all right?"

For a moment, she had to consider things. She didn't

have a coin to her name. She had no legal guardian to take care of her. She had so little, yet—

"I've always wanted to travel on this path," Alliana said, truth ringing with every word, her smile glowing as bright as the rising sun.

The witch grinned back, letting out a whoop. "Hurrah!" Then she snorted. "Why did you say I transformed Kabo from a pigeon?"

"Let her think he's a pigeon." Alliana laughed. "All the better for us, and especially for Kabo. We're the only ones who need to know he truly exists; their tall tales will ensure no one will go looking for him."

But Alliana knew the truth as she looked around: The crystal pigeon had disappeared. Alliana had always suspected that her mother and father—and Grandmother Mari—had wished for her happiness, even if it meant leaving the last place they'd been together. And, as much as it stung to miss the cooing, chirping bird, it felt like a reassurance that Alliana had finally begun to fulfill their wishes.

Birds have wings. Am I a bird? The nightdragon looked at them, his eyes wide with interest, too.

"The best fire-breathing bird I've ever had the honor of befriending." Alliana reached out and patted his thick hide, and Kabo let out a happy dragon grin, baring his very real, sharp teeth. Below, Alliana could see his emerald-and-gold bracelet, entwined around his wrist. The arrow pointed straight up, at her, and her heart warmed. With Nela's magic, Kabo had still felt her signal, and come to Alliana in her time of need. With her two dear friends, Alliana had been able to find her own path.

Slowly, Alliana reached out with her arms, feeling the winds flow around her clothes, cool and serene. And then they flew over the crossroads, the path that she'd walked time and time again, only to go toward the town or down to the abyss, or to return to the inn.

She glanced behind them. The inn had shrunk from towering over her to nothing more than a pinprick of dust, covered up by the soft white clouds.

Now, finally, she was heading down the last path, the path she'd only been able to dream about for years on end.

To the capital...

Alliana was on the path of dreams.

CHAPTER TWENTY-SEVEN

THE TOWN OF LIGHTS

Thick, cool mist shrouded Alliana's view, but Kabo kept flying onward, steady as ever, guided by Nela. When the clouds parted, ever so briefly, a glimmer of light caught Alliana's eye. "Is that a city?"

From her side, Nela laughed. "Just wait a minute, you'll see. Can you ask Kabo to descend?"

Alliana nodded. With a pat on the dragon's thick hide and a gentle nudge on the harness, Kabo tilted his wings. They tunneled through the clouds, icy on the skin, and then burst into open air, and—

Alliana breathed in with delight. "It's like a queen's tiara!"

A cozy town was nestled against the cliffs, with blue and gilded roofs like sapphires interwoven through a gold crown. But if the town was a tiara, the ocean beyond was a chest full of jewels; water sparkled under the midday sun.

"This town's called Auteri," Nela said. "You know, the place that hosts the Festival of Lights. I haven't heard much about them, though; they don't have a town witch or wizard right now."

"I wish I was a Guild member. I'd want to live here!" Alliana said with a laugh.

"I wish you could be a witch, too! See, if you were a witch, you could live in this spot." Nela guided her and Kabo to a tiny cottage set high into the cliffs, hidden from the town's view. "It's one of the Guild of Magic's cottages, where any witch or wizard can stay. But no one's here right now, so we're safe—and we've made it in plenty of time to get to the boat."

They landed in the rock meadow in front of the cottage. The tiny house looked quite neglected, as if it was missing someone to care for it.

Alliana slid off Kabo, her heart thumping as she pulled the knapsack off her shoulders. "If we have a moment..."

"What is it?" Nela asked. "Go on, spit it out."

Alliana pulled the embroidery box from the bag. "Grandmother's box is breaking, but I don't want it to fall apart. Would you be able to fix it?"

Nela chewed on her lip as she joined Alliana in

prodding the space behind the bottom drawer. "Huh. That's strange. It doesn't quite feel the same as the other areas. I can try, though I'm not very good at repair magic."

They sat on the top step in front of the cottage. Alliana set the embroidery box in her lap, her fingers protectively curving around the paper sides. As she held it closer to her chest, there was a metallic *clink!*, like something had gotten loose during the ride.

"What kind of spell..." Nela frowned. Alliana could almost see a book in Nela's mind, flipping through all sorts of enchantments she'd used in the past. But this new spell was like a blank page, uncharted territory.

Kabo curled around the bottom of the stairs, his long neck twisting around Alliana and peeking over her shoulder. He sniffed at the box, so she gently reminded him, "No flames for this."

Nela sat up, brushing dust off her skirt. "I know! Think of your grandmother, what she means to you." The witch placed one hand over Alliana's, tight around the embroidery box.

What did Grandmother Mari mean to Alliana?

There was no one word that described the truth. It was more than just *she means a lot* or *I miss her.*

To Alliana, Grandmother Mari burned brighter than candlelight in darkness. She was salty rice crackers right when her stomach grumbled with hunger, or cool barley tea after scrubbing the inn top to bottom. The old woman was the gentlest, most welcoming of hugs after the toughest of days. She was starry nights and blazing bright sunrises. Together, they'd formed memories that were tucked away in Alliana's heart, treasured and fondly remembered.

The old woman's eyes brightening when Alliana poked her head through the attic door.

Walking side by side to the meadow by the abyss— going ever so slow, but Alliana had never wanted to speed up a second of their time together.

The magic-like thrill of Grandmother starting a story with, "Once upon a time…" With just a few words, Alliana felt like she was traveling through the realm.

Late nights helping Grandmother Mari thread her needle and trying to tackle the never-ending stack of shirts to mend, but reveling in the quiet joy of every moment.

Kabo snuggled closer on her shoulder, echoing the warmth of the old woman's comforting hugs, and her heart ached.

I miss you. I miss you so much, Grandmother Mari.

"I can feel your love for her; it's written all over your face." Nela smiled softly, and waved her wand in a circle over the box. *"Clear as crystal, bright as light; with haste and speed, repair what is in need."*

Glittering specks poured out of her wand, like crystal snow, delicately sprinkling over the paper. Where the magic touched, the paper glowed, turning clear as glass. It revealed the odds and ends: spools and paper packets of needles and glossy skeins of embroidery thread and—

The paper of that peculiar drawer turned clear, and Alliana sucked in a breath.

A small, thin package, wrapped in cloth, lay underneath the back panel of the embroidery box. It was just about the size of her two hands placed together, but the fabric shielded the view of whatever may lay inside.

"It's not broken—it's a secret compartment!" Nela gasped. "Alliana, I think you can open it through the drawer."

Her fingertips were already skimming against the back of the drawer, searching, searching. . . .

Then—there it was—a barely noticeable loop of thread crammed into the edge, like a handle meant to be pulled. If Alliana hadn't known about the secret compartment through Nela's spell, she never would've looked, but—

She gave it a tug, and the thread broke. Alliana's heartbeat stuttered.

She'd spun up castles of air in her heart. Perhaps Grandmother had never meant this for her. Maybe she should bring this back to Stepmother; Grandmother had likely meant this for her own family.

Then Kabo leaned forward and nudged at the back with his muzzle. *Look, look.*

Alliana couldn't let the box go up in flames. "Oh, wait, it'll break—"

The back panel of the embroidery box swung open to a thin compartment, no deeper than the width of a finger, and revealed a small fabric bundle. Alliana met the witch's eyes over the box, frozen with shock.

"Go on, open it," Nela said, her dark eyes gentle and kind. Kabo breathed softly on her now-cold hands, warming them up from their frozen state.

She reached out to touch the fabric; it was smooth, just like the silk backings of the tapestries. Her hands felt like they'd been coated in freshly churned butter: slippery and unable to grasp the fabric.

Nela set the embroidery box into her lap and cupped her hands under Alliana's, giving her a place to rest until her hands could stay steady.

"Th-thank you," Alliana whispered, her voice carried away by the sea breeze. "I...I just can't believe...I can't believe it's been here all this time."

"Sometimes, things show up just when they're needed the most," Nela said. "A friend, a gift...even a dragon, right?"

The fabric fell open to reveal a lushly embroidered miniature tapestry, no longer than Alliana's forearm, and tears blurred her sight.

The background glittered with midnight blues and candlelight gold, like a window into the past. In the center, two hands were clasped together: one mottled with age and wrinkled, the other smooth and young, with a scar on the thumb.

Grandmother Mari...and her.

Back at the inn, she'd never been the subject of a painting. Alliana had never stared down from the hallway walls, made of swirls of oil and color.

This bit of cloth was embroidered lovingly, stitch by stitch, by someone who had cherished their time together just as much as Alliana had.

Grandmother Mari had made a tapestry just for her.

She could've stared at the tapestry for hours, running her fingertips over every stitch. But Kabo leaned over her shoulder again and nudged at one of the other small packages that the tapestry had been wrapped around, knocking it off her lap.

Nela swiftly caught it; the insides clinked as she returned a small pouch to Alliana's hand. When Alliana loosened the string, something bright and shiny as the sun slid into her palm.

The crystal necklace.

Shock reverberated through Alliana's nerves. A thin piece of paper crinkled underneath. Her hands fumbled as she smoothed out the creases.

Dearest Alliana—

I have written this many times. But there are sometimes not enough words to properly explain my thoughts. For, if you are reading this, it means I have passed on. But let us not dwell on that; I write this now, for you. For you to continue on, after I am long gone.

Do you remember how, so late in the night, you asked me what I dreamed of?

Alliana, I dream of—

This beginning...

Alliana pulled out the well-read, worn-to-bits letter she'd carried close to her heart for all this time, and put it side by side with this new one.

The gentle handwriting, the very words, even the thin paper the color of sun-soaked barley—it matched the letter that Stepmother had forged, all the way up to this point. Without doubt, Alliana knew Stepmother had picked up one of Grandmother's drafts from the rubbish bin, and made it into her own version, twisting the message so Alliana would stay and work.

Alliana's eyes burned. She'd *known* there had been something utterly like Grandmother Mari about it—that had been why she could never simply disregard the letter, even when she'd wanted to doubt it.

But that line was where the letter changed.

Alliana, I dream of—

Alliana closed her eyes, breathing in a sharp, unsteady gasp of air. At her sides, Nela and Kabo leaned in for just a moment. The witch hugged her, and the nightdragon rested his head on her shoulder and huffed out a warm puff. Then they retreated to overlook the ocean at the edge of the cliff, leaving her to read the rest of the letter in peace.

Slowly, she focused on the words, though the paper wobbled in her trembling hands.

Alliana, I dream of your future. I dream of you finding your true happiness. I want, more than anything, for you to realize that you stand at a crossroads, and a journey awaits—but, my dear, you must be brave.

Chase the fairy tales that have always charmed you. It is time to release the tapestry of the past and keep your hands on the threads of the present. Follow your own path into a story untold. And remember, your future is an untold story, and you decide how the tale unravels. But, my dear, your tale is a beautiful one already, and no tapestry could ever do it justice.

You will always be my family, my dear. And, wherever your road may take you, remember that you have all my love, now and forever. Let the light shine, brighter, always. The darkness is out there, but shine bright.

Your grandmother,
Mari Sakamaki

Alliana carefully held the letter to her chest and put on the necklace, pressing it close like she could feel the phantom touch of the old woman's arms, holding her in a hug. As she read over the words again and again, bittersweet as they were, she soaked in the sunlight, the brightness of the blue sky, the gentle weight of the crystal necklace. She had begun to fulfill Grandmother Mari's wish. She had stood at the crossroads of her life, and taken the path she had longed for—

And to finally know that it had been what the old woman had wanted for her—

She couldn't wait for the rest of her adventure to begin.

Which reminded her... Alliana looked around, as she slowly remembered where she was, like she was waking from a beautiful, mesmerizing dream. "How much longer until we have to board?"

The witch hurried over to the edge and peered around

the rock cliff. "The boat's loading up passengers—it'll be leaving soon!"

Alliana knocked her hand against one of the night-dragon's spiky points. "Ouch! But—I can't leave Kabo here."

You have to go. The dragon worriedly nudged her hand, breathing his warm air over the sore spot, soothing away the pain, and Alliana leaned against Kabo. Just as she'd finally made peace with Grandmother Mari's wishes, she was losing someone else, so soon. Yet Kabo couldn't stay in Rivelle; he was like her, without a place to truly belong.

"There's a spot into the abyss only an hour or two from here, I think," Nela said.

"Can you make it to the abyss alone?" Alliana asked Kabo, her heart aching. She tried to cover it with a smile. "You promise you'll make it back safely?"

The dragon bent his head in a nod, letting out a snort of ash and embers. *Of course. I can make it back anytime, but—*

"Once a year." Alliana reached out to run her fingers along his bumpy, thick hide. "Let's meet again, at the abyss, once a year."

Nela waved her wand, and a familiar emerald strand draped from Alliana's neck. "There—to replace the one you're missing."

The dragon's muzzle parted in a sharp-toothed smile,

before he rubbed his forehead against Alliana's shoulder, nearly toppling her over. *Promise?*

Her chest ached.

This was where she belonged. She didn't have a home in Narashino; she never had. Kabo had found a place in her heart and she in his; when they were together, it felt like she belonged. Just like how she'd felt at Grandmother Mari's side, or with Isao or Nela: It was with them that Alliana felt at home. The girl circled her arms around the dragon's neck, and she pressed her forehead into his. Kabo was right in front of her, yet she missed him so much already. *"Promise."*

Moments later, far too soon, Kabo backed away, nudging her toward the cliffside path down to the boat. The nightdragon spread his wings, stirring up dust, and shot into the sky. He circled once, and Alliana wanted to cry out, *Please stay*, but she breathed in a sharp breath of cold air instead.

She raised her hand up, pressing the necklace to her heart. Necklace or no necklace, she'd never forget Kabo—just as she would never forget Nela, Isao, and, of course, Grandmother Mari. She hoped, too, they would never forget her.

Alliana watched and watched as the nightdragon turned toward the abyss and flew onward, until the witch tugged her down the winding cliffside path, and they raced to the boat before it set off without them.

PART FIVE

Three Moons Later

EPILOGUE

The bell above the door chimed, and the charmed book sparked under Alliana's fingertips. This one was about Queen Natsumi's first Royal Ball, where she'd met her fellow students of the Royal Academy—including a student who would become her rival. Books about the Royal Ball were flying off the shelf since this year's Royal Ball was at the end of the week. Rivelleans from all around the realm had traveled into Okayama just for the chance to get a glimpse of Queen Natsumi welcoming the newest class to the Royal Academy. Alliana already had plans to wake early and hurry over to the castle on the day of the ball. She couldn't seem to tear her gaze away from the riveting tale as she called, "I'm sorry, I thought I'd locked the door. The store's closed now, but we'll open again at—"

"Ten o'clock, I heard."

The familiar voice made her head snap up. "Isao!" She slid off her stool and hurried to the door, throwing her arms around him. He'd grown a little taller in the past three moons, his shoulders broader from all the heavy lifting and countless loaves he was kneading as part of his baker's apprenticeship.

Isao ruffled her hair teasingly. "Looks like you've found a good place to work." He looked appreciatively around the small, cozy shop filled with tables and shelves crammed with books, both magical and non-magical alike, and his eyes lit up when he saw the cookbook section. "It feels like these books were written just for me!"

"How's Miyada? Have you created any new yuzu pastries yet?"

Her friend laughed. "There'll be plenty of time for catching up later—well, maybe. I've got to head over to the castle to help my master prepare for tomorrow night's festivities. But first..." He motioned over his shoulder.

Two others stood in the doorframe, the morning rays shining brightly in a halo around them, as dust motes gently floated through the air. For a moment, Alliana thought one of the enchanted books had come to life.

"Nela? Taichi?"

She'd missed her friends. All four of them had been terribly busy since Alliana had come to Okayama. The witch and wizard grinned as they stepped into the shop; they both had bronze pins to mark their newly minted

Novice status. Unsurprisingly, they'd passed their first official Guild of Magic quest with flying colors. The bell chimed one more time as the door closed, and the air seemed to shimmer with a hint of magic, thrumming with the excitement of something yet to come.

Taichi pushed his wavy black hair out of his eyes, clearing his throat as he looked at her. It turned out that he lived close by—on the day her boat had landed, Taichi had brought her and Nela to what he'd declared as one of the best shops in the realm, this very bookstore. The kindhearted owner, a childhood friend of Taichi's parents, had hired Alliana on the spot, as she went off to the West in search of a rare magical tome.

On those first few days together, when Alliana had some free time, they went across the street to the magical goods shop to scour the aisles for the latest enchanted trinkets, or down to the shop on the corner to slurp up fresh, handmade noodles in thick, rich broth. This time, though, even with Isao here, they weren't budging.

Alliana studied the three of them. "Is something the matter?"

Taichi cleared his throat. "It's...the judgment is complete."

"Oh." Alliana's throat tightened. Kyo, the head steward to Royal Advisor Miwa, had been assigned with investigating her father's death and the treatment Alliana had received during her years at the inn.

"The letter came through to the Guild of Magic, and Taichi and I both volunteered to bring the news to you." Nela pulled out a thin paper from her pocket, smoothing out its folded edges, and offered it to Alliana.

She shook her head. "Do you mind—do you mind telling it to me?"

Alliana had had enough of letters from Stepmother.

Nela tucked the paper away and spoke softly. "She's guilty of mistreating you and in your father's death, of course. Your stepmother has been tasked with serving the inn's guests for the rest of her life, but without a coin in pay and no more than the food and clothes she allotted you. Master Yamane will be checking in regularly, and he's devised a few spells to help her remember *exactly* how she treated you and what happened to your father. Reizo admitted he was guilty of adding to your awful living conditions, so he'll be sent to apprentice at the healers' guild to learn about selfless care. Reina has been sent to live with her father's extended family in the West."

Alliana breathed out. The weight her stepfamily had left on her life was still heavy, and no matter what the Royal Advisor decreed, nothing would bring back her father. But, day by day, and after weekly talks with a healer in the city, she didn't wake up at the crack of dawn anymore, expecting to get her ears boxed and her breakfast taken away.

"Thank you for bringing me the news." She tried to force cheer into her voice. "Shall we go down the street for bowls of noodles? Isao, you have to try the house specialty; that rich broth topped with spring onions is absolute perfection."

The baker glanced over at the witch and wizard.

"Wait. Isn't all of that about Stepmother what you'd come by to tell me?" Alliana asked, looking between the three of them. They guiltily shot each other grins, and Alliana crossed her arms suspiciously.

Then the bell chimed again, and the door swung open, but no one stood there waiting. Over her friends' shoulders, a black dot fluttered through the sky.

Alliana furrowed her brow. "Nela, it's one of your bird-letters."

Her three friends spun around, and Nela laughed. "Ah, I've been waiting for that. Actually, that's what I'm here for. I'd heard it was arriving today."

The bird-letter soared down, out of the clouds, and fluttered around them. Yet Nela didn't reach out for it like she normally would. Instead, the witch tilted her head toward the bird. "It's for you."

"Me?" Alliana lifted up her hand and the bird-letter soared down promptly. Its beak tapped Alliana on the palm, as if checking it was really her. "Ouch!"

"Oh, behave!" Nela scolded the bird.

Taichi snorted. "Hayato probably sent this one. He always puts too much magic into his letters, just to show off."

"What is this letter for?" Alliana asked. "I thought Stepmother's decision was complete."

"Ask it to open," Nela urged.

A fold in the paper looked like a beady, judging eye. Alliana swallowed. "Um, open, please."

Isao grinned. "Ask with the strength of the girl who stopped a nightdragon from burning down the Farmlands; that'll do the trick."

"Or with the power of a girl who *befriended* a nightdragon," Nela murmured, so just Alliana could hear.

Alliana rolled her shoulders back so she was standing straighter, and said, clear as crystal, "Please, open *now*."

The bird-letter jolted straight up—and unfurled into her palm.

A ROYAL INVITATION
DECLARED BY QUEEN NATSUMI

TO ALLIANA OF RIVELLE REALM

YOU ARE FORMALLY INVITED
TO THE ROYAL ACADEMY

FIRST YEAR CLASSES BEGIN
ON THE FIFTH MOON, EIGHTEENTH DAY

Alliana's head spun. "*The* Royal Academy?" She leaned against one of the tables as she stared at her name, written in pitch-black ink. "But...could this be a trick?"

What if—what if Reizo had sent this invite as one last cruel prank, so she'd show up and no one would let her in?

"It *is* for you—and only you." The corner of Nela's mouth tipped up in a sly smile. "I sent word of your help to the capital—and there're quite a few folks who are very grateful for your assistance. The way you helped all of the Farmlands, well, it's something that only a witch or wizard or one of the Royal Advisors could have done, usually. So you're due a thank-you or two, and I thought—I thought this might be a good way to share their appreciation."

"Anyone would've done the same. I don't deserve—"

"You deserve it." Nela's voice burned with conviction.

Taichi added, "Say yes?"

Alliana turned out toward the city, the rooftops shimmering bright outside the windows. This was the world Grandmother had always wanted her to see; she just hadn't realized it for years. But, finally, she had cut through Stepmother's lies and found the world as it truly was.

And the truth was just as she'd once hoped.

Your future is an untold story, and you decide how the tale unravels.

Grandmother Mari's promise rang out, crystal clear, shimmering in her heart and throughout the beautiful world around her. Alliana had a feeling that, if she could see under the stitching of the tapestry Grandmother Mari had embroidered for her, she might find that very phrase sewn onto the cloth.

Alliana's parents and Grandmother Mari had loved her, and had given Alliana exactly what she needed to take her own path into the world. Alliana only wished they were still here to see her finally become who she was meant to be, but she knew that wherever her parents or the old woman were now, they would be cheering Alliana on, no matter what. For their love ran deeper than time and goodbyes; their love was with Alliana, no matter how many years passed.

"So"—Nela looked a touch nervous—"you'll enroll, right?"

"Yes," Alliana whispered. Tears burned at her eyes. Then she raised her chin and said, louder, "Yes, I'd be delighted to attend the Royal Academy."

Her friends whooped with delight, tugging her out the door and down the street to celebrate over hearty bowls of noodles.

Yes, Alliana would attend the Royal Academy, as she'd always dreamed.

Yes, this world, her *life*, was finally a story all her own.

Alliana ran her fingers against the paper and ink once more, and her heart flew as high as the birds that soared above the capital city, swooping and pinwheeling through the sapphire-blue sky. Beyond the cobblestone paths, the castle—and Royal Academy—awaited her. She had finally begun to unravel her own tale, her own future, one step, one day at a time.

ACKNOWLEDGMENTS

Thank you, dear reader. Every reader who has stumbled upon one of my books at the store and it sparked your curiosity so you brought it home, or if you were walking through the library and your fingers brushed across the spine, or if you shared my books with a friend...thank you so much for fiercely rooting for and championing my stories. I hope you, too, will unravel your tale and find your own path.

A gigantic dragon hug and thank-you to Sarah Landis, Alvina Ling, and Ruqayyah Daud. You were at my side when I was at a crossroads, and guided me to my path of dreams.

Special thanks to the Little, Brown Books for Young Readers team, LB School, NOVL, and the Hachette family, including Megan Tingley, Jackie Engel, Tom Guerin, Siena Koncsol, Janelle DeLuise, Hannah Koerner, Karina Granda, Sarah Van Bonn, Jen Graham, Andy Ball, Nyamekye Waliyaya, Emilie Polster, Stefanie Hoffman, Savannah Kennelly, Mara Brashem, Bill Grace, Rick Cobban, Christie Michel, Victoria Stapleton, Marisa Russell, Paula Benjamin-Barner, Shawn Foster, Michelle

Campbell, Danielle Cantarella, Hannah Bucchin—from editorial to copyediting, marketing to sales, contracting to foreign rights—you have given Eva and Alliana wings to fly, and I appreciate your love for Rivelle Realm with all my heart.

To my family, my dear friends, and book community—sending hugs whether you are far or near.

A special thank-you to Chelsea Ichaso, without whom this story might never have been written. I owe you a unimercorn.

The early readers and cheerleaders deserve croissants and mochi for helping me find my way from a dusty start: Alyssa Colman, CW, Eunice Kim, June Tan, Karina Evans, Melissa Seymour, Sarah Suk, the Wavy Discord, and the Rivelle Guard.

Thank you to Emily and Eugene, with all my love.

The heart of *Alliana* was sparked by my own Grandmother Mari. There are never enough chapters to explain what you mean to me, but I hope this is a start.

This story is for all the Grandmother Maris, the fiery Kabos, the Nelas and Isaos, and the unstoppable Allianas of our world—our chosen thunder.

Julie Vu

JULIE ABE

has lived in Silicon Valley, spent many humid summers in Japan, and currently basks in the sunshine of Southern California (with never enough books or tea), where she creates stories about magical adventures. Of her debut novel, *Eva Evergreen, Semi-Magical Witch*, *Kirkus* said in a starred review: "**Bewitching... a must-read for fantasy lovers.**" Julie is also the author of *Eva Evergreen and the Cursed Witch* and *Alliana, Girl of Dragons*. She invites you to visit her online at julieabebooks.com.